2019
Elayna Silvas

Shining Sea

A Novel

ANNE KORKEAKIVI

Little, Brown and Company
New York Boston London

Copyright © 2016 by Anne Korkeakivi

Little, Brown and Company
Hachette Book Group
1290 Avenue of the Americas, New York, NY 10104
littlebrown.com

First Edition: August 2016

Little, Brown and Company is a division of Hachette Book Group, Inc. The Little, Brown name and logo are trademarks of Hachette Book Group, Inc.

The publisher is not responsible for websites (or their content) that are not owned by the publisher.

The Hachette Speakers Bureau provides a wide range of authors for speaking events. To find out more, go to hachettespeakersbureau.com or call (866) 376-6591.

Excerpt from "Rocca San Giovanni" by George Fraser Gallie. Used with permission. Excerpt from "I Feel Like I'm Fixin' to Die Rag." Words and Music by Joe McDonald. Copyright © 1965, renewed 1993 by Alkatraz Corner Music. Used by permission.
Scripture from the Holy Bible, New International Version®, NIV®. Copyright © 1973, 1978, 1984, 2011 by Biblica, Inc.™ Used by permission of Zondervan. All rights reserved worldwide. www.zondervan.com. The "NIV" and "New International Version" are trademarks registered in the United States Patent and Trademark Office by Biblica, Inc.™
Haiku by Erin Coughlin Hollowell. Used with permission.

ISBN 978-0-316-30784-0

LCCN 2015958604

10 9 8 7 6 5 4 3 2 1

RRD-C

Printed in the United States of America

For Antti, of course

BOOK ONE

1962

Again it is peaceful, the valley is silent,
Only the birds and the stream have their noise,
The twittering, bubbling sounds of nature.
Apart from this—silence which nothing destroys.

—George Fraser Gallie, 1943

Good Friday / April 20, 1962

MICHAEL

A CROWD OF SPARROWS flies up, peppering the California sky overhead. His heart constricts, and Michael Gannon thinks: *Today is the day I am going to die.*

"Look at that cloud," Luke says, lowering his paintbrush. "It's going to rain."

"It's not going to rain," he tells his middle son, struggling to catch his breath. "Don't give up in the home stretch, Luke. Another hour, and the house will be done."

His heart squeezes; his fingers and jaw stiffen. *You'll be all right, corpsman,* the doctor at Letterman told him, signing his release sixteen years ago. There were more than seventy thousand of them moving through Letterman Army Hospital in Frisco that year. *If you could make it through the Bataan march and three years in the hands of the Japs, you can make it now. You'll be all right.*

But heart failure can be a sneaky enemy, quietly waiting to strike the fatal blow. He had plenty of opportunities to see its tricks, barely out of medical school, trying to keep his fellow prisoners alive in the Pacific. People say it's the brain that keeps you alive—*Give up, and you are done for*—but who is to say that the will doesn't have its home in the heart? And if that heart just won't function?

3

He climbs carefully down the ladder and leans his back against a panel that has dried. All he and the boys have left is a bit of trim around four windows and under an eave, and the paint should be good for another ten years. Last December, he finished paying off the mortgage.

At least, this.

But *no*. Death no longer flits overhead, waiting to brush his neck with its frigid fingers, to breathe its mortal fog into his mouth. He left death behind on an island in the Pacific and then on a cot in Letterman hospital. He is strong now. Tomorrow, with the painting done, the kids will dye the eggs for Easter. He'll put the crib back up for the new baby. Barbara will bake a coconut cake to have ready for Easter dinner. Life will continue, as it should do.

The pain is becoming heavier, pressing down against his throat and clavicle. If this is the real thing, the sooner he can get help the better his chances.

Give in, though, and it's as good as giving up.

"Dad," Mike Jr. says, peering sideways at him from atop the stepladder, paintbrush poised in midair. "Are you okay? You look a little funny."

He slides down against the side of the building into a crouch. No. He has lived through so much. Nothing can beat him. He won't let it. He—

———

1942. He keeps his head down. Any untoward movement, any sign of weakness, any act of petition elicits a bark in Japanese, a bayonet flashing. He will not think of Hughes or D'Auteuil, lying in the dirt a few miles back. He will think of the living. He will think *of* living. He focuses on the Filipino dust, the detritus of other men who have trod before him along this hellish road up the Bataan peninsula. His socks have worn through, his feet blistering inside his ruined boots. The last halt they were given, he used a sharp stone to remove the leather over his toes, a rude sandal. Now pebbles and dried blood— not his, but from those who couldn't make it, from those who have fallen, from the young blond kid to whom he offered a precious sip from his canteen but too late, the boy fell to his knees, and then the *hohei* ran up, shouting . . . —encrust his feet. He takes what is left of his shirt off and wraps it around his head.

Blessed is he that watcheth, and keepeth his garments, lest he walk naked, and they see his shame. Revelation 16:15.

He is but mud, but filth, but hunger.

The trick is to set goals. The abandoned cart ahead. That distant banana grove.

The flies are thick, big as hummingbirds, heavy with the refuse of human carcasses. Waves of them, and then the mosquitoes. He wants to slap at them, to slap the sun, to slap away the sound of men pleading, grunting, moaning. But he can barely move one foot in front of the other.

The fever returns, waves of it, hot and then cold, racking his body, a heavy pendulum swinging in and out of the Ice Age, knocking the fiery center of the earth from one side of his frame to the other. A thousand porcupine quills tipped with burning then freezing poison penetrate his neck, his back, his groin, his calves. A dark murky burning wash pours over him, like swimming through phosphorus.

The world is melting off his face, sliding down his nose, cheeks, neck, shoulders.

His mouth swells so thick and sticky it almost chokes him.

Water. Please, God, water.

Ike! The *hohei* screams at him, pointing.

A trough of river, shallow and oily and littered with limbs attached to lifeless bodies. He descends as directed, lowers his face into the wet, pushes a corpse away. His body shakes with revulsion and pleasure. The water, the water. He dunks his canteen in swiftly. The *hohei* shouts at him from the bank above, and he reaches for the bobbing helmet he's been sent down to salvage.

There he is, his reflection looking up at his self.

Climb out of here. Climb up those banks and keep on climbing.

Breathe, stay calm, pray. Believe God does whatever he does for a reason.

———

His heart doubles over.

He relaxes into the pain, as he learned to do in the Pacific, tossed from one POW camp to another, fed little more than a small ball of dirty infested rice a day, his body riveted with disease. As he learned to do in order to survive.

A veil of sweat breaks out along his hairline.

"Dad?" Mike Jr. repeats.

"Just need a sec, buddy," he manages. "Hot."

"Do you want something to drink, Daddy?" Patty Ann says, stepping out of the kitchen door, pink pedal pushers poking out from beneath her mother's apron. Her dark ponytail shines in the sunlight. "Mommy and I made lemonade."

"That would be swell, sweetheart," he says, forcing his tongue to cooperate. Patty Ann, his precious first child, his only daughter.

And he said unto them, Ye will surely say unto me this proverb, Physician, heal thyself.

But his heart muscle presses down against his rib cage, hard, harder.

And then, just as suddenly, it releases.

His breath frees. The heaviness vanishes.

"Fresh lemonade!" Barbara says, stepping out the kitchen door now, the old white pitcher in her hand. Her round belly lifts the apron she is wearing. It won't be long before the new baby arrives—not more than four weeks. Maybe a second daughter, maybe a fourth boy. They each hope it's another girl. Neither of them says so, but both of them know it.

"Look at Daddy," Patty Ann says. "I told you he wouldn't mind, that we shouldn't wait until they're all finished. The body is sixty percent water—just a loss of one and a half percent already begins to bring dehydration."

"Thank you very much, Miss Smarty-Pants," Barbara says, smiling. "Oh, Michael! The house looks so fresh and clean and bright, like a baby chick. And just in time for Easter, like you promised!"

How beautiful she is. His Barbara.

"Why yellow again, Dad?" Luke says.

"Yellow is a nice color for a house," Barbara says. "A happy color for a happy family."

"I think yellow is a good color," Mike Jr. says.

"Yellow is pretty," Patty Ann says. "Don't you like yellow, Lukie?"

"I never said it wasn't nice," Luke says. "I was just curious why the same color twice. Why not white? Or blue? I'm just wondering."

"That's enough, Luke," Barbara says. "I love the yellow."

The world suddenly upends itself, spinning.

"It has to be yellow," he says, dropping his head between his arms.

———

1945. She's wearing bright red lipstick, a little too old for her, and a crisp yellow dress. Not a nurse but a local girl, volunteering. A very pretty local girl, with shiny dark hair and a round face.

Where you from, soldier?

When the first B-29 flew over Jinsen dropping supply packages, he and the guys burst open the packets of Spam and chocolate bars and sucked out every last sweet drop from the cans of peaches, cans of fruit cocktail, the sticky liquid dripping down their cracked lips into the sores on their necks. Over three years as a prisoner, he'd lost almost one hundred pounds from his six-foot frame. Anything, everything, was like manna. But it wasn't until he was picked up by a transport plane three weeks later and dropped in Honolulu that he could keep a meal down. For another three weeks, the nurses stuffed him with an endless feast of sulfanilamide, Atabrine, pork, and oranges to fight the beriberi, the malaria, the dysentery before sending him on. Then the mainland. This girl.

Does she notice how his bones still press through his shirt, the dry red patches on his skin, the uneven patter of his weakened heart?

Massachusetts, he says.

Bet you can't wait to get back there. You have a sweetheart waiting for you?

I'm not going back. I'm going to spend the next two years at the University of California in Los Angeles. I joined up the day I finished medical school. But I still have two years to go before I'm a full-fledged doctor.

The touch of her little hand on his shoulder sends sparks all the way down to his bloated ankles. Thank the Lord the swelling in his scrotum has faded.

A doctor! But the University of California in Los Angeles—that must be expensive.

Uncle Sam's dime.

Is that a fact? Well, Lord knows that's the least we can do for you, after all you boys have been through. And then corrects herself: *After all you boys have done for us.*

She lowers the tray stacked with books and magazines so he can go through them without sitting further up. He takes his time, although he's ready to read anything. The written English language looks as beautiful to him as this girl.

Well, almost. Nothing could be as beautiful as this bright-eyed girl. She is life itself.

She doesn't hurry him. Instead she smiles some more and starts to play at helping him choose. *How about this one?* she says, holding up a copy of *White Fang.* He read it as a boy: a fighting dog, cold, capture. He shakes his head.

Or this? She picks up a copy of *Life* magazine with the words BALLET SWIMMER and a girl in a two-piece swimsuit underwater on the cover.

That looks nicer, he says.

She takes a closer look at the cover image and frowns. *No, not this. This looks terrible.*

And then she shoots him an even more brilliant smile that lets him know, at least to this beautiful girl, he is by some miracle still whole.

Will you come back again tomorrow? he asks her.

She frowns for just one brief moment, maybe deciding whether it is worth losing her job or skipping school or whatever coming back tomorrow will cost her.

You bet. I'll come back to see you as often as you'd like me to.

And she does.

Her name is Barbara, and she is nineteen years old, one year out of high school and working as a receptionist. She lives at home alone with her folks; her only brother fell on D-day and is buried in

Normandy. *My mother's family is French. So at least in a way he's home,* she tells him, and he understands right away that this is how she survives, that this is the way she has chosen to navigate this world. That she is a girl who will fight to the end, fight to remain cheerful no matter what life throws at her.

That's a good way to think about it, he says.

It's the only way to think about it, she says.

After ten days, he is ready to go outside for a walk. In a light warm drizzle, they stroll through the Presidio to the waterfront.

She leads the way, pointing out the Golden Gate Bridge, Torpedo Wharf, Anita Rock, the yacht club. *We used to come down here most every morning when I was younger. Looking for something to put in the pot.*

At the yacht club?

If we'd been that type of people we wouldn't have needed to fish for our supper! But it was okay. We'd go before school and, with the day opening up over the water, I always felt . . . I don't know, like something good might arrive with all the light.

The edges of her mouth turn up. It's the dearest mouth he's ever seen.

Would you miss it? he asks, taking her small cool hand in his.

If what? she says, still looking out to sea.

If you married me and moved down to Los Angeles.

She turns to look at him. *Nope,* she says, her eyes sparkling like the water at their feet. *I wouldn't miss it a bit.*

He could kiss her all day, and all night, too, but he doesn't want to make a spectacle of her in public. Not his Barbara. So he kisses her once, just once, and there have been a few other girls, but it's the best kiss he's ever known.

Are you sure you're ready to throw your lot in with an old man like me? Ten days isn't very long to know someone. He is twenty-six years old, nearly seven years older than she. And being in the war ages a man.

She stretches up onto her tiptoes and kisses him again.

We'll have a lifetime to get to know each other, soldier.

She's been in the war, too. Not in the same way, but still.

———

"Michael?" Barbara says, holding a glass of lemonade out toward him. "Everything okay?"

His head is still light, his arms feel strange, uncomfortable, but the pain hasn't returned. Maybe this attack, whatever it was, is passing.

"I'm the one who is supposed to be asking you that," he says, working to keep his voice even. If he were to lay his hand on her belly, he would sense the heartbeat of his fifth child. For that he doesn't need his stethoscope.

Oh, Barbara! Every night he relives that magical first kiss by the water. Her small vibrant body never loses its warmth and mystery.

She laughs. "It takes more than a baby to stop me. Here: drink."

How cold the glass feels in his hand. Gingerly he lifts it to his lips and lets the cool, bitterly sweet liquid trickle down his throat. In an instant, the hair on his arms—not on his chest, for some reason he's never grown hair there—and legs stands up. His skull prickles. Fingertips of ice crawl up his body, prying into his every pore and crevice.

He sets the glass down on the lawn. But the chill has lodged; an icicle has made it to his right ventricle. His heart freezes up around it.

Is this it? Is it—

———

1933. Snow squeezes under his feet. White flakes scatter down from the trees and sneak under his collar. His feet slide as he tries to pull Jeanne on the sled up the hill; at twelve, his younger sister is already almost as tall as he is at fifteen.

But there's the house, peeking through the barren oaks over the hillside. Just ten minutes more. He needs to get Jeanne home before she catches pneumonia.

Let me walk, Michael.

No, no, Jeanne. We'll patch up the soles of your boots again this evening. For now, you stay put.

I can warm my feet up once we get home. It's all right. Jeanne jumps off the sled this time, not waiting for him to answer. Her frost-covered mittens reach for the sled's rope. *How about this? I'll pull the sled with our pails on it the rest of the way. You run ahead to start the fire.*

Jeanne!

Come on, Michael. It won't take me any longer than it would for you to pull me on the sled, so if you run ahead and get the fire going my feet will be able to start warming up sooner. They're already *soaked.*

There's no point in arguing. Jeanne is right. Mother goes on Father's rounds with him now that they have the car, which means the kitchen will be cold and empty, and it'll be up to him to get the fire going and supper started. Mother's the one who learned how to drive the car; she says their father became a different man after going off to the Great War—eight months before they became first-time parents, before they even knew he was going to be born—so she has had to become a different woman. But Father still attends to patients all day. Even though the first months of 1933 have been even worse than 1932 and most people have no cash to pay for his services.

He slip-slides the rest of his way up the hill. He'll have Jeanne read her lessons aloud while he starts on supper. He's going to be a physician, like his father; that's set in stone. Jeanne—she could be anything. She's a genius.

His arms stacked with wood, he uses an elbow to unlatch the kitchen door. Someone has left a basket of beets in lieu of payment on the kitchen table; before going to bed, his mother will carefully mark the beets down in her ledger, and that will be that. The beets are fine. He'll make beet-and-potato soup for dinner. But if only someone would leave some boots for Jeanne instead of leaving beets. Not even new boots, just better old ones than the hand-me-downs from him she's now wearing, their worn soles lined with cardboard. At almost six feet tall, Jeanne is outgrowing her shoes too fast to keep up with.

Stamp up and down, he tells her when she busts in the door, carrying their snow-covered lunch pails and satchels. *I'll have the room warm in a jiffy.*

He leaves the beets, kneels by the woodstove, and blows hard. Slowly the lick of flame grows. He draws the bench close and, just for a moment, sits on it beside his big little sister, savoring the warmth of the fire.

———

A bead of sweat runs down his forehead. The chill is gone from his arms and chest. In its place, a ball of heat, rising from his abdomen.

"That cloud's coming this way," Luke says. "Look—if you watch long enough, you can see it moving."

"Daddy says it won't rain." Francis's voice is so soft it's barely audible.

Francis—such a beautiful baby and now such a beautiful boy,

13

always a little apart from his older brothers and sister although only sixteen months younger than eleven-year-old Luke, nearly as close in age to Luke as Luke is to Mike Jr. Last night, he found Francis sitting alone in the half-dark of the garden shed, the book of Greek myths open on his lap. *What are you doing in here?* he asked.

Francis looked up at him and said sadly, *I could never be brave like you, Daddy. Save people.*

You mean be a doctor?

No. I mean brave like you were . . . over there.

Maybe they've been talking about the war in school. Or maybe it was just that book, sent to them at Christmas by Jeanne. All the bows and arrows, battles in it. Like Jeanne, the author, a man named Robert Graves, is a classicist.

You can be brave.

Francis shook his delicate head. *I want to be like you, Daddy, but I could never be a hero.*

Son, he said, *you never know how you'll be until you are tested.*

Blood rushes from his heart. Whoosh. And then, snap. The pain is back, this time a blow of thunder in his chest cavity.

"If your father says it won't rain, it won't rain." Barbara's voice sounds far, far away. "That tiny little cloud, Luke? You're worrying over that?"

The world grows dark, very dark. His head hits the lawn, knocking the glass of lemonade all over.

———

The oak trees on campus while he walks to the science laboratory, books in his arms, friends on either side of him. The breeze that flies through, shattering the leaves.

The rain, cold and alive and green.

14

———

"Stay with us, Michael! Stay with us!" Barbara is on her knees, be-side him. The bulge of her abdomen hits his chest; still, her arms circle his neck and draw him toward her. "Call an ambulance, Patty Ann!"

His heart is pounding, too loud, too jagged.

———

A cool breeze. Then calm. He is not sure where he is. He is no longer walking along a body-strewn road in the Philippines. He is no longer passing through winter, autumn, one season after another. He lays his whole body down flat; the breeze brushes over him. The ground beneath him feels soft and mossy. Rain begins to fall, and it is tender, warm, it is the sound of his sister's voice whispering to him to wake up on a school morning with the dawn just cracking through the windowpanes. It is Barbara. Her bright eyes wide-set and lustrous, her swift, light, determined steps, her way of clasping her hands together when laughing.

He is home. He is home.

BOOK TWO

1962–1973

Don't bother Max's cows. Let them moo in peace.

—Sign at Woodstock festival, 1969

Easter Sunday / April 22, 1962

BARBARA

A BROWN-SUGARED HAM is waiting in the fridge. Two dozen white eggs are lined up in two long cardboard cartons for the kids to dye for Easter.

It's not as though you wake up Good Friday morning and think: *When I go to bed tonight, my energetic forty-three-year-old husband will no longer be living.*

"Well," she says, tucking her handkerchief inside her shirtsleeve and using both hands to propel her belly-heavy body up from the sofa. "The wake will begin in an hour. I better start making sandwiches."

"You don't have to do that," Jeanne says, her voice wobbling toward the end of her sentence. Her sister-in-law's tears are like raindrops hanging off the end of a branch, waiting to fall. The anticipation is exhausting. "We could put out the things brought by your neighbors last evening."

"It makes her feel better to do something," Luke says. He's switched the television on, and filmy images of hundreds of British people halfway across the world in a Ban the Bomb march flit across the screen.

She lights a cigarette. She's going to make sandwiches. She'll use

that damn ham for them. "Can't you watch *Bullwinkle* or something that normal eleven-year-old boys watch, Luke? Where are
your brothers and sister? Go find Patty Ann and tell her to help you
dye the Easter eggs."

"No one wants to dye eggs, Mom."

If Michael were here, he would tell Luke off for speaking to her
like that. She draws on her cigarette so hard the smoke hurts her
lungs. But Michael isn't here.

"Okay, Luke," she says. "It was just a suggestion."

In the kitchen, she ties on an apron and hoists the ham out of
the fridge. Normally, Michael would be carving this up. They'd be
just back from church, the table would be all set, and they would
be sitting down together to Easter dinner. One of the kids would
give a blessing. Another of the kids would crack an Easter egg on an
unsuspecting brother's head—probably Luke on Mike Jr.'s. Michael
would gently reprimand Luke while she tried not to laugh, and
then they'd inspect the remaining Easter eggs, admiring their bright
colors and prettiness.

That's how it would be. That's how it *should* be.

"Here—let me do that," Jeanne says, following her into the
kitchen.

But that's *not* how it is. Because Michael is not here.

But the kids are. And Michael's sister, Jeanne, and their eight-
year-old niece, Molly, who have flown across the country to
join them, are, too. Her parents, who have never been more
than fifty miles outside of San Francisco before, will arrive by
overnight bus tomorrow in time for the funeral. Father O'Malley,
their neighbors and friends, Michael's colleagues from the hospital, possibly the milkman and newspaper delivery boy, perhaps
someone from the Veterans Administration, although she declined
to request a space for Michael in the already overcrowded Los

Angeles National Cemetery. They will all soon arrive to share their condolences.

And then there will be the day after. And then the day after that. And after that, until the day she joins Michael six feet under.

Jeanne's husband, Paul, walked out a few years ago and never came back, but Jeanne's only got the one kid and has a good job teaching Greek and Latin at a fancy girls' college on the East Coast. She, on the other hand, is almost thirty-seven with almost five kids and not even a college diploma. What does she know how to do, other than be a wife to Michael and a mother to their children? God in heaven, at least let there be a decent pension or whatever it is that goes to a widow. Somehow she has to keep this family going.

The baby pokes her gut, hard. She pats the solid knob that is either the baby's head or the butt. Butt, fingers crossed—by now the baby should be in position for entering the world.

Time isn't going to stand still while she figures things out.

"Is he moving?" Jeanne says, her long pale face an artless blend of concern and envy. At forty-one, there's no chance of Jeanne having a second child now. Not with her lousy husband MIA. "Are you okay?"

"Oh, he's gotten too big to move. Just an elbow or knee every now and then." *She she she,* she thinks. She and Michael have both been hoping for a second girl.

"Far along as you are, Barbara, you still look so light."

Light? She feels so heavy she could fall right through to the other side of the world and come out in China. Maybe light to Jeanne— Jeanne, Lord bless her, is as tall as a man. Taller than most men, actually. Taller than Jeanne's husband, Paul, was. "Thank you, I guess."

But she would not come out in China. Nowhere on that side of the Pacific. She'd sooner burn up at the center of the earth.

While Jeanne hacks at the ham, she lines up slices of white bread, opens jars of Kraft mayonnaise and French's mustard, tears off big crinkly leaves of lettuce. It feels good to do something manageable. With four kids, plus Francis's friend Eugene always around, and any other of the kids' friends who may happen to be over at any given time, she's used to feeding the troops. She picks up the cigarette she set down in the seashell ashtray Luke made for her in second grade and inhales slowly then exhales, letting the smoke stream out her nostrils.

The baby grinds down hard against her pelvis.

She stabs the butt of the cigarette into the ashtray and takes out the Melmac serving platter, white with a spray of spindly blue, green, and pink flowers around the edge. She and Michael bought a full dinner set when they moved down from San Francisco. So young, so inexperienced. So proud to be picking out housewares with her handsome new husband. *How many plates should I get?* she asked. *The entire set,* Michael told her. And in this way it was agreed they would fill their home together with children and life, and everything that had happened over the last years would be left behind them. That was the plan, anyhow.

She whacks the platter down on the counter. "They got him in the end. The Japs."

Jeanne sighs. "Oh, Barbara."

If she didn't have the kids around, if her sister-in-law hadn't flown across the country to stand beside her in her kitchen, if a river of well-meaning well-wishers wouldn't soon begin to stream through their home, she would throw the platter across the room.

Although it wouldn't break. *Melmac.*

"I guess I should cut the crusts off the bread. Make them look nicer." But she doesn't; after all these years, she still can't bring herself to waste food. After what he went through in the Pacific,

Michael couldn't throw food away, either. They were completely in tune about this. They were in tune about everything.

She uses a spoon to air-drop mayonnaise across half of the slices of bread, then slaps a piece of ham and a leaf of lettuce on top of each.

A perfect, perfect man. A perfect husband.

Last evening, one of the neighbors brought over a tentlike black dress for her. *I don't mean to intrude, dear. But I thought it might be handy.*

I'm not going to wear black on Monday. I'm going to wear yellow.

Be reasonable, dear. You can't wear yellow to your husband's funeral.

Michael.

She *loved* him. God almighty, how she loved him.

She smashes the other half of the slices of bread on top, then picks up the meat cleaver, because it's the closest to her, and quarters the sandwiches. The cleaver leaves fissures on the cutting board. She's wearing the yellow maternity dress now. She bought it to wear for Easter, and she's going to wear it today, on Easter. She'll wear it again tomorrow for the funeral, too, if she wants.

"Can I help, Mom?" Mike Jr. keeps a careful distance from her. "I've put away everything from . . . outside."

Poor Mike Jr. He doesn't want to talk about the sun on their backs, the lemonade tinkling in the pitcher, everyone so happy. The last moments of life as it was. Mike Jr. went out as the sun was going down yesterday and finished the painting, without a word to anyone as to what he was doing.

"That's a good boy," she says, laying the knife down and ruffling his short tawny hair. "Where are your sister and brothers?"

"I told Luke to help me clean up, but he said he was thinking. Patty Ann is in her bedroom with the door shut. I guess Francis is over at Eugene's."

"Well, go tell Patty Ann to come give me a hand."

"Molly, too," Jeanne says. "Your cousin can help, too."

"Molly went with Francis," Mike says.

"Who is Eugene?" Jeanne asks, looking up. "Is he that curly-haired boy?"

She picks up the cleaver again. A few months ago at lunch, two ladies started talking about how having Eugene's parents in the neighborhood is an embarrassment. *I hear the husband takes a shotgun up into the hills to hunt rabbits toward the end of the month,* one of the ladies said. *Kick a fella when he's down, why don't you? They're decent people,* she said, standing up from the table. It's no one's fault the father lost his right thumb and, with it, his job as a plumber. In a way, Eugene's parents remind her of her own, struggling all those years just to keep food on the table. Her father still works in the cigar-box factory; during the worst years, he couldn't even get that. The kids make a funny pair—Francis, fair and quiet, and Eugene, with his mother's black ringlets and a mouth that won't stop—but it's good Francis has a best friend to keep him company through this.

She's just not gentle enough for Francis. Michael could be so patient.

"Yes," she says, wielding the cleaver on the last of the sandwiches. "A good kid. Look, let's boil up those eggs also. We'll devil them."

She doesn't want to have to see them in there later, all lined up and ready for a family life that now will never be lived.

Oh, Michael!

At three on the dot, the doorbell rings. Father O'Malley with his shadow, Mrs. Dawson, the woman who runs catechism for the parish.

"My dear child," Father O'Malley says, taking her hand into his soft one. "We can only be glad our Michael has gone to a better place."

Something inside her rises up. A better place? Than here with her and their children? She has to refrain from kicking him.

"Thank you, Father," she says, leading him into the living room. She has to pull herself together. In the end, this awful day isn't about her. It's about Michael. Michael, who struggled so hard to survive and ended up like this. "Patty Ann will get you tea. This is Michael's sister, Jeanne. She has come out from New York."

"New York City?" Mrs. Dawson says, frowning.

"Poughkeepsie," Jeanne says. "It's about an hour and a half north by train."

Father installs himself on the brown leather recliner, where Michael liked to sit and read the paper after dinner. Mrs. Dawson roosts on the sofa next to Father and sets in on Jeanne. Mrs. Dawson is the congregation's most insufferable gossip, never far from Father O'Malley's ear—so devoted, but with a heart like a hollow chocolate. It's hard to know whom Mrs. Dawson tormented more, Patty Ann or Luke, during the two years of First Communion preparation. Or Francis, for that matter, although Francis never said a word about it—apparently, he never said a word during the classes, either. *Does he ever talk?* Mrs. Dawson stopped them after church to ask once. *Of course he talks,* Michael said. *When there's someone who is actually listening.*

How is Francis going to manage without his father to defend him? To show him how to be a man? Of the three boys, Francis will need Michael the most.

The doorbell again.

The living room begins to fill. Everyone seems to have heard and come out, even on an Easter afternoon, to pay his or her respects. Everyone who ever meets Michael remembers and likes him.

Met.

Liked.

Patty Ann and Mike Jr.'s homeroom teachers arrive together. Patty Ann's teacher says, "Such a smart, popular girl. I am sure she will be all right."

Mike Jr.'s teacher nods. "Such a solid, responsible boy. Mike will be fine."

"Thank you so much," she says. "They're good kids."

Luke's teacher isn't with them—probably too embarrassed to show up after giving Luke a D in comportment. Michael thought they should consider switching Luke to a private school next year, where there would be fewer students and more time for teachers to talk with them.

But private schools are expensive. How is she going to do that now?

Eugene's parents, Mr. and Mrs. Kozma, hesitate just outside the front door. Molly and Eugene stand behind them, whispering something, maybe encouraging them to step in. It can't be easy for the Kozmas to come today, knowing that so many people in the neighborhood who look down on them will be here. The kids at school probably pick on Eugene also.

But that's right. Francis's teacher hasn't shown up, either. Maybe Francis is so quiet at school his teacher has forgotten he's in her class.

"Please come in," she says, making her way around a group of guests to shake the Kozmas' hands. "Where's Francis?" she asks Eugene.

Eugene pushes up on his glasses. "He's not here?"

"We were playing marbles," Molly says. "He suddenly walked away."

"We figured he'd come home, Mrs. Gannon." Eugene lifts the cloth bag. "I brought his marbles for him."

Is she losing control so swiftly? She could have sworn Francis hasn't come in. "How long ago?"

Molly and Eugene look at each other.

"Maybe three hours?" Eugene says.

Molly nods. At eight, Molly is the image of her mother, already taller than Eugene, although he's a year older. Not taller than Francis, though—those Gannon genes. Such a nice girl, too. Even under this visit's terrible circumstance, she and Francis fell right back in together. And Francis doesn't usually fall right in with anyone, other than Eugene. He gets invited onto the teams and to all the other kids' birthday parties, but it doesn't seem to mean much to him. Michael says it's just the way Francis is. Some people like to be part of a crowd. Francis doesn't.

Said.

"Your dad popped his head out back to let you know they were home from Easter mass," Molly says. "And it was just after that."

"We don't take Eugene to mass, anymore. You know, ma'am, the incense," Mr. Kozma says.

Mrs. Kozma nods, the homemade net on her hat bobbing. "It's not good for his asthma."

On Sundays, her mother also wore a hat like Mrs. Kozma's, with a homemade net that sprung up and down during reception of the sacrament. But for her, with a baby in her arms or at least a toddler, little hands reaching up to play with anything available, hat wearing always was too impractical. Soon, very soon, there will be another baby. Michael will never get to know whether it's another boy or the second girl. She touches her stomach, feels that hard roundness, the life in there.

"Yes, of course," she says. Last Sunday, after Palm Sunday mass, Michael had gotten out the camera. *Oh, for heaven's sake. I look like a cow,* she protested. *You look beautiful,* Michael said and gave the camera to Eugene, who'd been waiting on the front step for them to return from church. *Can you take a photo of us all, son? I'll show you how. You just press here.* Thank God, now, Michael had Eugene take that picture. When she gets the film developed, she'll have copies made for all the children. She'll have the original framed and set it in the living room. "Please help yourself to refreshments. Thank you for coming."

She beckons to Patty Ann. "Is Francis in the boys' bedroom?"

Patty Ann has tried to hide the puffiness of her eyes with the heavy use of a compact, presumably hers. Patty Ann has been forbidden to own makeup before turning sixteen. "I haven't seen him."

"Can you please go take a look? And Patty Ann, I think not the powder."

Patty Ann returns a few minutes later, powder still present, a sullen look added. "He's not there, Mom."

Francis knew what time the wake was starting. There's no excuse for him staying out to play. There's no excuse for him playing at all today. And yet she can't find the vim inside herself to get angry. "All right," she tells Patty Ann. "Go find Mike Jr., then, and tell him to check the school playground. You go look in the toolshed."

"But Mom—"

"Oh, for Pete's sake, Patty Ann," she says, seeing Mrs. Dawson heading toward them, turning away from her daughter. "Not *now*."

"Well, at least," Mrs. Dawson says, reaching for her hand, "a person who leaves us on Good Friday goes straight to heaven."

"What the hell are you talking about?" she says, pulling her hand back, something snapping deep inside. "Michael would go straight to heaven no matter what day he died."

Mrs. Dawson pretends not to have heard, busying herself with extracting gloves from her boxy purse and then carefully fitting each finger in its place. "I'm so sorry to have to leave already, dear. My parents. Easter. But I'll be back to fetch Father."

She put her own white gloves aside, laying them in the top

drawer of her dresser next to the children's baptismal candles some-time between her first and fourth baby, with the blessing of Michael, who liked to feel the smooth skin of her hand in his.

Michael's hand in hers. His grip, warm and promising.

"Please don't trouble yourself about Father," she says, collecting herself. She can do better than this. "We will make sure someone brings him back to the rectory."

"Oh, dear, no. Please don't even think about it."

"No, *really*. You take care of your folks. We will take care of Father."

"I can't find him Mom," Mike Jr. says, coming through the door. In his Sunday suit and with his wrinkled brow, at thirteen, Mike Jr. already looks like a little man. "He's not in the yard. He's not in the car. I went all the way around the block plus down to the school and didn't see him."

"Oh, heavens! Did you lose one of your children, Mrs. Gannon?" Mrs. Dawson says.

From the book of Job: *Gird up now thy loins like a man; for I will demand of thee, and answer thou me.*

"No. The . . . dog."

"You have a dog, too?"

"No. I mean, yes," she says, ignoring Mike Jr.'s startled expression. "I mean our neighbor's dog. We look out for him."

"Really? As if you don't already have enough to think about!"

She places a hand firmly on Mrs. Dawson's arm and steers her through the door. "Do not worry about the dog, Mrs. Dawson. Or about Father. We will get them both home safely."

She closes the door.

"Mom?"

"Oh, don't ask. Where in the dickens is your little brother?"

Although the baby of the family, Francis has always demanded the least attention from her, happy riding his bike around with Eugene or trailing after his father. Why does he have to cause trouble right now? "Go talk to Eugene. Maybe he'll have some other ideas."

More people stream in, and still more. Some are dressed in their Easter clothes, some have changed into something more somber. Michael's kind elderly partner, Dr. Zimmerman, and his wife arrive, looking shell-shocked.

"Shouldn't you be sitting, Barbara?" he says.

But she can't sit. She knows she is supposed to preside on the sofa while people take turns perching beside her, pressing her hand, offering up remembrances. *Once when I had a flat tire, Michael . . . Such a nice baritone voice; we'll miss hearing it on Sundays . . . Michael was the smartest of us interns at the hospital, but he shared notes with everyone.* They want to talk at her. They want her to help them with their shock, their own sadness, unloading their memories upon her. But who will be brave enough to acknowledge that while Michael's gone, she's still here, her heart ripped out?

In one corner, several men are discussing President Kennedy and the Soviets and Cuba. They stop when she draws near. By the dining room table, a group of mothers grows silent when she approaches. School, kids, politics, America. The weather. *I'm still here,* she wants to tell them. *I have to keep going. Please help me to pretend life is normal.*

If she sits down, she will fall apart. Her body will give out; her heart will give out. She will never ever get up again.

The room swirls around her, a blur of pale faces and somber colors, like sick flooding her home.

"Allow me to offer my sincerest condolences," a smooth-skinned man in a neat blue suit says, intercepting her passage, extending a hand.

Who is this? There is something familiar about him, but he's too well dressed to be the milkman or postman out of uniform.

"You and I haven't been introduced," he continues, "but I've had the pleasure of speaking with your husband after church—while you were otherwise engaged—on several occasions. Ronnie McCloskey."

"I was running after the kids, probably."

He smiles and extracts a business card from his inner pocket. "Look. If you need help, something you need a man for..." His face reddens, and he adds quickly, "Maybe to move something or fix something, please don't hesitate to call me. I don't have a family of my own. I have time. I will be glad to help."

The card lies dumbly in her hand: RONALD M. MCCLOSKEY, PRESIDENT, MCCLOSKEY AIR CONDITIONERS.

"The boys will be as big as men soon," she says, realizing even as she says it how rude she sounds. Mr. McCloskey is just trying to be nice. They're all just trying to be nice.

"Yes, of course," he says, shifting a little in his handsome suit.

She stuffs the card into the pocket of her dress and turns away. Los Angeles was the special home she and Michael carved out for themselves, just themselves, their own personal history. Here she is now, alone, miles away from family. But what family does she have anywhere who could help her? Her brother is dead. Her parents barely manage. Both were first-generation Americans; there are some cousins in northern California, but none she's seen or even spoken with in years. And then there's Jeanne, clear across the continent. Not long after she and Michael married, her in-laws both succumbed to the polio epidemic.

Someone ushers her toward the sofa. "The eulogies are going to begin now, Barbara." She stops to stand beside Father O'Malley's chair. Mike Jr. joins her; she leans against his shoulder. Luke takes his place on the other side of her.

"We shouldn't call it a living room today," Luke whispers. "We should call it a dying room."

"Shh. *Luke.*"

It's just a dream. An awful dream. Tomorrow morning, dawn will creep in between the drapes, and Michael's warm body will stir in the bed next to her. He will put his arms around her. They will make love before the children awaken. He will dress for work. She will hurry to get breakfast on the table.

The baby suddenly drives down hard. She balls her fist in her mouth to keep from gasping.

"There, there, dear," someone says from behind her, patting her back.

"When we give tribute to Michael," Father O'Malley says, "we also have to give tribute to the great faith that kept him going during even the darkest days of the war. Throughout, he ceaselessly strove to save the lives of his fellow soldiers. He never gave up. He never gave in. Michael Gannon was a true hero. And our Lord was his hero."

"I need to sit down," she says.

Space is hurriedly made for her on the sofa next to Patty Ann, Jeanne, and Molly. Luke crowds in beside her. Mike Jr. stands over them. Someone brings her a glass of water.

With her family resettled, Father O'Malley continues. When he is done, Dr. Zimmerman starts speaking. And then someone else. The words drum against her, but she won't let them inside. The only way to keep going is to pretend it isn't happening.

Finally, all the words stop.

People begin to take their leave. They come up to her, kiss her cheek, press her upper arm. Patty Ann gets up brusquely from the sofa and walks away.

"May heaven comfort you," Dr. Zimmerman says, taking her hand, before she can go after Patty Ann, try to say something that could make this all less terrible.

"You can count on us," Mrs. Zimmerman says.

"Thank you," she says. "Thank you for coming."

Women she is friendly with from the neighborhood, from the school, from church will bring casseroles for a week or two. When the baby is born they will bring still more. There will be meetings with Dr. Zimmerman, and maybe someone at the VA, and with a lawyer. But in the end, there will just be her and Patty Ann and Mike Jr. and Luke and Francis and the baby.

Oh, God.

"Are you sure Francis didn't say anything about where he was going?" she asks Molly. "Nothing at all?"

"What's going on?" Jeanne says.

"Aunt Barbara can't find Francis."

"Since when?"

"Since a little after we went to Eugene's."

"But Barbara," Jeanne says. "That was *hours* ago."

She catches sight of the well-dressed man from earlier, the one who gave her a business card, one of the last to file out the door. "Mike Jr.," she says. "See that man? Can you please ask him to take Father O'Malley back to the rectory? Where's Patty Ann gone?"

"Maybe you should call someone, Mom," Mike Jr. says.

Call someone? Whom? There is only she.

"I'll go see about Patty Ann," Jeanne says. "You just sit."

So, so heavy. The baby is grinding down against her pelvis again. *Stop that! Not now! Not already!* "That's okay, Jeanne. I have to get up to look for Francis anyhow."

"Patty Ann is talking to the police," Molly announces, pointing.

"What?" She and Jeanne swivel in the direction of Molly's finger.

There on the front step is Patty Ann, the powder on her face streaked with tears, speaking with a young police officer.

She hoists herself to her feet, Jeanne rising beside her. "What's going on?" she says, bracing herself with a hand on the doorjamb. She looks past Patty Ann and the officer to the street, at the mourners getting into their cars or walking home along the sidewalk. And at the curb in front, a police car, the back door open. Francis stands beside it, held firmly in place by a second police officer.

"Oh, no," Jeanne says.

Francis looks a little dusty, a little embarrassed. No blood, no bruises.

"Oh, for Pete's sake," she says, relief warming her face and hands.

"We found your son, ma'am, at the bus station," the young officer says, looking back and forth between her and Jeanne. "He won't say how he got there. He wouldn't say where he was trying to go, either. That *is* your son? One of you is Mrs. Michael Gannon?"

The bus station? "Oh, Francis!"

Francis looks down at his feet. A smudge of dirt shadows his delicate cheekbone.

"Yes," she says. "That's my son. I'm sorry, officer."

"Ma'am—" the officer begins.

"Oh, leave her alone," Luke says. "My dad just died, okay? This is his wake."

"Luke! Don't speak to the officer that way."

The young policeman glances at her stomach, looks at Luke and then at Mike Jr., Patty Ann, and Molly. Then he looks at Francis. "My condolences, ma'am."

"She's not mine," she says reflexively, of Molly.

"Excuse me?" the police officer says.

"Oh, never mind." She smothers a sob.

"Here, Mom," Patty Ann says, handing her a soiled tissue.

"No, no," she says, extracting the handkerchief from within her shirtsleeve.

The other police officer releases Francis. He shuffles toward the house, still avoiding her eyes, as the policemen get back into their car.

"I'm sorry," he says.

"Where, Francis?" she says, touching his thin shoulder.

He scuffs the ground. "Nowhere."

"All right." Because what else is she supposed to say? Because how could he run away right now, just when the going gets tough? Because who wouldn't want to run away from this—but how is it conceivable that one of Michael's children would? Michael never ran away from anything in his life. Not running away *was* Michael. She lets her hand drop. There's going to be work ahead. "Okay. Get into the house now."

The kids file back into the house, Luke following Patty Ann and Mike Jr., Francis following Luke. Molly brings up the rear. This is what it will look like tomorrow, she thinks. All of them behind Michael's casket.

She stops in front of the open door, breathes deeply.

"What will you do?" Jeanne asks in a soft voice.

"That," she says, "is the question."

Not today. Not tomorrow. But the day after. And every day after that.

A Marriage / August 26, 1965

FRANCIS

FRANCIS STIRS HIS FINGERS through the sand, combing for flat pebbles. It's not so hot as it has been, and the sudden cool feels like a billboard announcing the first day of school. He'll be turning east up Brookhaven, in the opposite direction from the beach, come Monday morning. Another nine and a half months cooped up in a classroom.

"Let's go out onto the pier."

Eugene shakes his head. "I don't have any money."

"Doesn't matter. To look at the water." They have the whole sea in front of them here on the beach, so he adds, "Let's see if anyone's caught anything."

He needs to get up and move.

They drag their bikes through the sand, lean them against a pillar, and tie their tennis shoes around the handlebars. Then they look at each other and, without speaking, break into a sprint.

He hits the middle of the pier way ahead. It's really not fair to race. After all, Eugene's got the asthma.

"Here," he says, pulling up short. "I'll buy us Cokes."

"Boss!" Eugene says, dropping his hands onto his knees beside him, panting.

"Ugh. Don't say that."

"Why not?"

"Cause it makes you sound like a candy-ass."

The pier feels empty—they find no fishermen and none of the usual couples, either. Two or three tourists wander around looking sun-struck, although today's almost cloudy. The whole beach is quieter than usual for an afternoon in August, especially for the last Thursday before school starts back up. People are keeping to themselves since that Negro neighborhood went crazy. Even his mom, whom nothing ever scares, told him not to wander too far from home when he left this morning. And not because she thought he might try to run away yet again.

There's only enough change in his pocket for one soda. He pops the top and hands the bottle to Eugene. "Share?"

"Yeah."

They lean their stomachs against the pier railing, passing the bottle back and forth between them. Up toward Pacific Palisades, surfers bob on the swells, little specks in the distance, like brightly colored seagulls. It takes more than riots to keep the surfers away.

"You think we should learn to surf?" Eugene says.

"Nope."

"Why not?"

He shrugs. "I don't dig the sea enough."

"Oh, come on. Who doesn't dig the sea? Well, except David Balfour."

"Who?"

"You know. In *Kidnapped,* the summer book. The one we were supposed to read."

"You *read* that? Since when do you do the summer reading?"

Eugene looks sheepish. "My mom made me."

"Did she read it to you, too?"

Eugene punches him in the arm, but not hard. "It was a good book. Well, not that bad."

They walk down toward the end of the pier. A collection of trawlers plows slowly through the Pacific a few miles out.

"What do you see?" Eugene asks, squinting. "With those eagle eyes of yours."

The sun has made its way toward the horizon. It glints off the mast of one of the boats; there is action below, something being pulled onto the deck. The sun-way along the sea's surface makes the water seem even darker, almost metallic.

"Nothing. Boats."

He has better than twenty-twenty vision. Unlike Eugene, who has to wear glasses.

"Maybe I'll become a sailor," Eugene says, "when I leave school. Get out of here, see the world."

"Not me, man. Being trapped out in the middle of the sea on a boat is about the worst thing I can think of."

"That's stupid. Worse than having your fingernails pulled out? Or being pinned above a bamboo plant until it grows right through you?"

"Shut up, Eugene."

Eugene picks at a scab on his wrist. "I'm sorry. I didn't mean to say that."

He and Eugene never talk about the stuff that was done to prisoners of war in the Pacific. Some of the other boys at school do, though, trading the stories back and forth as though they were baseball cards.

A tern soars by, its sharp orange beak and feet narrowly missing their heads. It flaps its wings hard and dives. He takes one of the pebbles from his pocket and pitches it into the sea.

"If your father was alive," Eugene says, "he could show us how to skip it."

Eugene's dad can't skip stones. Eugene's dad lost his right thumb and can't hold anything properly. Including a job—or so the kids at school like to say. But his own dad was a master at skipping stones. Even from up high here on the Santa Monica Pier. His dad could do anything.

His dad was a *hero*.

Thirty feet below, the Pacific swirls and swells, the water deep green-blue and unknowable. There must be things living inside it, a whole other world, but nothing is visible. The tide is in; the sea is at its highest. He spits as hard as he can. He and Eugene crane over to watch the gob fall.

He starts unbuttoning his shirt. "Let's jump."

"No way."

He stuffs his shirt into his back pocket.

"Come on, Francis," Eugene says, frowning. "I don't want to die."

The air feels soft on his bare chest. He pulls himself up on the railing and throws a leg over. "So, don't. Meet me back by the bi-cycles."

"If the lifeguard sees he'll skin us alive."

"Not a problem if we've died."

"If we don't bust into a million pieces when we hit, we still have to swim all the way back to the beach. There are great whites out here."

"It's not so far. Surfers come out this far."

"So? You know how your feet look after you've been sitting in a bathtub for a long time? All loose and shriveled? That's what surfers' brains look like."

"Pff."

"It's true."

He swings his other leg over the railing and stands on the thin wooden ledge directly above the water, holding on to the pier with just one hand behind him. The breeze licks the back of his neck

39

and down his thin shoulder blades. The water seethes way below, completely indifferent to him.

Silently, he lets go. His feet slice the air; his heart lifts and rises right out of his body. He doesn't care if he dies, doesn't care if his body explodes into a million pieces when it touches the water. For a moment, he is like the tern—fast, free, soaring.

Slap.

He goes under, his mouth filling with the Pacific. The water is shockingly cold. His legs begin to kick. They fight his way back up to the light.

"Yeeeee-hawwww!" Eugene hits the water a few feet away, his dark curls disappearing underneath its surface.

He swims over, fumbling in the water to find his friend. The sea really is cold out here, much colder than he expected.

"Aaarugh," Eugene sputters, emerging, spitting water.

They look at each other and begin to laugh. They roll with the waves, laughing, until their lips start to turn blue. Then they swim as hard as they can back toward the shore.

They bike home through the waning afternoon. Eugene sounds out of breath, so he slows his pedaling. Eugene's glasses, swiftly crammed inside his pants during the dive, are crooked. If their mothers find out what they did, there will be trouble.

"You coming over?" he asks when they reach his house.

"Nah. I promised my mom I'd be home before sundown. You know."

He does know. Talk about the riots is everywhere. On the television, on the radio, in his house.

Luke at the table, last night: *They have good reason to complain. People treat Negroes like dirt here in Los Angeles.*

Mike: *That doesn't give them a reason to tear up their own neighborhood.*

Patty Ann: *Oh, shut up, both of you. We're starting a world war over in Vietnam. Why not set our own backyard on fire?*

Which made his mom stand up from the table, sharply enough to rattle the dishes.

Patricia Ann, his mom said, *that's enough. You do not know what you are talking about. I'd like to see* you *live under the Communists.*

It's enough to make him want to hide under a rock when they get started like that. Luke with Mike, Patty Ann with his mom. When his dad was alive, no one ever argued. Or at least very rarely. When Luke didn't help wash the car. Or Patty Ann held hands with a boy in grade school. Patty Ann was his dad's, Luke his mom's. Mike was everyone's. That left no one for him, but at least there was a balance in the house. Nowadays, it's like an ongoing game of Chinese checkers, the rest of them jumping over one another, clickety-clack, no one ever winning. His little sister, Sissy, at only three, folds her arms over her chest like a mini Buddha and tut-tut-tuts. Sometimes it makes his mom stop quarreling and laugh. Sometimes no one seems to hear her. But he hears her. He hears everyone.

Sissy is sitting on their mom's bedroom floor as he slips past it to the boys' room at the end of the hall, facing the bathroom. She looks up at him, and he puts a finger to his lips. She won't give him away. For a three-year-old, Sissy's all right.

"Francis!" his mom calls out.

He drops his wet shorts on his bedroom floor and pulls a dry pair out of his dresser drawer. Luke is lying on his bed reading *God Bless You, Mr. Rosewater,* a novel by Kurt Vonnegut. Luke says Kurt Vonnegut is a genius and his books should be required reading for the whole world.

"Mom called you," Luke says, turning a page.

"Yes, I did." His mom is standing in the doorway. "Didn't you hear me? I want you to carry some boxes to the car for the Labor Day church sale."

He follows her back down the hall. Two boxes of neatly folded clothes stand on the floor of her bedroom. "This, too," she says, taking one last dress from the closet. He can see his dad's four suits hanging in there, as though waiting for his dad to appear in his undershirt and boxers and black socks to button up a dress shirt and put one of them on for work. His dad's dress shoes, still shiny, wait below them.

The dress in her hand is the one she wore to the wake. Yellow, like the paint they had just put on the house.

It has to be yellow. Almost the last thing his dad said.

He takes the dress from his mom and stuffs it under the other clothes.

"Come on, Francis. Not like that. It will get all wrinkled."

His mom pulls it back out, folds it in half, then quarters it. She lays it on top of the box. Then she looks at it.

"Never mind," she says, picking it up again and shaking it smooth. A calling card falls out of the pocket. "I'll keep this one a little longer."

He picks up the card and reads it silently: RONALD M. MCCLOSKEY, PRESIDENT, MCCLOSKEY AIR CONDITIONERS.

"Oh, look at that," his mom says, taking it from him. "That man goes to our church. I forgot he gave me his card."

"Are you going to give away Dad's things, too?"

His mom smiles—not her strong, happy smile, but the other, softer one she's developed since his dad died—and shakes her head. "Just my maternity clothes. I won't need them anymore, but someday you may want your father's things. You're going to be just like him. Maybe even taller."

He bows his head. Maybe he'll be as tall as his dad. Everyone says he looks like him. But he'll never *be* like his dad. He'll never be brave. He'll never be a hero. He never would have made it out of the Philippines alive, much less helped anyone else survive. He practically got both him and Eugene killed on the pier earlier today, just by being an idiot as usual.

"Oh, don't look so down, Francis. I know it's hard. It's hard for everyone. Here," she says, rummaging on the shelf above the clothing rack. "Why don't you take this now?"

It's his dad's old army canteen. Once, when he was little, his dad took the canteen out and showed it to him and Luke and Mike Jr., saying: *This canteen meant the difference between life and death for me during the war. Without it I would never have made it up Bataan, much less through the three years that followed. Sometimes it's the littlest things, boys.* It was unusual for his dad even to talk about the war, so they all knew what he was telling them was something important.

Shouldn't one of his brothers have the canteen? Wouldn't they be mad if they found out their mom gave it to him? He screws the top off and peeks carefully inside, as though a little bit of his dad might be distilled within.

"Mommy," Sissy says from where she is lying on the carpet furiously coloring, her hair a shout of red-gold around her round, freckly face. Everything his baby sister does, she seems to do furiously. "Will you read to me now?"

His mom is strangely still, far away. It takes her at least a minute to answer. "Ask Luke, dear. I have to get started on dinner now. Mike and Patty Ann will be home soon."

Mike has a full-time summer job bagging groceries at the Safeway. Patty Ann is waitressing at Peter B's Galley, in the bowling alley. She got Luke a job in the alley also, on Friday and Saturday nights, plus Luke has taken over mowing the lawn for the church and rectory while Mike is bagging groceries. Next summer, his mom says, he should get a job, too: *With you getting bigger, you're going to want more pocket money. Anyhow, it's important to learn how to work, as important as book learning.*

Francis should get a job bagging groceries like Mike, Luke said. *All the ladies will head for the register he's working and tip him double if he carries their bags to their cars. He'll earn enough for his own set of wheels twice as fast as Mike will.*

Hush, his mom said, laughing. *That's no way to talk. He's still a baby.*

If anyone can set his mom laughing, it's Luke. But he's not a baby. He's not a man, but he's not a baby, either.

He stuffs the canteen into the top of his pants, bundles the two boxes up with string, and carries them, one by one, out to the car. He didn't even understand what was so funny about what Luke said. Maybe it didn't mean anything. Maybe it was Luke making fun of Mike somehow.

In the kitchen, his mom is trying to get the oven to light. The oven hasn't worked properly for more than a year. Sissy follows him down the hall to his bedroom. "Read me this?" she says, climbing onto Luke's bed and sticking the book in her hand between Luke's face and novel.

Luke pushes the book's bright green, red, yellow, and blue cover away. "I'm already reading something. And *Goodnight Moon* is a baby book. You're not a baby."

"I like it."

"It's a going-to-bed book."

"Please, Luke." Sissy crawls up beside him and tucks her bright head against his shoulder. "Luke, Luke, Lukie-Luke."

Luke sighs and sets his book down.

He shoves the canteen under his mattress. It makes a big lump. His mom should have given the canteen to Mike. Mike plans to join the army in two years, or at least go ROTC. He may be the only one tall enough ever to wear his dad's suits, but Mike's the one who will *be* like their father.

"A bowl of mush?" Luke says, looking up from his reading. "Why is there mush in the room where the bunny is going to sleep, anyhow?"

He hastens to lie down over the lump the canteen has made in his mattress, to conceal it.

"What's mush?" Sissy asks.

"Some gross thing Mom probably ate during the war when there was rationing."

"What's rationing?"

"What you should do with your questions."

Sissy purses her little mouth. Her red locks stick up in the air. "So you mean mush is like tapioca pudding?"

"Exactly."

"Hey!" Mike says, marching into the room in his grocery-store shirt, making straight for his piggy bank. Clink-clink goes his tip money. His big brother is saving to buy a car for college. Patty Ann is supposed to be saving her tips for use at college, too, but their mom says she wastes it on buying sodas and hamburgers for her good-for-nothing boyfriend. Luke spent most of his last paycheck on books, including two novels by Kurt Vonnegut. "Why aren't you listening to the game? The Dodgers are playing the Mets."

"That's it, kiddo," Luke says, dislodging Sissy. Baseball is one thing Luke and Mike never disagree about. Neither of them misses a game. "I'll read the rest to you tonight before you go to sleep."

"You're almost done!"

"I'll finish what I haven't read after the game, and then I'll read it all the way through again. Deal?"

Sissy smiles and jumps up. For a three-year-old, Sissy knows how to drive a good bargain.

Alone in the bedroom now, he extracts the canteen from under his mattress. The surface is smooth and silver in his hand, flat on two sides and rounded on the others, with small dents here and there where it must have banged hard against a Far Eastern rock or a ship deck. Only the chain securing the cap is rusted, a little bit along the seam where the curved top joins with the bottom.

It was once in his dad's hands. His dad lifted it to his mouth and drank from it. Other soldiers may have, too.

"Aren't you going to join your brothers listening to the game?" His mom stands in the doorway, watching him.

He slides the canteen back under his pillow. His mom is always trying to get him to do stuff with the others.

"Francis?"

His mom's dark hair bounces gently against her chin. She tips her head and smiles at him. He can almost imagine her stepping off the pier herself, throwing herself into the air, way above the water, her sudden grin, the toss of her head. She'd be mighty unhappy if she knew he'd done it, though. People have killed themselves jumping off the pier.

"Okay, Mom."

He follows her into the living room, sprawling on the floor next to Luke. Mike is sitting on the sofa with Sissy stretched out beside him.

By the third inning, his little sister has begun gently snoring. Even though it's August, and warm, his mom lays a cotton blanket over her.

"I can't believe it!" Mike says when the game ends. Through the open window, they can hear the next-door neighbor cursing: *The Mets beat Koufax! The lousy Mets! Son of a bitch!*

Sissy jumps up, pretending she wasn't asleep, shaking her golden red sprouts of hair. She knocks over the framed photo of their family, that last one from Palm Sunday, his dad standing directly behind him with one hand on his shoulder, Sissy still in his mom's tummy. He gets up onto his knees and rights it.

Luke clutches a pillow to his stomach and groans. "Who is this new pitcher, anyhow? Tug McGraw? Who's ever heard of *him?*"

"We're going to hear about him now," Mike says grimly.

His mom shuts the living room window against the neighbor's shouting. "You didn't hear *that,* I'm sure." She looks meaningfully at Sissy. "Dinner is ready. Where has Patty Ann gotten to?"

"She's not home yet?" Mike says.

"Uh...duh," Luke says. "Like she could have gone through to the girls' room without your seeing her."

Mike ignores him. "I thought her shift was done at four today, like mine. That's what she told me this morning."

His two brothers look at each other. Whole blocks burned down in Watts. People were even killed.

"Don't worry, Mom," Mike adds quickly. "Lee was picking Patty Ann up. Nothing could have happened to her."

Lee is Patty Ann's steady. Skinny and dark-haired, in jeans and boots even when it's hot out, Lee's only job this summer seems to be driving Patty Ann to work and taking her parking after. Their mom says the worst part about Patty Ann not getting a scholarship to Vassar is that it means not putting the whole of the United States of America between the two of them. She says if their father were still alive, he'd have sent Lee packing a long time ago. Their mom doesn't like Lee much.

She and Patty Ann had a fight about him again just this morning: in fact, Lee is what they mostly fight about. *At least CSU will get Patty Ann to a different part of town,* his mom said after Patty Ann went running out the door into Lee's Dodge Matador. *With a different sort of boy.*

"Right," his mom says now. "She's with Lee. That makes me feel miles better."

There's no way to reach Patty Ann if she's left the coffee shop. Maybe she and Lee went to the movies, or maybe they're just hanging out in Lee's car—although, normally, Patty Ann would have said if she weren't coming home for dinner. If anything, Patty Ann seems to enjoy telling his mom when she's staying out with Lee.

They go ahead and eat. Afterward Mike does the dishes without protest, even though tonight is supposed to be Patty Ann's turn. His mom bathes Sissy and tucks her into bed, and Luke goes to read to Sissy as promised while he stays in the kitchen to dry the dishes and help Mike put them away. When the kitchen is all cleaned up, he and Mike return to sit in the living room again, Mike pulling out a deck of cards. Soon, his mom joins them.

As the night crawls in, his mom gets more and more irritable. She smokes one cigarette, and then lights another. A little before ten, Mike taps the cards neatly into a pile, slides them back into their cardboard box.

"Good night, Mom," Mike says and disappears to their bedroom, yawning and stretching.

The house is quiet around him and his mom now, just the radio, the crickets outside, the low hum of the fridge. She starts folding laundry on the dining room table, something she normally never does at this hour. He sits in his dad's old armchair, listening to KHJ. The DJ is talking about the Beatles playing the Hollywood Bowl this weekend. His favorite band is the Byrds, though, and he waits patiently for their new song, "Mr. Tambourine Man," to come on. He knows it will eventually. McGuinn's voice sounds like no one else's, and his guitar is reedy and twangy, almost like the little piano-organ at church. He's never heard a guitar sound like it before. If only he had a record player, he'd buy the 45 for "Mr. Tambourine Man" and listen to it over and over again.

Maybe he'll get a job after school this year, so he can buy a guitar and learn to play it himself. So he won't have to wait for it to come on the radio.

But what kind of job can he get during the school year that'll pay enough for a guitar? Could he start bagging groceries on weekends already? Or washing cars after school? Delivering newspapers before school?

Eugene will have an idea. Eugene always needs money.

At eleven, the phone rings.

"Can you get that, Francis?" his mom says, looking hard at him from the sill of the dining room. She reaches into a pocket for her cigarettes.

She doesn't follow him to the phone, but he can feel her expectation trail after him.

"Hello," he says into the receiver.

"Francis? Is that you?" Patty Ann's voice sounds funny—faint and crackly—but it's definitely Patty Ann. He glances at his mom. She has her hands on her hips, smoke trailing from her cigarette, watching him.

He speaks low into the receiver. "You missed dinner."

Patty Ann laughs. "That's not the half of it. Guess where I am?"

From outside the house, he can hear night sounds, a creak of a screen door, a lone car driving past. There's noise behind Patty Ann's voice, too, over the telephone line, but he can't make it out. "I don't know. With Lee."

Patty Ann laughs again. "And how! We're in *Las Vegas*."

He turns away from his mom, as though she might otherwise be able to hear, and the receiver slips in his hand. He grabs it before it hits the floor. This time Patty Ann is really going to catch it.

"Francis? Are you there?"

He looks out the picture window, through his reflection and into the dark glow of the street lamps, avoiding the feel of his mom's eyes on his back. Why did he stay up? He should have gone to bed when Mike did. He really would rather not be around when she finds out about this. "Yes."

"Were you guys listening to the radio this evening?"

"Yes. It was a bad game."

"No, I mean *the news*. Did you hear the news? Did Mom hear the news?"

"I don't know. I don't think so. We were listening to the baseball game. She was listening with us."

"Well, Lee and I weren't. We were sitting in his car...and a newscast came on. President Johnson signed an executive order this afternoon saying couples married after midnight tonight will no longer be eligible for the draft deferment for married men without children."

"So?"

"So we drove straight to Las Vegas. Me and Lee. We got married."

For a few moments earlier today, he was air, he was lighter than air, he was as free as the tern that skimmed right over his and Eugene's heads. He felt no fear. He felt no weight. There was nothing but his body moving through the sky and then into the water.

And then he plunged into the cold, and the sea pushed him back up.

"Hold on," he says. He can't slip out the door unseen now. Could he hand over the phone and make straight for his bedroom? Or the bathroom, like he needs to pee? He'd need to be peeing for a long time, though. What comes next isn't going to end swiftly. "I'll put Mom on the phone."

"And Francis! Don't tell her. I want to tell her myself."

That will not be a problem. He cups his hand over the receiver. "It's for you, Mom. I mean, it's Patty Ann."

He holds the phone out, stretching his hand into the night, waiting for his mom to take it. Figuring out how he can make like air. Like water.

Memorial Day / May 29, 1967

BARBARA

THE DODGE MATADOR PULLS up to the sidewalk in front of the florist's. Behind the steering wheel, Patty Ann's face, too pale for Southern California, strains over the head of the baby to see out the passenger window.

"Mom," Patty Ann says.

She bends down to look in at her daughter. "I was starting to worry."

She stows the basket of daisies, daffodils, and blue carnations in the backseat, then tucks the bouquet of roses and baby's breath in next to it, pushing them close together for stability. They look like odd lovers snuggled there, one sunny, the other red and formal, against the dirty vinyl. She lifts a wad of papers and other trash off the front seat and slips in, scooping the baby onto her lap.

"Jeepers, Patty Ann. A person could catch something just sitting here."

"So which bouquet is for which?" Patty Ann says, ignoring her complaint, surveying the flowers through the rearview mirror. "I mean, don't you think it's a little *weird?*"

With that, Patty Ann tears away from the sidewalk.

She clutches the door handle to keep herself and the baby from

jerking sideways. The baby plays with the cheek curls of her bouf-
fant, then grabs for her cigarette. So maybe the timing is a little
strange. The bottom line is Jeanne couldn't come out to California
twice but was determined to be here for both events, to show no hard
feelings about her getting remarried. Also, Father O'Malley wasn't
available any other afternoon over the Memorial Day weekend.

She takes a last puff of her cigarette and tosses it out the window.
"Ronnie doesn't like my smoking."

"No?" Patty Ann screws up her nose. *Ronnie.*

She won't point out that if it weren't for Patty Ann, she probably
wouldn't be marrying Ronnie McCloskey later today, a few hours
after they get back from the cemetery. She might never have picked
up the phone to ask him for help with the oven. After Patty Ann
ran off to Las Vegas to get married, she was just too tired with trying to make everything work on her own.

"That's enough, Patty Ann. I am lucky to have Ronnie."

"Nothing to me," Patty Ann says, reaching over to turn the dial
up on the radio. "I won't ever have to live with him."

Blue skies, only you for me
Only youuuu . . .

The streets of Los Angeles roll by, the jacarandas in full bloom.
She would watch the wings on this car before Patty Ann ran
off, day after day, as it pulled up in front of the house and Lee
honked. She'd say to Patty Ann: *Hmm. What has wings and honks?*
A duck. But Patty Ann would gather up her sweater and books
and rush out. The Dodge has started to take on a rusty look since,
and now there's the baby sitting up front with Patty Ann—while
Lee is off picking up a few dollars here or there, anything but a
decent day's work.

Someday Patty Ann will go to Vassar with her aunt Jeanne, Michael used to say. *Or any college she wants. My smart girl.*

She couldn't have tied Patty Ann up inside the house, though. She couldn't pick the cost of tuition at Vassar off a lemon tree. If only she'd called Ronnie sooner. Maybe he would have fixed more than her stove. Maybe he would have fixed her oldest daughter also. It will be such a relief, not having to do all this on her own anymore.

"The jacarandas throw the whole city into a purple haze," she says.

Patty Ann laughs. "Purple haze, Mom?"

The baby—Kennedy, Patty Ann named him, like some sort of joke—sneezes, and a stream of snot rolls from his little nose. It glides freely, spooling into the down of his upper lip, into the sweet of his mouth. Patty Ann looks over at him, and suddenly the car is lurching toward the curb. Her daughter jumps out, short skirt pulling against her thigh, just a bit plumper than it was in high school, runs to the metal-weave garbage can on the street corner, and vomits.

Her heart sinks. And then, because this should be a joyous thing but there's no way it can be, her heart sinks a little further.

When Patty Ann slides back into the car, she hands her the hankie she used for Kennedy, neatly folded over the wet spot. "How long?"

"I don't want to talk about it."

"How long?"

"I don't know. Five weeks."

"Does he know?"

"Of course."

"And?"

"And Lee's fine with it. We're both fine with it. We're happy!"

But her daughter sounds anything but happy. At the christening, Lee and Patty Ann told everyone they had the baby cause President Kennedy had put married men with children on the very bottom of the call-up list for the draft and LBJ hadn't changed at least *that* yet. But Patty Ann's tone turned from triumphant to defensive soon after. A second baby can't be good news when they can barely keep the first one in disposable diapers. And forget using cloth—Patty Ann and Lee's tiny bungalow, in Venice, doesn't have a washing machine. Patty Ann and Lee's tiny bungalow doesn't have anything.

With Ronnie moving in his leather living room set, she can give them the sofa. She can give them the Melmac plates and rocking chair also. Too bad Ronnie's apartment doesn't have its own washing machine. She could have given them that, too. Ronnie wouldn't have minded. Ronnie is generous to a fault.

"You know," she says, "what's done is done. But there are things you can do to avoid this happening a third time, Patty Ann. Easy, effective ways that are now legal."

Patty Ann slams on the brake. The baby jolts forward and lets out a wail.

"Mom!"

She rubs Kenny's back and checks over her shoulder to make sure the flowers are all right. "Well, I'm just saying. You're modern in all these other ways. Why not be modern in a way that's useful?"

"*Mom.* Anyhow, what about *you?* You're certainly no model of family planning."

"We are not talking about me. Your father was a man of faith, and the only method the pope approves is the rhythm method. Which doesn't work unless, like the pope, you're celibate. Proof positive: Francis, Sissy." She ignores Patty Ann's grimace. The kids want to do all this love business themselves but don't want to think their parents ever have. "Besides, and most important, you were all wanted. And we were able to care for you. We didn't know your father was suddenly going to die. That's not something we *chose,* Patricia Ann."

"We want our babies, too. Money is not everything, Mom. *Love* counts for something also."

She takes the baby's fingers out of her hair again, turns him around, and sits him down on her lap facing forward. She won't rise to the bait. Marriage is a lifelong partnership, not just a weekend adventure. That's the part Patty Ann overlooked. If only Lee *had* gone to Vietnam. Not only would Patty Ann not be in this mess, the army might have made a man of him. And Patty Ann would be in college, as planned. *Everything* would be different.

But a house can't be built on "if onlys." Nothing can be.

They drive past the Woolworth's and turn right. Two girls stand on the street corner, waiting for the light to change, laughing. One, in a short pink skirt, holds a tiny white dog in her arms. She was once a girl like that, not in a short skirt but a freshly ironed yellow dress, passing out magazines to the returning soldiers, dreaming— without for a second actually imagining—that her future husband might be among them. And then there Michael was, propped up in a hospital bed, gaunt but so calm, so handsome.

This life of hers as a grown woman happened, bang, just like that.

Patty Ann should be a girl like those girls, a little dog in her hands rather than a baby, and dreams in her head of a future yet to happen. Why didn't she and Patty Ann have this conversation *before* Patty Ann went and got knocked up? And still before *that,* before her daughter went running out to that stupid car, honk honk honk, with Lee sitting behind the steering wheel? Why is it women aren't allowed to talk about private things with their daughters when they can still use the knowledge?

"I tried the Pill," Patty Ann says. "It made me fat."

"Having kids makes you fat," she says.

She jogs her feet up and down to make Kenny giggle. His warm, chubby hands grasp at her fingers. Having babies hasn't made her fat. At forty-one, she feels lighter than she did as a girl, as though each child she's given birth to has taken away several pounds of her flesh. She thought Ronnie might want to have a child with her, too, while it was still possible, but he insists being stepfather to her children will be enough to make him happy. With Ronnie, the rhythm method seems likely to work just fine. She and Michael could barely keep their hands off each other long enough to sign their marriage certificate. Ronnie holds her hand, then kisses her cheek good night.

It's been five years since she became a widow. Five years is a long time. She really wouldn't have minded a little more than a kiss on the cheek from Ronnie, especially now she's agreed to marry him.

She flicks the thought away as though an ash from her cigarette. In some ways, Ronnie feels more like a friend than a soon-to-be new husband. But a friend is good. A friend is what she needs. The last thing she wants is to try to replace Michael.

"You know, Mom," Patty Ann says, "you didn't go to college. You were barely any older than I was, and you were perfectly happy married to Dad, right? And it's not like *you* didn't rush into marriage. I mean, at least I *knew* Lee."

She snaps out of her dirty thoughts. "Don't you compare your father's and my marriage to your and Lee's. Don't you ever."

They have arrived. Patty Ann drives through the front gates of Holy Cross Cemetery, and they continue in silence toward the mortuary. The parking lot is full today. Young families button sweaters over little kids, middle-aged children assist wobbly grandparents. Everyone looks impossibly alive. In the first row of cars, Mike leans against Ronnie's Chevy—her station wagon is in the shop again.

Sissy plays on the ground by his feet. The top of Luke's head is just visible, slunk down inside.

A few feet away, Jeanne and Molly stand on the lawn. Molly is holding the flowers Jeanne bought at the airport with one hand, her mother's arm with the other. Jeanne's doing a bad job of not crying. It's her sister-in-law's first time back to the cemetery since Michael was buried.

The rest of them—they come every Sunday after church. Sometimes she stops by during the week also, just to make sure everything is being taken care of properly. Sissy knows this place as well as the school's playground.

"I can't believe Ronnie let Mike drive his big fancy car," Patty Ann says, maneuvering through the lot, looking for a free space. "He hasn't had a real license for even a year yet."

"It's not half what Mike could be driving someday."

"Damn, Mom! How can you let him?"

"Do what? Serve his country? He'll still start at Claremont McKenna in the autumn. The ROTC will even put him through medical school."

"He'll get sent over."

"He'll get sent over anyhow."

"Not if he's in school and not ROTC. He could get a deferment."

"How do you know they aren't going to change that rule tomorrow? They've changed the rules on graduates. And on married men, for that matter."

Patty Ann angles her clunker into the last open space. "I *don't* know. The SOBs. But if he goes ROTC, Mike will be trapped for certain."

"Not trapped, Patricia Ann. *Committed.* Now, don't you dare say one more word to me about it."

She pulls up on the door handle. Not on this day, of all days, and not from Patty Ann, of all people. What was the point of Michael's death if service isn't worthy? She checked his chart after they met: malaria, beriberi, starvation. There were so many things listed she can't even remember them all. And the pills they had him take! Maybe it took fifteen years to happen, but Michael died for his country. The war ruined his heart. That's the long and short of it. His service has to mean something.

"Where is Francis?" she says to Mike, handing him the bouquet of daisies. The roses are alone now in the backseat of Patty Ann's car.

"I'm sorry, Mom. I couldn't find him."

She sighs. "Why is there always one or another of you missing?"

"That's not fair."

"You're right." Mike is reliable. So, in their own ways, are Luke and Sissy, stubborn but predictable. Even Patty Ann—except for that one time. It's Francis. Always Francis. "I'm sorry."

Sissy looks up from moving pebbles strategically around in the dirt, some game whose rules no one else knows. "Francis is scared to come to Daddy's grave."

It kills her how Sissy calls Michael "Daddy" despite never having met him. She'd like to pick her five-year-old daughter up and give her a squeeze, but she's still got Kenny on her hip.

"What's there to be scared of? There's no such thing as ghosts. And even if there were, your father would be the nicest ghost who ever existed."

Sissy hops another pebble. "Not of ghosts. He's scared of Daddy being dead."

Desiree—the name was Michael's idea: *In case the baby turns out to be a girl.*

"Look at you, Desiree," she says, handing Kenny to Patty Ann and lifting Sissy onto her feet. She starts to brush the dust off Sissy's smocked pinafore, but at the sound of her hated real first name, Sissy balls her hands into fists and steps away.

"You haven't told him, have you?" she says over Sissy's head to Patty Ann.

Patty Ann sighs and shakes her head. "No."

"Told who what?" Sissy asks.

She taps Sissy's upturned nose. "Aren't you the one with the buzzing ears?" She gives Patty Ann a warning look. Sissy is the kind who hears everything and, even if beyond her comprehension, remembers it.

The white stone of the cemetery shoots sun at her. She slides her sunglasses down over her eyes. "Luke! Do you think I don't see you?"

Luke drags his lanky bell-bottomed legs out of the car.

She turns toward the cemetery path. She's a marshal now. A small female marshal, leading the troops. Such a short time ago she was a twinkly-eyed virgin in a crisp yellow dress, starstruck at the sight of the haggard but gallant veteran just back from the Pacific islands.

How do people get from point A to point B in their lives? When did this happen?

"We're our own Memorial Day parade," she says to Mike, taking his arm. She doesn't need to; she knows how to make this walk on her own. But Mike likes her to lean on him. When Mike is done with his army service, he'll be a doctor, just like his father before him and his father's father before that. And he'll have done it without paying a penny. The army will take good care of Mike. Patty Ann will see. She was overjoyed when Mike told her he wanted to enlist in the ROTC. *Overjoyed.*

"Are we gonna see the real parade after?" Sissy says.

"You hear me talking about parades with your brother? How'd

you hear me say that?" She takes Sissy's hand in her other hand. The ears on that girl. "Not this year we won't go, remember? This afternoon we're going to have a special party. For Mommy and Ronnie. And then afterward, we'll all be a big family together."

Jeanne and Molly walk slowly back toward them. A little boy, three or four, dressed in a mini sailor suit, races in front of them, chased by a tense-looking mother. The woman glances toward her and breaks into a small surprised smile. Canary yellow isn't the norm to wear to the cemetery on Memorial Day, but she's allowed her one little private exchange still with Michael. She can have that much. She smiles back at the woman.

"A lot of people here today," Jeanne says, stopping in front of them.

Even before she agreed to marry Ronnie, Jeanne wanted to come out to Los Angeles this Memorial Day weekend in honor of the fifth anniversary of Michael's death. So, of course, she had to work out how to package the two events together. It's a long way from Poughkeepsie.

"More than last year," Mike says somberly, nodding.

"Vietnam," Luke mutters.

"That's right," Patty Ann says, shifting Kenny to her other hip, the better to glare at her. "And I'd rather be married to a draft evader than to a body in a box."

"Shut up, Patty Ann," Mike says.

All around them families are laying flowers, planting American flags. Some of the mounds look fresh, too fresh; mothers about her age stand beside them, tears rolling freely down their faces.

And so it continues.

Every day alive is a precious day. And she has to live this life for both of them, herself and Michael.

"Come on," she says. "Let's go find your father."

———

No one says much on the way back from the cemetery. She rides with Mike and Jeanne and Sissy in Ronnie's car, Kenny in her lap again. Luke and Molly go in the Dodge with Patty Ann, promising to pick up the wedding cake after they've picked up Lee. The wedding dinner will be at Trader Vic's in Beverly Hills. *We're a small group,* Ronnie said when she protested about the cost. *Only your kids and your son-in-law, and your sister-in-law and her kid, and Patrick and Johnny, and Father O'Malley. And us, of course.*

Patrick and Johnny are friends of Ronnie. He didn't invite any of his family. *Not close* is all he's said about them. She didn't pry; Ronnie's a grown man and entitled to his privacy. Her own mother is too poorly to leave the house, much less travel this far outside San Francisco for the first time since Michael's funeral and the second time ever, and her father won't come down without her mother. Fifteen people total. Well, Ronnie is paying the bill. It's his decision to make.

Francis is sitting in the living room when they arrive at the house, already dressed in the dark blue jacket and white button-down shirt she bought for him, bent over that beloved guitar he bought working on the pier with Eugene.

"You should have come to your father's grave," she tells him, setting Kenny down on the floor beside him.

In his typical maddening way, Francis stares up at her and says nothing. He doesn't apologize or try to explain his behavior. But with his grown-up clothes on, his dark gold hair washed and slicked back, he looks so much like Michael and yet so much himself, such a startlingly handsome young man, it's hard to scold him.

She sighs. "I'm going to go get ready. Watch your nephew."

"What time do we need to leave for the church?" Jeanne asks, fussing with her handbag, averting her eyes as though approaching a delicate subject. "I mean, just to be sure Molly and I are ready in time. Well, you know what I mean."

He's a nice man, her sister-in-law told her last night, after Ronnie had said good night. And then, faltering just a little, *I'm happy for you.*

What does a sister-in-law become when the person who unites them is no longer living? Is Jeanne still her in-law, even? *And you?* she asked cheerfully, skipping right past the unspoken words, the thought that Michael would in some way be replaced this evening. Because he won't. Michael will never be replaced. Just because he died doesn't mean he stopped being her husband. She'll just have two husbands. Barbara the bigamist. *Are there any nice men in Poughkeepsie?*

Jeanne looked embarrassed. *Oh, Barbara. You know I am still married. I tell Molly I'm like Penelope from* The Odyssey. *When Paul gets back, I'll be waiting.*

Paul—ten years without sending so much as a postcard—is, for all intents and purposes, as gone as Michael is. The nuns taught *The Odyssey* in high school, and she remembers the story; Paul isn't coming back and she's willing to bet there are no suitors banging on Jeanne's door like they were on Penelope's, either. Poor Jeanne! Stuck with a husband who isn't a husband. Probably everyone but Jeanne realized that Paul married her to get a green card—when they came out together to visit that one time, before Paul took off, he as much as told Michael so. He even made eyes at *her,* his own sister-in-law, when no one was looking.

You think he's gone back to Canada? Although, of course, Paul didn't go back to Canada. Why would he have married Jeanne for a green card and then gone back to Canada?

But Jeanne didn't answer, and she understood suddenly: the way

Jeanne deals with the failure of her marriage is not to think about Paul as flesh and blood, walking on earth, his wife and child forgotten. It's easier to make a constellation out of her lost husband, a Greek myth, something abstract.

If that makes it easier for Jeanne, then fine. She's certainly not one to argue with that. It's hard, this life.

"We have an hour before we need to leave," she says. "When Molly gets back, let her help herself in the kitchen. The ceremony won't take long, but your inner clocks must be out of whack, what with the time difference."

In the quiet of her bedroom, she gets Sissy's stiff green dress from the closet.

"Don't want to," Sissy says, sitting on the bed, kicking the bed skirt.

"Oh, come on. You're my flower girl. I want you to look pretty."

Sissy folds her chubby arms over her chest. "I'll look like Jell-O."

"Green is lovely with red hair."

It's the wrong thing to say. Sissy, whose brothers—and probably the kids in the playground, too—have teased her more than once about her ginger crop, scowls. But then her spunky little daughter suddenly relents, lifting her arms up, as though somehow intuiting this is not the moment to give her added trouble. Because it is true—now that the time is getting so near, now that she's back in this bedroom, knowing she'll soon be again sharing it with a husband—her nerves are getting a little raw. She runs her free hand over her stomach, not big but not as flat as it was before giving birth to five children. What will it *be* like with Ronnie? She's into her forties now, long past being the girl she was when she and Michael married.

She won't find out tonight. With Jeanne and Molly occupying the girls' room, Sissy has been sleeping with her. *We could go spend the night in a hotel,* she told Ronnie, laughing, as they made their plans. *The honeymoon suite.*

Ronnie laughed, too: *Don't worry about it. I'll wait until after Jeanne and Molly have gone to move in. Maybe that's better. It will be easier for Jeanne.*

She was laughing, but in fact she wasn't joking about checking into a hotel. The idea of exploring another man's body for the first time with the kids down the hall—she would have liked to do that someplace private, anonymous. Didn't he want that also? Wasn't he eager to be alone with her?

But Ronnie is always so thoughtful. There can't be many men who would be so considerate—she should be thanking her lucky stars is what she should be doing. Of course, it will be easier for Jeanne not to see her going off for the night with a man other than Michael. One thing at a time; the wedding is already enough.

"Help me, Mommy?" Sissy says, her voice muffled by cloth.

"You need to take the dress you are wearing off first," she says to Sissy, smiling.

While Sissy wriggles out of her cemetery dress, she slides out of her own clothes. She ordered a light blue suit with a matching pill-box hat for the wedding; with five kids, she wasn't going to act the fool and dress in white, like a virgin. She removes its wrapper now and runs her fingers down the front of it. She'll slip it on in a few minutes, once she's rolled hose up her legs and put on her makeup.

With him in the room or not, when she takes the suit off again tonight, she will no longer be Mrs. Michael Gannon. She'll be Mrs. Ronald McCloskey. That's what is going to happen.

Independence Day / July 4, 1968

BARBARA

YOU AREN'T REALLY GOING to leave Los Angeles?" Patty Ann says, staring over the kitchen sink into the backyard, where Ronnie is talking with Mike and Mike's girlfriend by the grill.

Ronnie is switching the focus of his company from individual air-conditioning units to central air, and he says it means he needs to switch his office location as well: *People in Southern California are too reliant on the sea breeze. The desert is where to get a foothold.*

As far as she can tell there's not much sea breeze to be had in LA, certainly not east of the new 405 highway. But she did tell Ronnie before they married, *I'm not moving to a new house in LA. And I'm not going to have the exterior repainted. It's the last thing Michael did, and I like it.* If Ronnie simply doesn't like living in another man's home and this is a way to get her to move, who is to blame him?

"If Ronnie's loan comes through," she says, "and he decides to go, we're going. And soon, before school starts back up. He's paying the bills, Patty Ann. It's not for me to argue."

"Just up and leave your home like that?"

"I up and left my home twenty years ago to follow your father."

"Twenty-three." Patty Ann points to the hammock draped with

66

Luke's lanky seventeen-year-old body, seemingly asleep despite all the cap rockets going off and the loud music from the neighbors. "Why'd Ronnie put that up in our backyard if he's just planning to make you sell the house?"

Patty Ann has been out of the house for three years, but it's still "our" backyard. It's enough to break her heart. With the house sold, does Patty Ann feel as though her childhood will be once and for all out of reach? There were days after Michael's death when her hands shook so much with rage—this perfect life dropped in her lap only to be snatched up again—that it was hard to zip the younger boys' Windbreakers or attach a barrette in baby Sissy's fine red hair. Maybe the real reason Patty Ann ran off with that good-for-nothing Lee was out of a similar anger, snubbing her nose at fate for what it had done to them.

Where is Lee today? It seems like just Patty Ann and the babies these days.

"You and the boys can always come visit. It's not that far."

"For Luke? He put the hammock up for Luke?"

"I told Luke last week if he's going to just loaf around, I wish at least he would loaf around at home, where I could keep an eye on him. Luke laughed. But Ronnie came home with the hammock."

"And Luke has barely left it since."

"I don't think Luke likes his friends much more than I do."

"Superman Ronnie."

"He has a way."

"Like I said. Superman."

"I don't know what you have against your stepfather, Patty Ann. Ronnie's been nothing but nice to you. He even tried to help Lee land a job—not that Lee followed him up on it."

"It wasn't the right fit," Patty Ann says, looking down at her beer.

"Right. Well. Ronnie tried."

"He always tries. That's just it. Like he's *too* nice. Like he's hiding something. You never really know *who* he is."

If he's such a nice guy and loves kids so much, why hasn't he had any of his own? Why hasn't he ever even married? Patty Ann said after the first time Ronnie joined them for Sunday dinner. *He's a good-looking guy. I mean, for a middle-aged square.*

It's a question, like a song she can't shake, that she hears again each night when Ronnie kisses her on her forehead, puts out the light, and turns over onto his side, facing away from her. She's sure he loves her. It was his idea they marry, not hers. It's not like he had anything to gain from it—she'd hardly an extra penny in the bank. And he's an honorable man. He served in World War II, just like Michael did. And yet she could count on two hands the number of times he has turned to her in the dark. Being married to Ronnie is great, but it's not exactly how she imagined it.

But maybe that's how it is with most men. Just because their private life isn't like the one she had with Michael doesn't mean it's not normal. They're neither of them kids anymore, after all. *She's* no longer a kid.

She wouldn't mind if he were to turn to her sometimes, though.

"That's what he is, Patty Ann—*nice.* Some people are." She picks up the plate of raw steak and heads for the door. "I think the baby has woken up."

The late afternoon air smells of eucalyptus and car exhaust and barbecue. She sets the plate down by the grill. "Another ten minutes?"

"Fifteen," Ronnie says. He's wearing the new madras shirt she picked out for him; it makes his hair seem even darker and thicker. He really is a nice-looking man.

"Well, the salads are ready. And the corn on the cob is done."

"I'm starved," Eugene says, looking up from a pile of firecrackers.

A body would think she didn't have enough children already without Eugene making himself at home here. Then again, Eugene's been an honorary member of the family longer than Ronnie has—it'll be strange leaving him behind if they move to Phoenix. In some ways, she understands him better than she understands Francis, her own son.

Right now, Francis is leaning against the coral tree picking on his guitar, paying no mind to Eugene or the firecrackers. Ronnie must have given the boys the money for them. He's the one who came up with the plan for Francis and Eugene to spend the summer working for Jeanne, helping fix up her rattling old wooden house. When they went East at Thanksgiving, Ronnie saw how badly it needed painting. *The college would pay for it, right?* he said on the plane ride home. *Jeanne just hasn't gotten around to asking them?*

Francis and Eugene will be on a bus heading toward New York State this time on Saturday. Ronnie, of course, bought their tickets. The college will let Jeanne hire her nephew, but it's not going to pay for his transportation across the country.

"Me, too," Kenny says, swaying on his chubby little legs, glancing adoringly at Eugene and Francis. "Hungry."

Sissy slams her book shut. "Let's play hide-and-seek!"

No one pays her any mind. Francis keeps fiddling with his guitar. Eugene continues fiddling with his firecrackers. Luke might as well be a corpse over there in the hammock.

Sissy puts her hands on her hips. "Come on!"

"I'm sorry, sweetheart. I have to tend the barbecue," Ronnie says, forgetting again that Sissy doesn't like being called by endearments. He can't help it. Endearments come naturally to him. "Boys, play with your little sister."

Sissy glares at him, then stalks over to the hammock and pulls up hard on its side, flipping Luke over onto the ground.

"Hey!" Luke says, coming to life, rolling up onto his knees and grabbing for her. Mike puts his beer down, ready to step in.

Sissy jumps back. "Play hide-and-seek. Come on, Luke. Everyone here is so boring."

Luke wipes his hands on his legs. He laughs. "Okay, squirt."

Mike picks his beer back up.

"Okay, Sissy. We'll play, too," Eugene says, punching Francis.

"Yeah, okay," Francis mumbles, looking up. "What are we doing?"

Sissy sticks her tongue out at him.

"No sticking your tongue out, Sissy," she says—though as far as she's concerned, Sissy is within her rights. Those *boys*. "That's not ladylike."

"Hide seek," little Kenny says.

"You're too small to play," six-year-old Sissy says.

Kenny's tiny face crumples. He doesn't cry, just looks down at his feet. It rips her in two. "I don't know what you're talking about, Sissy," she says. "Kenny's going to play with me, and as a team we're going to beat all of you." She takes Kenny's hand in hers. He looks up at her, his eyes round and shiny.

She gives Francis a look.

"Oh, don't worry," he mutters. When it comes to hiding, Francis has them all beat when he wants.

"You're it!" Sissy says, tagging Luke.

Luke laughs again and sits back down on the hammock. He covers his eyes. "One...two..."

She scoops Kenny up onto her hip. "Come on. I have a great hiding place for us." She runs through the grass around the house, carrying him. "Shh," she says. She tiptoes through the front door and back toward the kitchen.

"Six, seven, eighhhhht..."

She places Kenny on the floor. "We'll crawl under the table and pull the chairs in. He'll never find us."

Kenny sticks his thumb in his mouth.

"Don't do that, Kenny. It'll give you rabbit teeth."

He takes his thumb out.

She folds a chocolate chip cookie into a napkin and gets down on her knees beside him. "There are cookies to eat while we wait. Quick." Together, they crawl under the table. He leans against her shoulder. She kisses the top of his head.

"Ten. Ready or not, hipsters, here I come!"

Luke finds Eugene first. It's easy—something in the garden shed sets Eugene off on a coughing fit. In the last few months, Eugene's asthma seems to have disappeared, but his lungs are still fragile.

"Aw, hell, Luke," Eugene says.

"Now, no need for that language, Eugene," Ronnie says. "Come give us a hand with the barbecue."

Luke next finds Francis, who hasn't bothered to hide at all, just climbed into the backseat of Ronnie's car with his guitar.

Kenny starts to squirm. She hands him the cookie.

"Let me guess where Mom and Kenny are," Luke says loudly, entering the kitchen. He opens the oven door. "Are they in here?"

Kenny stifles a giggle. He has a dab of chocolate on his upper lip, and she wipes it off while holding a finger in front of her mouth.

Luke opens the fridge. "Are they in here?"

Kenny cries out, "Silly!"

"Aha! Do I hear something?" Luke lifts the top of the cookie jar. "They couldn't have fit in here. Nah, not Kenny. He's much too fat."

Kenny giggles. She smiles at him.

"Oh, now I definitely hear something." Luke pulls away one of the chairs and sticks his face under the table.

She waits for Kenny to crawl out first. "How'd you find us so fast?" she says, smoothing her red-and-white skirt. She made it herself, and the side seam isn't hanging quite right. The little blue blouse is nice, though. "Did you peek?"

Luke laughs. "I knew I'd find you in the kitchen, Mom. That wasn't hard. That's where you always go to hide."

Luke! Maybe if they leave Los Angeles, things will be better for him. All the kids are smart, like their father, but Luke is the smartest. She just has to get him away from that crowd he's running with. In truth, getting Luke away is half the reason she's supported moving to Phoenix.

"Well, it still was a great hiding place, wasn't it, Kenny? Almost everyone else has been found. Plus we got cookies."

Kenny nods. "Lost."

"No, buddy. Not lost." Luke picks him up. "Even when you're not with family, family is still with you. And family *never* loses family."

And there is her seventeen-year-old son tossing her toddler grandson in the air. Both babies, her babies. She reaches out for Kenny. "Better go find Sissy. I bet the steaks are on the grill now. Ronnie likes them done just right."

She sets Kenny down on the floor and gets the potato salad out from the fridge, the bean salad, and then the green salad, laying them on a big tray.

"Patty Ann! Come in here and help."

She picks up the second tray, with all the plates and napkins and silverware, using her hip to open the screen door onto the back patio.

"Hello? Happy Fourth!" Their neighbor Gary O'Connor appears around the house, gripping two six-packs. His wife, June, crowds in behind him with a cake.

"Oh, Barbara," June says. "I am so sorry we are so late."

Ronnie turns the last steak on the grill, then frees Gary from the six-packs, claps him on the shoulder. "Perfect timing! I was slow getting the grill going."

She gives June a peck on the cheek and accepts the cake. "Let me get some glasses," she says, nodding at the beers. "Where's Meg?"

Meg is the O'Connors' teenage daughter, in the same grade as Francis at school, and usually as fast as a shooting star at finding an excuse to come over. It's embarrassing, really. Girls don't have the pride they used to.

Gary and June look at each other uneasily.

"We had a little trouble with Meg," Gary says. "That's why we're late."

"We had to go get her from the police station!" June blurts out.

Gary gives June a look. He says, "She's gotten all involved with these peaceniks. You know we don't support it. We forbade her to go, but—"

"She snuck out." June looks about ready to cry. "Meg was such a sweet little girl. But lately . . ."

"We were told a large protest was planned for today up at the school," Mike says. His girlfriend takes hold of his upper arm.

Gary and June exchange glances.

"We're sorry, Mike."

"We just can't seem to control her."

The kitchen screen door slams. In his playpen, baby Sean startles or maybe wakes—it's hard to tell; Patty Ann's second child is such a quiet baby—and throws his hands in the air. Patty Ann lays the tray of salads down hard on the table next to the old white pitcher, then picks Sean up. "Hello, Mr. and Mrs. O'Connor."

June chucks the baby under his chin, nervously. And little wonder—Patty Ann looks ready to bite her. "Isn't he darling?"

The baby shrinks from her touch. Patty Ann shifts him away from June.

"Well," Ronnie says amiably, "Meg still has to eat."

June twists her hands. "She . . . she didn't feel like socializing."

So Meg doesn't want to eat with Mike, because he is ROTC. Mike probably puts up with stuff like that all the time on campus. In fact, if he weren't their brother, Patty Ann and Luke would probably be treating him as though he had a disease, too.

Luke. Where *is* Luke?

"You can bring a plate for Meg later," she says. "Unless she'd think it would contain *napalm*."

"Oh, Barbara, never—"

"I was just joking. Listen, is beer okay, June? Something else? We were just finishing a game of hide-and-seek. Practicing for that jungle combat! Luke? Luke!" She turns to Mike. "Where's your brother gone?"

"I'm here," Luke says ambling around the side of the house, a whiff of sweet smoky aroma accompanying him. He nods at the O'Connors without saying hello, something Michael would have sent him to his room for were he still here. Ronnie doesn't try to be a father to the boys—more like a wise older friend. A friend to all of them. But it's good. Really, it is. No matter what Patty Ann says. The boys like him. Even Sissy tolerates him. It's only Patty Ann who seems to have it out for him. "But I can't find Sissy."

"Oh, she has a good hiding place. She wouldn't have suggested playing otherwise," Patty Ann says, rocking baby Sean in her arms. Kenny sits down in the grass and sticks his thumb in his mouth. He was such a sweet baby. Sean is a different story, quieter but fussier. "She's probably been thinking about it for days."

"Should I put the steaks in the oven to stay hot?" Ronnie asks.

"Sissy!" she shouts. "You've won! Now, come out!"

Evening is starting to fall, just a little bit, just a touch of veil over the sunlight. The smell of the lemon trees winds in and out through the smoke of the barbecue. Where did she put the sparklers? There's no point in arguing with anyone, not today. Not with Luke. Not with Patty Ann. Not with the neighbors' daughter. It's a perfect afternoon, a perfect evening. They're together, still a family.

"Come on, Sissy," Luke says. "I give up."

"I'm up here." Sissy's freckled face leans over the edge of the roof.

"For God's sake, Sissy!" she cries. "How did you get up there?"

Sissy smiles. Her red hair flashes in the late sun. "I flew."

Woodstock / August 16, 1969

FRANCIS

THIS IS BEAUTIFUL," THE girl in the beige bra says, pulling him further and further into the lake, further away from Molly and Eugene. The girl's laughter breaks over him in murky, rhythmic waves. "It's like the river Jordan, man. It's like everything bad that's ever happened is being washed away."

Somewhere in the near distance, cows are mooing, their moans plaited with the sound of more laughter; farther away guitars, people singing, the concert. Water fills the hollows of his knees, slipping against his naked thighs. Something soft but determined is clutching at his neck, a clinging slopping strangling water lily, a reed, the arms of an octopus. He pulls on it and, when he's finally freed, hands the bandanna to the girl in the beige bra and high white panties, throwing his lanky sunburned seventeen-year-old arms open wide.

The girl swirls the bandanna across the surface of the thick, green water in a trail of purple. She lifts it to write on the sky, and the letters appear as surely as if the cloth and the sky were made of pen and paper: B-E-A-U-T-I-F-U-L. She comes in close and ties the drenched cloth around his forehead, her body a tingle of flesh against his, and her nipples are right there in their beige nets, so close they are fish reaching out to nibble at him. He wants to look away, but his hand glides like an eel through the water. The girl kisses his mouth, makes a peace sign, flips onto her back, and floats away.

Her lips stay on his lips, soft and warm and silky.

He floats as well, first on his stomach, but that's the dead man's float. He turns over and stretches on his back, staring into the sky. The water is a million tiny velvety hands, holding him up, tickling his ribs and thighs and forehead. He shuts his eyes. The lake is a huge mouth, a big silken tongue, swallowing him. Rain is falling again, crystal drops, breaking against his face, hard, hurtful.

The girl in the beige bra is standing over him, her cupped hands spilling water onto his face.

"You're really freakin' out, aren't you?" she says, smiling. "What're you on?"

Her long brown hair snakes over the water. He grabs a mass and swirls it against his wrist. It becomes a paintbrush, the one he used over and over in first grade; the one with his name written on a piece of tape stuck to it. The one he used over and over at Aunt Jeanne's house this summer and last. He paints his wrist, his forearm, his face. Brown of the sand on the beach. Brown of the wood in his guitar. Brown of the seats in the car Aunt Jeanne lent them.

"You're beautiful, man," the girl says. "What's your name?"

Letting go of her hair, he glides again onto his back. The sky presses down: it throws its arms and legs over him and pushes, like Uranus, the sky god, on top of green-tinted Gaia, the young mother earth, with her voluptuous hills and valleys and bodies of water; he is stuck between the couple, enveloped by their union, Uranus all handsome and masterful and Gaia with stars in her eyes for her new husband with his beard and broad shoulders, or maybe they are reflections of the stars in his eyes. *He looks so kind,* he told Molly when they thumbed through her worn book of Greek mythology, passing a joint back and forth between them. They were alone; Eugene was showing Aunt Jeanne the stuff they've gotten done so far this summer, talking up a storm, working toward Molly asking for the car. Aunt Jeanne's house looked like no one had picked up a hammer or screwdriver or paintbrush for fifteen years before he and Eugene arrived last summer; she teared up when they said they wanted to come back and work for her again this year.

Well, Molly said about kindly Uranus, before flipping to the next page. *He's getting what he came for.* Molly is the coolest.

Molly?

He stands up in the lake. "Where's Molly?"

The girl sprinkles him with water. "Is Molly your old lady?"

The idea of his cousin being mistaken for his girlfriend rips him up inside. His too-tall, too-funny cousin. Whom he and Eugene should not have brought along with them to Woodstock, because she's a girl and younger and so he's responsible for her and how could he be responsible for anyone? He pats the water, searching for an explanation. His reflection looks back up at him, his deep-set eyes, his wavy chin-length hair wet and plastered against his thin face and sharp cheeks, a trace of stubble on his chin. Almost a man.

But so far from a man. He returns to floating on his back. There's the lake, a big warm mattress. He shakes his head, and water whooshes in his ears.

The girl crouches down next to him, knees tucked up, arms spinning in the water in circles like the wings of a sodden butterfly.

"Sleeping Beauty," she says. "That's your name."

"Hey, man! There you are!" It's Eugene, plowing into the water from the shore, a beer in hand, his curly dark hair shining in the sun. Eugene, an arrow shot from real life. Eugene, his best friend since always, his best friend still, though the desert now separates them most of the year, his best friend forever.

Eugene will know where Molly is.

"Are you Sleeping Beauty's friend?" the girl calls out, standing up in the waist-high water, her beautiful breasts emerging, the tips of her long hair emerging, her soft rounded stomach. Now that she has turned her brilliant smile away, toward Eugene, he can look at her face. Her hair is parted in the middle, and her eyes sit light and close in the tent of her hairline. Beneath them, her cheeks are smooth and pale and slightly swollen, as though she has just awoken.

"When the child of morning, rosy-fingered Dawn, appeared," he says too softly to be heard, but she hears something because she turns her smile back on him. "This is Dawn," he says more loudly to Eugene, splashing his way toward them.

Eugene's dark-haired legs disappear into the silty, khaki-colored lake water. *I'll spill my all-American blood in a rice field,* Eugene said on the drive over to Woodstock, or to Bethel, as it turned out, balling his hands up and pow-powing at the windshield. Eugene's parents won't have the money to pay for college, not even CSU-LA, and Eugene won't have the grades to qualify for a scholarship. *Why doesn't Eugene fuck up enough to have an extra year of high school?* Patty Ann wrote him, but what would be the point? Eugene would either become eligible one year later or get thrown out of high school without having earned even that diploma. If it were that easy half the boys in the US would be actively flunking twelfth grade.

Yessiree, one more for you, Uncle Sam, Eugene said. *At least I'll die high on Southeast Asian wacky weed. They say it's even better than Acapulco Gold.*

FAMILIES FOR PEACE. STOP THE WAR. END THE WAR IN VIETNAM. A phalanx of signs on the way to the concert grounds, after the grilled local corn stand and before the straw-hat stand. *No coolie hats? No paddy hats?* Eugene shouted at the two girls selling the hats. *Shut up,*

Eugene, Molly said, waving her arms like she was fending off horse-flies. *Hey, man, just ignore him.*

He bundles his hands into fists and rubs his eyes.

When he looks again, the lake is the color of an olive, the kind his mom would slice and mix with cream cheese then spread on slices of bread for his lunch. *That's all I've got in the house right now, Francis,* she'd say back before she married Ronnie. Sometimes it would be jelly. He'd get a scholarship, though, if he had to: there's always a girl willing to help him with a lab or paper, and he has a good memory. But he won't have to now because Ronnie's promised to pay his tuition. He doesn't even have to go to CSU. He can go to UCLA and live in a dorm in Westwood.

Cool, Eugene said. *I'll be your lowlife townie off-campus connection. Until I get sent over.*

Maybe you won't. Or maybe I will. Aunt Jeanne says they're going to change the draft. Anyone will be eligible to get called up—no more defer-ments.

Maybe, maybe.

Something told him that Eugene was certain only one of them would ever get sent over. And that Eugene was right. At least he himself will still be able to get the one-year student deferment. Eugene could be knee-deep in a rice paddy by then. Or worse.

The girl laughs. "Groovy. I can be Dawn." She has something in her hand, something white and oval. She rolls it over his collarbone and shoulders. "Soap yourself," she says. "Wash it all away."

His hand slides over the suds, gathers them up like shaving cream. He only began shaving this past year, buying the Noxzema and razor himself. Luke saw his face over the breakfast table and hooted: *Little brother's been to the barber! His cheeks look like a baby's butt!* His mom smacked Luke on the head, but she was laughing. He touches his face, fingers the fuzz on his chin that has sprouted overnight. His beard grows faster all the time, lighter blond than the hair on his head. He spreads the soap foam under his arms and over his chest, where hair hasn't started to grow. His hard-on pushes up through the surface of the water, but it feels strangely separate from him, weirdly undemanding.

Come on, Francis, his ex-girlfriend Joan said when they were still going together. *Come on. It's just love.* Joan, with her long eyelashes and stubby fingers, with her yellow hair, her way of whistling between her teeth when she was thinking.

Joan, who knitted him two sweaters and a vest this winter, each one uglier than the last, who called him on the phone every evening, who always asked what he was thinking. *What are you thinking, Francis? What are you thinking?* That Joan.

You might get, you know . . . he told her. *I don't want to get you in trouble.* But that wasn't the real reason he wouldn't do it with her. He watched Joan for weeks after moving to Phoenix before sliding into the seat next to her at the movies, the way her hair slipped over her shoulder, the confident way she poured from test tubes in chemistry class. So focused, so self-sufficient. So independent. But once they were going out, she turned out to be just like Lisa and Susan and Becky and all the girls who followed him around his new high school, made him brownies, slipped him joints, offered to sew patches on his jeans. Acting as though they were giving him something when the truth was they wanted and wanted and wanted. They wanted so much from him. The more Joan brought up doing it, the less he felt able to do it with her even if he tried, even if he wanted to try, and, of course, part of him wanted to, the part of him he held in his hand in the dark at night. But no, because once they did it, Joan would own him.

The hard-on is gone now. He is a tiny thing, a minnow, a tadpole, a worm.

Here is Eugene, a shit-eating grin on his face, offering him a drink of his beer. Eugene! Who cheerfully chases all the Susans and Beckys and Lisas. Who would laugh but not laugh at him over what happened with Joan and what didn't. Who can even find a way to laugh at the possibility of being sent over.

"Eugene, meet Dawn," he says, touching her long, dripping hair. "And now as Dawn rose . . . harbinger of light alike to mortals and immortals . . ."

Eugene laughs his loud laugh. "*The Odyssey? The Iliad?*"

"Sing, O goddess, the anger of Achilles . . . but not here in Bethel, cause no one is fighting here . . ."

"*Iliad,* meet rock 'n' roll!" Laughing again, Eugene makes a peace sign, then turns to the girl. "He can remember anything. Like new songs but also math and history and Latin and old Greek myths. We're living with his aunt. She teaches that stuff."

"Out of sight," the girl says. "I can dig the old stuff. The old stuff is like old, but new, but old. You know what I mean?"

He lies facedown in the water and floats away, letting the soap suds trail off his skin. Eugene's and the girl's voices become tiny ants crawling through his outer eardrum into his inner eardrum, through his brain. He rolls onto his back, slaps the water, shakes his head. His hand hits something hard—a knee. He looks up into the face of a chanting boy sitting on a surfboard. There are others; they are all crowded on the surfboard, singing. He pushes away from them.

Now he is standing on the edge of the lake, bulrushes tickling his legs, water streaming down his naked body. Someone has laid a cloth of many colors around his shoulders, deep blue with pink and brown and green explosions of paisley all over. But he needs his clothes, his blanket, and the banged-up steel army canteen that once belonged to his father, the black Bakelite stopper attached by a little chain in a way that seemed miraculous when he was younger. He once believed war had to be a magic thing, littering such treasures in its wake—he didn't yet understand that the treasures littered by war are people's lives. Like his father's. Like maybe that of Mike, over in Vietnam right now, or Luke, if their mom can't wrestle him back to school fast, or Eugene. Or maybe of his own self, if the president ends educational exemptions.

Welcome to Woodstock, canteen. Welcome to the sixties.

There are his clothes. The arm of his shirt is thrown back as though waving to him. "I'm sorry, man," he mumbles, slipping his long, thin legs into his jeans, losing the cloth of many colors. "I wasn't just gonna forget about you."

Watch out or you'll end up like your uncle Paul, his mom said one time when he didn't come home for dinner and didn't call, either, when he just couldn't bring himself to join the others. But it always just looks as though he's running away, because he has yet to find anything to run toward. She wouldn't have said that if he could find someplace he belongs. Something he could be good for.

"I wouldn't leave you here," he says, louder.

Music has started up in the distance, a rumbling echo, and he fumbles his feet into his sneakers, shoves his T-shirt into the back of his pants, picks up his blanket and the canteen, swings the cloth of many colors back around his torso. His movements become swifter and swifter until the cloth trails purple and green through the air in front of him, enveloping him in color, a cocoon of colors, like the blankets their mom wrapped Sissy in when she was still little, blankets worn thin from having swaddled his own baby body before Sissy's, and Luke's and Mike's and Patty Ann's before his.

Family. He is sure he did not leave Molly, not on purpose. They were sitting on the great heaving hill listening to the music; he, Molly, and Eugene. And when Joan Baez finished singing, no more than a sunflower-seed speck leagues away whom only he with his twenty-fifteen eyesight could make out, but with a voice louder than thunder, and the stage went dark, the three of them moved through the swarm of people as far as they could, settled Molly's plastic tarp in a field, popped the two-person tent, bound themselves in their individual blankets, and squeezed inside together. *Hey, man,* Eugene said. *Look at that: we're bivouacking!* and practically drowned in his own laughter. Sometime in the morning, awakened by the heaviness of the air in the tent, the risen sun on the canvas, they went looking for the portable toilets and fresh food, and all of that took what felt like hours, and while he was on line for something, some guy handed him something, which he took because they're at the Woodstock rock festival and that's how it is here, and then there was rain again and they started back to the tent but headed into the trees instead and Eugene said, *Hey, man, where's Molly?* And that was it. Molly was gone.

Eugene doesn't know where Molly is, either.

He shouldn't have brought Molly. He should not have brought her. He. Should. Not. Have. He told her so from the beginning. There are about ten million freaks rolling around on this hillside, and Molly is one tiny drop of water somewhere among them. But she insisted: *Francis, you gotta take me. Mom will be cool.* And he said: *I don't know, Molly. You aren't even sixteen.* Molly laughed. *I'll be sixteen in ten days! Jesus, Francis, you're only seventeen. C'mon, I'll die if I don't go. Country Joe and the Fish, and Canned Heat, and Janis Joplin. They say there'll be, like, thirty thousand kids there! If you won't take me, I'll go on my own. I'll hitch a ride. Maybe I'll get stabbed and murdered, like Sharon Tate.*

"Whoa, cat. Who you talkin' to?"

The guy has a beard and glasses with edges that drop down onto his fat cheeks. A pipe made out of tinfoil is in his hand. Hair is flying off his arms and shoulders; it's moving and swinging and jumping out at him, dark and springy.

He swipes the air to fend it off.

The guy puts up the hand not holding the pipe, and a thousand hands follow. The hair is waving. It's alive. The guy's arm is a caterpillar, orange and black, spotted.

He steps back, shields himself.

"Whoa, cat. Everything cool?"

His thoughts must have grown voices. He will never be able to have a secret again. He backs away from the caterpillar guy, trying hard not to think any thoughts, thoughts that could be heard. "No one. I was talking to no one."

"Hey, just checking everything's okay, friend. You look a little freaked out." The guy walks on past the pond toward the trees.

Without knowing why, he follows. His feet rustle through the goldenrod, releasing breaths of tiny yellow seed. He stops when he reaches a clump of thin, gnarly apple trees to touch their bark, rough and alive against his palm. He no longer sees the guy, but he hears the music.

"Hey, Eugene," he says softly, turning. It feels as though he's traveled miles, but the lake is still there. "Let's go listen to the sounds."

Eugene is sitting with the girl on a rock on the edge of the water. The girl named Dawn. *Dawn...hasting from the streams of Oceanus, to bring light to mortals and immortals.*

He waves to them, and Eugene makes a peace sign back, his glasses glinting from the light off the lake. The girl is still smiling.

The music is louder now, a drum and a flute, and maybe a guitar. It's not coming from the direction of the stage, farther away. What he hears is closer, a delicate motif against a larger print. Maybe it will lead him to Molly! Through the cluster of trees, and here's a forest of little tents and a VW bus atop the mud in a clearing. The side door of the VW yawns, two guys sitting in its mouth. One taps on a drum, delicately but steadily, and the other holds a guitar. A girl with slippery braids and a puffy white shirt faces them, playing a flute, swaying. At first her face is hidden from him, but she turns and looks at him over the silvery tip of her instrument, and both her eyes and the glittery sound go straight into his chest.

"You know how to play?" The guy hands him the guitar. "I'm gone."

He accepts the guitar and sits down where the guy was sitting, pulling the guy's life around him like a new skin. Before his mom and Ronnie moved them to Phoenix, he worked weekends all one school year alongside Eugene, serving up cola and fish fries down by the pier, to save for his own guitar. *Don't be a fool and bring that,* Eugene said when they set out yesterday morning and Francis picked it up. *I'm not pushing another piece of cod again in my life.*

He starts strumming "Angel of the Morning," the first song to come to his head. The girl plays along on her flute. The afternoon slides into puddles of sound and people dancing, time passing like ripples made by a breeze. The music warps around him in huge ribbons until it begins to rain again and the drummer wanders off and the girl pulls him into the van and rolls shut the door.

In the obscurity, her eyes shine dark with a bright center. She pulls her white shirt off, and it flutters above her bare pale arms like a ghost. He rises to his knees and draws his shirt off as well. She pulls hard on his belt buckle, pulls down on his jeans. He lifts his hands wide and far like Jesus Christ on the cross and allows her to take his clothes; he will allow her to do anything. He is safe here with her in their Volkswagen capsule, the massive crowd kept outside. He pushes her down, lowers himself onto her. He lowers himself into her, fumbling until she puts her hand on his to help. She is soft, warm. He pushes hard, and the world explodes into a flash.

Everything, everyone that has ever worried him is gone. He himself is gone. He is a million trillion molecules thrown up in handfuls across the universe.

And yet he is whole; he is perfect. He could sob with relief.

"Baby," she says, stroking his hair. "Baby baby."

He hides his face in her neck. "I'm. I was. Jesus." He rolls off and lies naked on his back. She moves onto her side and kisses his bare chest. She starts to sit up, but he pulls her down. Her pulls her in close to him again, searching to return to that perfect place, holding the heat of his body against the heat of hers until they find it.

When they finally emerge from the van, the rain has stopped. The girl takes his hand. "Come on, baby," she says. "Let's hear the music."

He allows her to lead him into the mass of people, over the vast muddy field, into the swaying, gaily colored army spread across the alfalfa amphitheater. She knows exactly where they are going. She knows everything. She must know where Molly is. His heart lifts. She is taking him to Molly! They jump over hands and arms flung out, body parts. They skitter through more bodies, some sitting, some lying, some standing. This is what Civil War battlefields must have looked like, strewn with undulant soldiers, but with air sweet from the smell of blood rather than dope. Heaving magnitudes of life, so close—the further she leads him into the crowd, the more his stomach turns. Vietnam would be still worse, bodies sunk in jungle, tangled in vines. He would run back into the trees, he would head back toward the road. But he has to find Molly. He cannot leave without his cousin.

The girl points and, leaping over a kid sleeping on a towel in the mud, pulls him down onto a tarp. About fifty feet to their right is the first of three huge red towers, pulsing with sound.

And it's one two three,
What are we fighting for?
Don't ask me, I don't give a damn,
Next stop is Viet Nam . . .

The girl sings, too, clapping. Everyone is singing along with Country Joe and the Fish. He covers his ears to shutter the sound, but the shouting comes through his hands, through his skin, into his bones. He gives up. "Where's Molly, man?" he turns to say to Eugene, except Eugene isn't Eugene but some cat with colorless hair and a dark blue bandanna around his forehead and a pipe in his hand. He knows this cat. He's met him somewhere. "Molly's cool," the guy says, dragging on the pipe. "Molly's beautiful. Molly's in the sky with diamonds." The guy passes the pipe to him. He drags on it, then passes it on to the girl and lies back. Is Molly up in the sky? Instead, he sees his father's image—not as he last saw him, crumpled on the lawn, the blood drained from his bronzed face, but young and fresh-cheeked in the army portrait his mom keeps on her bed-side table, even now she's remarried.

His daddy is in the sky with diamonds. But not Molly.

Tears spill down his cheeks. They roll down his neck and into his T-shirt, all the way into his jeans. He is bathing in his tears. He is *not* a stand-up guy.

"He's having a bum trip," the girl says. He's laid his head down onto her lap. Raindrops. That is the wet. The music has stopped.

"Did you take the brown acid?" the guy who isn't Eugene says. "What are you on, man?"

"I brought my younger cousin," he says, staring up into the girl's sunspot eyes, shooting flames of chestnut from their black centers into green and gold. "Like, I should have made her stay home. She's only fifteen, man. I'm responsible for her, man." His voice is rising, he cannot stop it, he can feel his heart, his throat, everything inside him rising.

"It's cool, baby," the girl says. Her white blouse is transparent from the rain. "She's okay. It's beautiful. Everything's beautiful. Look at all these beautiful people."

"He's beautiful," the guy who isn't Eugene says, smiling at him but talking to the girl. "Like, I dunno, man, like, some kind of painting of Jesus. That's some kind of beautiful kid you found there."

"You found him," the girl with sunspot eyes says. "You handed him your guitar. And he's like honey sugar candy. Like Twinkies. Like Pixy Stix. Like a Tootsie Roll. Sweet sweet sweet."

"You like my old lady?" not-Eugene asks him.

"Your..." he begins, struggling with a new panic.

"So when are you going over, man? Are you going over?" not-Eugene is asking him now. "Is that it, man? Is that why you're freaking out? You been called up?"

"He's not going over," the girl says in a singsong voice. "He's a baby. Baby baby baby. Sweet baby."

"Not *yet*, you mean. Not yet. *Fuckers.*" The leather necklace around not-Eugene's throat bobs. "Who's Molly, then? She belong to you?"

The rain is falling harder, every single drop hits him and explodes, as though his face were a hill in the jungle and each raindrop a tiny liquid hand grenade. He jumps up, and the girl stands up with him, two in a sea of people. She takes his hand. "We'll find her," she says. "Your Molly."

She's leading him again through the unreal people, through the raindrops. The farther they walk, the more the crowd thins. They pass a grove of trees where a couple is cutting up a watermelon while listening to the concert on the radio. They offer up chunks of the bright pink fruit, and he feels the shock of food in his stomach. He hasn't eaten for hours, or maybe days. Is there anything left that bread could buy to eat here? No one is selling local corn or lunch-size cartons of chocolate milk made from local cows along this path anymore. Eugene packed most of their food in the army-issue brown-canvas rucksack his dad had given him to use as a suitcase again this summer. *It took my Dad through the Apennines,* Eugene said, stuffing a package of sliced American cheese, a jar of Jif peanut but-ter, and a loaf of Wonder Bread into the oversize rucksack while he and Molly sat at Aunt Jeanne's kitchen table. *It can get us to Woodstock.* They tossed some of the beer and cola in there, too, the rest in a box, the tent on top and everyone's blankets thrown over it, and he and Molly carried it between them. Somehow he still has the canteen around his shoulder. He still has his blanket. Eugene has probably given all the food and beer away by now. That's how Eugene is.

"Umm," the girl with sunspot eyes says, licking watermelon juice off her fingers. "Groovy."

And then suddenly she is gone. He is standing alone on the road, an open-mouthed endless yawn of crookedly parked abandoned cars, of puddles and swollen ditches. There is no crowd, hardly any sound louder than the sound of evening. Relief peels off layers of weight from his already lean body.

He hoists himself onto the hood of the nearest car and pulls his blanket around his torso. The glass of the windshield feels cool against his back and head. Above are stars, thousands of them, twin-kling. There is Uranus again, god of the sky, father of the creatures on earth. The air sprinkles a dust of amplified music and country sounds over him and the blanket. The smell of mud and motor oil rises. The breeze blends together the sweet hovering remnants of grass and hashish.

The globe is slowing. The sky is clearing. The world is reassembling. He tucks his blanket all the way up to his neck. Sleep tugs on him and drags him under. It brings no dreams with it.

"I don't know."

He struggles to open his eyes. It's still dark out; the stars are still shining. Hours may have passed or just minutes.

"That's the password," Molly says.

He touches her arm. It is solid.

He closes his eyes long enough to swallow the rush of his heart. "Password for what?"

"I don't know." She laughs. "The free concert. To get in. Can you believe we paid for our tickets? Such suckers."

She leans over the hood of the car, a dark silhouette in the heaviness of night.

"You look terrible," she says.

"You smell terrible." But she doesn't smell terrible. She just smells like Molly. "How did you find me?"

Molly lifts her ankle-length granny dress and clambers up onto the hood. At fifteen, she's taller than most boys her age. She's not taller than he is, but their legs stretch side by side on the hood of the Chevy. "That was easy."

"Yeah?"

"I just started walking *away* from the crowd, in the direction of the highway."

"I wasn't going to leave without you," he says. "I was looking for you."

"Yeah," she says.

"A lot of people here. More than thirty thousand."

"Yeah. A lot more. Ten times more." She smiles and slugs him. "Pretty far out."

He opens the flap of his blanket, and she squeezes under it. They lie there, looking at the stars, listening to the faraway sound of music.

"Bet your brother Luke wishes he were here," she says.

Maybe Luke is here. Who knows? "There's Sagittarius," he says.

She searches the sky. "You're sure?"

"Yes." He uses a finger to trace the archer for her. "See? There's his centaur body. There's his shield. There's his lifted arm."

Molly pulls the filthy blanket further up over her, claiming most of it. She tucks her chin in. In the dark, she looks even more like Aunt Jeanne than usual—long-faced, coconut-haired. "You know what I've always thought was kind of strange?"

"What?"

She giggles. "How can there only be male centaurs? I mean, wouldn't there have to be female centaurs, too? So there would be, you know, new centaurs?"

He remembers the girl with sunspot eyes. He thought getting it on with a girl would be the ultimate trap, but it turned out to be the opposite. For a brief minute—he winces; a very brief moment, the first time around—he disappeared entirely. Now he wants to do it again and again. He wants to find that girl. He wants to find all the girls. All the Joans. All the Lisas. He wants to disappear over and over again into them. They won't own him. They will free him.

"We'll have to ask your mom, the classics professor, to explain the reproductive lives of centaurs," he says.

Their laughter mixes with the sweet air and fades away. Molly props herself up on one elbow and looks at him. "Are you going to be a hippie now?"

"I already am a hippie."

"Seriously."

"Christ, Molly. No. Probably what I'm going to be is a shaved-headed soldier and then a shaved-headed corpse."

She sits all the way up. "Don't say that, Francis. That's just stupid."

"Well."

"Well, nothing." She throws the blanket off. "Hey, this is a downer. Come on, let's go back and listen to some music."

"No. I dunno."

"Eugene's waiting for us."

"You know where he is?"

"Of course I do, silly. You're the one who got lost. Not us." She kicks him.

He breathes in the night air. Hanging low to the west in the sky is the string of stars that make up the constellation Pisces.

He sits up. "Found."

Molly slides off the hood of the car, extending a hand to him in the semidarkness. "You'll be okay, Francis," she says. "Eugene and I will hold on to you."

He takes her hand. The peace it gives him won't last. It can't last. But for now, it will have to be enough.

Flu Season / February 9-11, 1972

BARBARA

SWIRLS OF BLUE AND pink and pale yellow, like a melted Bomb Pop, spread out over Squaw Peak toward the north. Outside the library's large glass windows, random palms blacken against the sky. Toward the downtown are the dark silhouettes of Phoenix's three or four tall buildings, and then nothing, the city fading out into endless desert, flat, flat, and more flat.

"Barbara," the librarian whispers, beckoning from the front desk. "Would you mind? I have to..."

She shelves the last book on her rolling cart and slips behind the circulation desk. It's almost closing time; probably no one will come in. But maybe someone will still come in. Or one of the few people left in the library will have a book to check out. There's the stamp—for a moment or two, she'll be the same as a real librarian, not a once-a-week volunteer shelving books, taping book covers, watering plants. Not just a transplanted housewife desperate to find something to do. With the Mexican girl whom Ronnie insisted she hire to clean the house and no one left at home but Sissy, her life is so easy now. It's enough to drive her nuts.

The library's glass front door opens. She straightens in her station. An elderly man in silver-rimmed glasses and a woolen cap shuffles in and up to the desk. He lays a well-worn copy of *The Sensuous Man* on the counter.

"Good evening," she says brightly, keeping her expression steady and professional. The effort not to laugh is almost painful. "Do you want to return this?"

"Yes."

She flips the book open and checks the card in the library pocket. "Sir," she says, "this book was due at the end of January."

The old man frowns and scratches his neck. The skin there is sun-stained and deeply etched, like the earth after one of Phoenix's rare but violent sudden rains. "Are you saying I need to pay a late fee? Because I didn't receive a notice from the library telling me when February started."

She's not going to laugh. She's definitely not going to laugh. She inspects *The Sensuous Man* for any new damage, turning it over in her hands. "The library doesn't do that, sir. Individuals are responsible for keeping track of how long the months go."

"Harrumph," the man says, opening a battered wallet. He counts out a couple of dimes from its coin compartment. "The library used to send out notices. I'm sure they did."

She opens the metal box and drops his change in, biting the inside of her lower lip. "Thank you, sir. You have a good evening."

"Thanks, Barbara," the librarian says, returning, glancing at the book, then tactfully looking away. "I guess it's time for you to go now. Did you check that in? Would you mind shelving it before you go?"

"Not at all."

The Sensuous Man: The How-To Book for the Man Who Wants to Improve His Lovemaking. The author is simply "M." Well, just "M" is easy enough to find. But which category? History? Science? She stifles a giggle. Sports and entertainment?

Maybe she should check the book out herself and leave it on Ronnie's bedside table. *How was the library today, hon?* Ronnie will ask when she gets home, giving her his nightly peck on the cheek. *Great!* she'll say. *I brought a book home . . .*

Sociology and anthropology: 301.41. She slips *The Sensuous Man* into its place on the shelves.

Back at the circulation desk, she gathers up her coat. "Good night, Barbara," the librarian says. "Thank you for your help. Will you be back next Wednesday?"

"Of course."

Her first lifeline after moving to Phoenix was the library's weekly Spanish class. *¡Buenos días, señor!* Within a few months, she could almost communicate with the housekeeper. And at Ronnie's favorite Mexican restaurant? For a change, she was the smart one in the family: *Take the* sopa. *It's soup.* Tortillas? *That just means "corn pancakes."* Not that there are so many more Spanish speakers in Phoenix than in Southern California, but it felt like a way to make a place for herself in this city. Even Luke—before he went off with the hippies—would turn to her to explain stuff. It was nice to know something none of the others knew—something educated, not just about cooking or cleaning or taking care of babies. That Spanish class was the first bright spot of her new existence in Phoenix.

She still felt like one of those Apollo 11 spacemen here, though, bouncing over the moon's surface, unable to plant her feet on the ground. All her life, she'd lived by the sea. Suddenly, she was a castaway in an ocean of sand. The Spanish class helped her interpret what was going on, but it didn't make her part of it. So when the Spanish teacher mentioned that the library was looking for volunteers, she put her hand up immediately. Anything to find her way into the heart of Phoenix. They'd bought a house here. The kids had begun in new schools here. She couldn't give up.

It's two minutes before 6:00 p.m. A lady wearing a thin-brimmed felt hat, her coat draped over a chair beside her, sits at one table, flipping through a magazine—waiting, perhaps, for someone to pick her up. At the other table, deep in a novel, is a girl wearing a miniskirt so short it'd be almost impossible not to see her panties.

Look, she feels like saying to the girl. *I see you in here all the time. Don't sell yourself short. And for God's sake, don't get into trouble.*

The hardest part about leaving Los Angeles, when it came down to it, was not the prospect of having to find her way in a new city. It was leaving Patty Ann. Saying good-bye to Mike was easier; he was likely to get sent over to Vietnam soon anyhow, and the army would take care of him. But who would take care of Patty Ann? She's asked Francis to keep an eye out, now that he's nearby, at UCLA, but Francis is useless for stuff like that. She hears more about Francis from Patty Ann than she does about Patty Ann from Francis.

"That looks like a nice book," she says to the girl. "Are you enjoying it?"

The girl looks up, her face like the light at an intersection: surprise, suspicion, shut. "I checked it out with the other librarian already."

"I'm not a librarian," she says and slips her handbag over her wrist.

She hasn't brought the car. With winter settled over the desert, it's cool enough outside to walk the half mile home in comfort, and she likes that fifteen minutes of being untethered. Tonight she's especially glad for it; she's felt oddly out of sorts all afternoon, as though on the verge of having a terrible headache.

Cars roll past her, their lights catching on the front windows of ranch houses, illuminating the bright yellow brittlebush, casting its herbal scent into the evening. She doesn't know why she's felt so strange today, lost in thought half the day, going over all the old stuff. Luke tried to convince her before he followed that raggle-taggle group of hippies into the desert: *It's real, Mom. They're building a self-sufficient city, a utopia in the desert. I want to be part of it.* She never thought he'd really do it. She looked the word up. *Utopia: An imaginary place in which the government, laws, and social conditions are perfect.*

Imaginary, indeed. Any place where life is perfect is imaginary. *America* is *a utopia,* she told Luke, *or at least as close as we can get on earth. Would you rather live in the Soviet Union?*

The strange waterless undersea landscape of the desert lured him. And the kids, the wrong kids. Until the army did what she couldn't and found him and dragged him back out. After his tour is done, he'll get his GED and follow his younger brother to college. Then he can go build his utopias if he still wants to.

"Hello, kiddo," Ronnie says, already in the kitchen, mixing pink liquid in the old white pitcher. He pecks her on the cheek. "Feel like a strawberry daiquiri?"

"Practicing already for when Nancy and George come over on Friday?"

Ronnie laughs. "Practice makes perfect."

She turns the oven on. "Dinner will be ready in a jiffy. I'm just going to check on Sissy. She in her room?"

"Yes. You know, she looks a little pale."

She smiles. "Sissy always looks a little pale."

But Sissy, lying on her bed with one of her notebooks open, does look even paler than usual. She sits down beside her nine-year-old daughter and touches her broad freckled forehead. "Heavens, Sissy. You're burning up."

Sissy pulls away. "I'm okay. I mean, I feel a little bad."

"Hmm."

Back in the kitchen, she takes the meat loaf out of the fridge and puts it in the now-warm oven. The night before library days she prepares a dinner she can heat up when she gets in. "Sissy's come down with that flu that's going around."

"Oh, jeez. Poor kid." Ronnie hands her a daiquiri. "Then we'll just have to celebrate on our own."

"You signed a new contract?" Ronnie was right about Phoenix being the place for his company. The city is growing like wildfire.

"A *big* contract. A new shopping mall going up in the north of town."

"Oh, Ronnie. That's wonderful."

He raises his glass to her and takes a drink. "I was talking to one of the partners in the mall, an older fellow. He said he grew up here in Phoenix, and when he was a boy he lived in an adobe house, just like the Indians. In the summer, they'd soak the walls and curtains with a hose, then set a fan on them. That was their air-conditioning."

"I guess it was cheap, anyhow." She sips from her drink. It tastes too sweet to her, strangely chemical. She sets it down.

Ronnie looks carefully at her. "Are you okay? You look a little pale, too."

She shrugs. "Maybe I'm fighting the flu also."

In the morning, Sissy's temperature reads 101 degrees. She gives her two orange St. Joseph aspirin and makes her drink a cup of weak tea. After Sissy's temperature drops, she bundles her up in a blanket and brings her out to the sofa.

"I'm going to make you some chicken soup now."

"My stomach hurts."

"I'll bring you some ginger ale. But not at the same time as the soup, because if you drink cold with hot your teeth may shatter."

Sissy sleeps most of the afternoon. She ladles herself a bowl of soup also and sits down to eat it, watching her youngest child's carrot-colored eyelashes flutter with dreams, her chest lift the blanket draped over it up and down. With the older kids, she never had the time for a moment like this. She hardly had the time to sit down to eat. They were happy kids, though. They were a happy family. Even after Michael was lost, although not as happy. How could they have been?

She feels her own forehead. Not hot, as far as she can tell. She's almost never been sick. When would she have had time for it?

And yet she still feels off.

She swallows the last of her soup. She's promised to help out with making costumes for Sissy's school play—she'll get started on that.

When Sissy wakes, her temperature is high again, but not as high. Ronnie comes home, and she sets about cooking liver and onions for dinner.

"I'm not going to eat that," Sissy says from her makeshift bed in the living room.

She laughs. "Glad to see you are feeling more yourself."

She makes Sissy a poached egg and toast and pours her a glass of ginger ale. After Sissy's done eating, she gives her one more aspirin. She takes one herself.

"Do you want to watch TV?"

"Will you watch with me?"

"Go ahead," Ronnie says. Sissy rarely asks for company. "I'll clean up."

She turns the TV on and nestles on the sofa, slipping Sissy's head onto her lap. The Winter Olympics are on; they are taking place in Japan. There's a crime show and a noisy variety hour. She turns the TV back off.

"You wanna help me with your costume for the play?"

Sissy nods, propping herself up into a sitting position. "Okay."

Ronnie joins them once he's done washing the dishes. He picks up the latest issue of *Life*. "Looks like this guy faked his whole story about Howard Hughes."

"Who's Howard Hughes?" Sissy asks.

"Rich fellow from Texas," Ronnie says. "Made out like a bandit during the Depression."

When Ronnie doesn't say anything more, Sissy looks to her. Ronnie never wants to talk about what he might have gone through during the Depression. Like Michael, he settled in California after his service and never went back to his home state. Not even one time, from what she can tell. *Not close* or *none* he's said the handful of times she's tried to ask whether he has any family still in Iowa.

"A few people did all right," she says. "But most people didn't."

Sissy lays down a piece of cloth, forgotten. "Did Daddy's family?"

"His people were fancier, but like everyone else during the bad years they had no money. When your father was little, his dad still made his doctor rounds in a horse-drawn buggy. By the Depression, they had a car—but not much money for gasoline.

"Of course I just heard all this from your father. I only met his parents one time, right after your father and me got married."

"Why only once?"

"That's just how it was. We didn't have much money at first for traveling, especially with your father finishing his medical studies, then we started having all of you, and there was a continent between us." She won't say it, but maybe, just as she didn't ever want to return to San Francisco, Michael wasn't interested in being reminded of his old life. This must be why Ronnie never goes home, either, although neither she nor Michael was quite so drastic. People created new lives after the Depression, then the war. It wasn't running away. It was running forward. All of America did it. "And then your grandmother got the polio. Your grandfather went right after. That was way before you were born."

"Before Daddy died?"

She thought she'd told this to Sissy before. With a tribe for a family, it's easy to forget what one child has been told and another hasn't. "Before your father died, yes. Come on, let's get you back into your own bed. We'll keep you home tomorrow."

In the morning, Sissy's fever is down to one hundred, but her stomach is still unsettled. She doesn't give Sissy any more aspirin, although she pops one herself.

"I'll run to the UtoteM to pick up another bottle of ginger ale," she says. "I'll get some saltines, too."

It's a warm February day. Although still morning, the sun drops its curious desert glare over the city, glinting off the roofs of cars and mailboxes. She buys two bottles of soda and rolls her window down on the way back. The pungent, camphorlike odor of the creosote plant fills the car. It must have rained during the night.

She turns onto East Avalon Drive. Sissy is standing out front their house, talking to two strange men. That girl! In her nightie, too.

The men are wearing uniforms.

She just keeps on driving, right past the house, right past Sissy's astonished expression, past the two men, their heads swiveling to look at her. She drives to the end of the block and rounds the corner, toward Camelback Mountain.

She'll keep on driving. She'll drive and drive until she's disappeared into the desert. Until everything has disappeared.

Her hands fall loose on the steering wheel. Sissy is there alone, on the doorstep.

She turns right at the next corner and then turns right again.

Maybe this time she'll turn onto East Avalon, and it will all have been a dream.

There will be no Sissy on the doorstep.

No anyone on the doorstep.

It will all have been a bad dream.

She turns the corner onto East Avalon very slowly, so slowly, as though somehow she can stretch time, make it long, elastic. Sissy is still there. The men are still there. She pulls up the driveway and opens the car door.

"Get into the house," she tells Sissy.

The younger of the two men steps forward. He has a wide face and brown eyes with almost no eyelashes. The left side of his chest bears a name tag. The right side shines in the late morning sun with badges and insignia.

"Excuse me, ma'am."

She hefts the two bottles of ginger ale into her arms and walks toward them, the heels of her shoes clicking on the stone walk.

"Ma'am," the young man begins again. "I'm Sergeant Major John Goode of the Eleventh Signal Group at Fort Huachuca. This is Chaplain Trenton."

The other, older man has a silver cross on each lapel. It is not a hot day, but sweat glistens on his forehead.

She shakes her head.

"Ma'am, are you Mrs. Ronald McCloskey, mother of Private Luke Patrick Gannon?" the young man says.

Luke. "Luke!"

"May we go into the house?" he says.

She pushes past the men into the house. Sissy steps back, out of the way, clutching the top of her nightie.

He's sick. Or missing in action. Or, no, he's gone AWOL. That's it. That's *it.* Luke's gone AWOL. Or sat down in the middle of the barracks and simply refused to move. That would be like Luke! He'll be court-martialed now. Will he go to prison? Or just be given a dishonorable discharge?

But he's safe! That's the main thing. Safe.

She turns to the soldiers and points at the living room sofa. "Sit."

The two men perch on the edge of the sofa, taking their hats off and clasping them between their hands. The younger one starts again, "Ma'am, the—"

She waves her hand. "Can I get you glasses of ginger ale?"

The sergeant major looks at the chaplain. The chaplain nods.

"Thank you, ma'am," the sergeant major says.

She carries the bottles of ginger ale into the kitchen and sets them down on the counter. She leans over the kitchen sink and vomits.

"Mommy! Do you have my flu?"

She looks up. Sissy is standing in the doorway to the kitchen, watching her. Seeing her face now, Sissy lets out a cry.

She reaches for her daughter and pulls her in tight. Tight, tight, tight, so tight it is hard to breathe.

"I'll tell them to go away," Sissy says into her chest.

She lets go and lowers herself down until she's eye to eye with her daughter. "Listen to me, Sissy. Your brother is with God. He is *with God.*"

Because she knows. *She knows.*

She ties on an apron, then rips it off. She fills two glasses with ice cubes.

Back in the living room, the soldiers sip once from their ginger ales, then set them down on the coffee table, carefully reaching for coasters to place them on. She sits stiffly on an armchair in the same room where she relaxed with Sissy last night. So careless. So thoughtless. When her son was somewhere dead, dying.

Luke.

Utopia.

"Ma'am, I have an important message to deliver from the secretary of the army," the young soldier says. "The secretary of the army has asked me to express his deep regret that your son Luke died in Phu Yen Province in Vietnam on February eighth. Ma'am, Private Gannon was a grounds casualty."

She shakes her head. "I don't understand," she says.

"He was killed by small-arms fire."

"No."

"It was at base camp, ma'am."

Luke. Luke.

"He's coming home now," the chaplain says. "He'll be arriving at the air force base tomorrow. We need...to discuss arrangements."

"No," she says, again.

"Ma'am, I'm sorry."

"No, he's not coming home. He's not coming home *ever."*

"Ma'am," the chaplain says.

"Are you Catholic? You're not even Catholic, are you?"

"No, ma'am. I'm Presbyterian. But the army will provide you with..."

She stands up with such force that the armchair rocks backwards. "The army couldn't even send a priest?"

Sissy claps her hands to her head. "Mommy!"

"Never mind. Never mind," she says. "What does it matter? What could it possibly matter?"

The two men have stood. "Ma'am, should we call your husband?"

"I'm Luke's only parent."

"I'll call Ronnie," Sissy says in a small, trembling voice.

Sissy leaves the room. She sits down again. The men take out their papers.

"Luke will go to Los Angeles," she says.

The chaplain lays his hand down on hers. "Ma'am—"

She pulls her hand away.

"Yes," she says. "Los Angeles. With his father. We already have a place there. Thanks to *you*, we already have a place there."

Separation / September 11-12, 1974

BARBARA

PATTY ANN AND LEE are arguing in the living room. Again. She turns over the top card on the deck between her and Kenny. The pile underneath slides out over Kenny's bed, and she tucks the stiff new cards back into a tower, tapping the sides to make them uniform. She and Kenny shouldn't be sitting on the bed—this is where she's sleeping while she's visiting. But Patty Ann and Lee have made the living room and kitchen no-go territory. Kenny's elementary school is closed for three days, since the janitor discovered a crack from last year's quake. Or maybe from the one in '71. Sean should have started at the same school, but apparently after the first day the teacher sent him home and told Patty Ann to wait another year.

Maybe that's why Patty Ann asked her to come. For help while all three boys are home. Two active little boys can be quite a handful when there's a new baby.

"War, Grandma!"

She snaps her cards down, counting loudly—"One, two, three, jack!"—to distract Kenny from the sound of his parents fighting.

"If you walk out that door, do not bother walking back in," Patty Ann shouts.

"You're so uptight, baby. When did you get so uptight? You weren't like this in high school," Lee shouts back.

"In high school I didn't have three brats and a broken oven and a doofus husband saying he was going to dump his latest jack-squat job to drive down to San Diego and then across the desert and then back to Anaheim, *Anaheim,* in our car-with-the-bumper-tied-on-by-a-shoestring-but-the-only-one-we-have to go to some rock concerts. David Bowie!"

"I'm not 'going to some rock concerts.' I'm not going for *Bowie.* It's work, man. And if the job's jack-squat, why you raggin' about my leaving it?"

"Cause it's the only fucking one you have. You're going to get fired again, Lee."

"I can turn over some good bread like this. Things were crazy at his show here this past week, just like I said they'd be. It's like a whole new level selling this stuff. *This* is my new job, babe. I'll come home with . . ."

"Shut up. Shut up! I don't even want to hear about it. That's fucked up, Lee. That's fucked up! Are you fucking crazy? My *mother* will hear."

My mother will hear? What planet do they think she's living on? Do they think she doesn't already *know* what Lee's up to? That she doesn't see his red eyes, his tapping fingers? That she thinks the package wrapped in foil in the back of the fridge marked DON'T TOUCH is a roast chicken? And all the rest of it: the empty bottles under the sink in the kitchen. The filth. Where does Patty Ann get the idea that it is acceptable to live this way, especially with children in the house? There are ways to behave and ways not to behave. It is that simple. Women don't *get* to give up. If they did the world would collapse.

Kennedy turns over his last card. "Queen! I win this war, Grandma!"

She hands him her lost cards. "So you did, Kenny."

The yelling is getting louder.

"You'll change your tune when I come back in a Cadillac," Lee shouts.

"*A Cadillac?* Like my mom's husband drives? I thought you said they were only for the Man. I thought you said they were only for pimps or fat-ass honkies. So: which one are you?"

Kenny jumps up from the bed. She lassoes him with her arms before he can run out of the room. *Grandma.* Born when she was not quite forty-one, just a few years after Sissy, he could be her own son. The new baby is sleeping peacefully in a crib in one corner of the bedroom. The little brother, Sean, is playing in another corner with the G.I. Joe she handed him after she'd stepped out of her car, a little dazed from the long drive from Phoenix. Patty Ann appeared behind the screen door, her face a shadowy web, the baby a dark bundle in her arms, and pushed the door open: *You're here. You came.* Then, spying the little plastic soldier and snatching it up from the stunned child, her face grew distant, a pale flat moon under the midday Southern California sun: *We don't let him play with stuff like that.*

Don't let him play with stuff like that? Like *what?* She gave the G.I. Joe back to the poor kid as soon as Patty Ann left them alone again, and he hasn't set it down since. He acts as though it's the only normal toy he's ever had. Maybe it is. He's gliding it through the air right now, making loops upon loops, accompanying the motion with soft sounds, almost the only sounds she's heard him make since arriving. All the boys seem oblivious to the shouting from the kitchen. Ugly scenes clearly are nothing new to them.

Life has taught her that there's no changing the past—or, really, the future. Free will doesn't mean free to choose what happens. It means free to be a good sport about it. But she has to protect the boys in what little way she can while she is here. That's *why* she's here, surely—Patty Ann can't be hoping for her help with Lee. *A lot of other fish in the sea,* she used to singsong while Patty Ann curled her finger around the telephone cord. *Just wait until you get to college. You'll see!*

She should have tied Patty Ann up with that telephone cord.

If only Michael had been still with them. *Patty Ann,* he'd have said after the very first time Lee came around, *that boy undoubtedly has his merits, like all of God's creatures. But he is not the right one for you.* And Patty Ann would have listened. Patty Ann always respected her father more than her mother; Michael was a doctor and a war hero. She herself doesn't even have a college degree. She could spend her life trying to prove she's worthy of bearing the name Gannon.

Of course, in real terms, that's water under the bridge. She's a McCloskey now.

"...the Man."

"Oh, fuck you, *the Man!* If the Man can get me a fucking stove that works, then bless his Man soul!"

"Yeah, that's just what you are, isn't it? You'd fuck the Man for a new fucking stove, wouldn't you?"

"Me? *Me!*"

She gets up and loudly closes the door to the kids' bedroom. Children should never hear the things she's heard since arriving the day before yesterday. It's worse here than she expected, and she'd expected bad.

Hey, Mom, what's up? Patty Ann said on the phone three days ago, as though seven months hadn't passed since they last spoke. *How's the weather in Phoenix? How's Sissy? Want to come visit for a few days? Want to come tomorrow?*

Even before they hung up she was reaching for her suitcase, because if Patty Ann was calling, Patty Ann must really need help. She thought Patty Ann would be forced to see her at Francis's graduation last spring, but then Francis got the job in a guitar shop and said he wasn't planning to attend his graduation, so there was no point in her coming. When she tries to call, it's always Kenny who answers: *Mommy can't talk right now,* he says. Which means she hasn't spoken to Patty Ann since the two-year memorial service for Luke last February.

She sits down on the bed and runs her hands over the sheets.

Two years, seven months, and three days.

Once a woman becomes a mother, the morning never comes when she wakes up, stretches her arms out, and feels light, like a teenager, again. Happy, yes. Weightless, never. The children grow up, they move out, they experience life in a way no amount of Mercurochrome, bandages, and a mother's kiss can make better. Becoming a mother means committing to a lifetime of worry.

Unless that child is lost. Forever.

And then you wish you could have all that worrying back. God, please, let me have it back! God, please, let me have *him* back. *Why did I waste all that time worrying instead of simply being grateful for this perfect person I put on this earth? Why can't I just have this perfect person back? Why why why.*

She reaches beside the bed for her purse and snaps it open. She rummages for a cigarette before remembering she quit again.

"You okay, Grandma?"

"Am I okay? Ha! You won that battle, but you haven't got me beat yet!"

They are an American family, and people have to stand by their country. Luke *had* to go over. It was no one's fault. Not hers, not Luke's, not their country's. Patty Ann is the one who had choices. And made them badly.

She flips over a card.

We've moved to a house, Patty Ann said on the phone. At least the last place had other apartment complexes around it, a sidewalk, a row of palm trees. Patty Ann's new home looks out on a FedMart gas station in a torn pocket of LA, a far cry from the orderly neighborhood where she and Michael brought Patty Ann up. Someone—presumably not Lee—has painted the squat bungalow a dubious blue that has nothing to do with the sky or a robin. The front door is on the side by the carport instead of in front; the interior is a box split in four. The kitchen door opens onto a back patio lined with broken cement. The only semblance of lawn is the scrub out front.

And the state of things inside…In her time, people *cleaned* their homes before having visitors, especially mothers or mothers-in-law. Wives turned the rugs, men washed the cars, together they hid any sign of desperation. When she first arrived from Phoenix, Patty Ann's house looked as though the Bomb had hit it. Soiled clothing lay on the beds and floors, dirty dishes on the counters and tables. An ashtray spilled ash and cigarette butts onto the sofa. A stuffed bear, flattened and chewed as though by a dog—although there isn't any dog—lay on the ragged carpeting. The musky odor of dirty bedding filled the air.

Even with kids popping out of her like Pop-Tarts from the toaster, she kept their house as neat as a pin. The day after Michael died, her heart heavier than an iron, she tucked in the corners of their empty bed, tight enough to pass any inspection. She pushed those sheets in under the mattress, firmly folded back the top sheet by the pillows, smoothed the now-barren land of her private life, then went out to the kitchen and tied on a clean apron.

The first thing she did at Patty Ann's—after pouring herself a glass of water and sizing up whether Patty Ann might possibly be pregnant again, which, thank God, doesn't seem to be the case—was to gather up those filthy sheets and take them to a Laundromat. *For Christ's sake, Mom,* Patty Ann said, lifting her shirt to feed the baby right in front of her, like some woman in *National Geographic* magazine. *You just got here, and already you're criticizing my housekeeping?*

Yes, Patty Ann. Yes, I am. You live in a pigsty. And look at you—you act like a suckling sow. On the way back from the Laundromat, she stopped at Sears and bought a vacuum cleaner. The abandoned Electrolux in Patty Ann's carport clearly would never hum its hum over anyone's floor again, probably stopped working months ago. Maybe it never worked.

Patty Ann is twenty-seven now, with three children. Lee's family was never much, but she brought Patty Ann up to be better than this.

Kenny turns over a card and rubs a sunburned knee. He fiddles with the edge of his shorts. "Mommy doesn't like it when we close the door to our bedroom, Grandma. She says it's sneaky. She says she can't keep an eye on us."

"That's okay," she says. "You just concentrate on your hand."

"Oh, Grandma. Everyone knows war's just a game of luck."

"You say that because I'm winning."

"No, you're not!"

They compare piles.

The front door slams.

"Okay, okay. Your pile is bigger," she says. "But it's not over till it's over. I'll whip your butt yet."

"Grandma!"

The front door opens and slams again. Patty's voice carries in through the windows: "That's it. That's it, Lee. I mean it!"

The old Dodge's engine turns over, stalls, turns over, catches. A roar fills the air, and then quiet.

"I guess Daddy's gone," Kenny says. He turns over a card.

"Keep your eyes on your cards. Never mind about your father."

"Mommy says we shouldn't play war, anyhow. She says we should play peace instead and make it so whoever turns over the lowest card wins the pile."

"Right. Well, never mind about your mother right now, either."

Two, three, four minutes pass. The freckles on her grandson's nose spill down its bridge and onto his wide cheekbones. His bright eyes become smaller with concentration.

The screen door slaps shut again. Patty Ann's footsteps are heavy in the kitchen. She lays down her last card and loses it to Kenny.

"Well," she says, "that's that. Time to get started on lunch."

———

Sunset spills Hi-C colors over the cracked backyard patio, warming the bland beige into something richer, almost rosy. She and Patty Ann sit on the two wooden garden chairs, towels thrown over the seats to keep splinters from entering their tushes, and sip burningly sweet lemonade mixed in the old white pitcher that once belonged to Michael's parents. Patty Ann has slipped some vodka into her own, as though she won't notice. The baby is down for the night, inside the house. The two boys—bathed and in clean pajamas—sit cross-legged on the scraggly lawn on a beach towel, eating Popsicles she walked across to the gas station to buy. It's peaceful now, without any chance of Lee stumbling back in.

Maybe Patty Ann will finally explain the phone call and why she was summoned.

"Don't drip on yourself," she says to the boys.

"Oh, let them be, Mom."

Kenny is licking the multicolored pop slowly, preciously, and the melting is getting the best of him. "There's a fresh roll of paper towels on the kitchen counter," she says.

Patty Ann waves her glass, creating an explosion of tinkling ice. "You see, that's just so typical. First you give a treat. Then you spoil it by nagging."

She takes a long drink. The air is soft and dry at this hour. Back in Phoenix, Ronnie will have his feet up on the footrest of the leather recliner, the remnants of dinner on a tray, a napkin neatly folded in his lap. Ronnie likes to eat in front of the television, a habit sprung probably from years as a bachelor. Sissy will be in her room, nose in a book or one of her journals.

Kenny looks up at her. A trembling Technicolor drop of liquid courses down a finger. "What did you say, Grandma?"

Patty Ann jingles her glass again. "You just can't let sleeping dogs lie."

"Okay, Patty Ann. That's enough."

She sets her glass down and goes into the kitchen for a paper towel. Kids have to learn to do stuff like this for themselves, but if Kenny comes in now, he's sure to leave a sticky-sweet trail of melted Popsicle across the kitchen floor she washed yesterday. God knows when it will get washed again.

Patty Ann stands in the doorway. "When are you going to visit Luke?"

She tears a sheet from the roll of Scott Towels. She bought a double pack for the house on her way back from the cemetery this morning, along with the playing cards, a bunch of bananas, some sandwich fixings, the pork chops they just had for dinner, a few steaks, potatoes, frozen succotash, frozen lemonade, four sticks of butter, and two gallons of milk. Plus a box of Bisquick and bottle of

Aunt Jemima syrup for pancakes. The boys gobbled that breakfast up like they'd never eaten before. She had to mix a second batch of batter.

"I already have."

"Mom!" In the obscurity of dusk, the hostility dropped briefly from her expression, her older daughter looks for a moment like the woman Patty Ann might have become—maybe trained as a nurse, married to a nice doctor, living in a nice house with two cars in the driveway—if not for Lee. If not for everything. "I would have come with you."

"You said you were done going with me to cemeteries."

But Patty Ann isn't that woman. Patty Ann's a wreck of a young woman, dangling in the ramshackle doorway like a loose tooth in a swollen mouth after a brawl. Her husband has run off, who knows for how long or doing what, leaving her behind with no job and no money but three children.

"I don't know why you left him to be all alone in Los Angeles," Patty Ann says, her expression closing up again.

"Luke is not alone. He's with your father."

Is that what this trip is about? Did Patty Ann bring her all this way to argue about Luke yet again? She turns away to pour more lemonade. If Luke hadn't run off with those hippies instead of going to college, he would have gotten a student deferment. He'd still have gotten called up—with number 013 in the lottery, that was for certain—but at a different time. *Everything* could have been different. She would have supported him in requesting a deferment: she's a mother; she knows her kids. Francis would have done better than Luke over there. *Patty Ann* is better cut out for the army. And getting a deferment isn't cheating. Just like it wasn't cheating that Francis didn't get sent over at all because he drew a high number. But Luke disappeared into the desert, and the army dragged him back out before she could. It's awful, but that's what happened.

She puts the pitcher of lemonade back in the fridge. "Also," she says, "Luke has his big sister here. And Francis."

"Francis is gone."

Patty Ann steps back into the night. She follows her out and hands the boys each a paper towel. "What do you mean he's gone? When'll he be back?"

Patty Ann shrugs. "He split. After Eugene committed suicide."

"After what? Eugene what?"

"Labor Day weekend. Eugene took a shotgun to his head."

"What?" She puts a finger to her lips and nods meaningfully at the boys.

Patty Ann shrugs. "I don't lie to my kids. They should know what war does to people."

The boys don't seem to be listening anyway, intent on the army of ants drawn by the sweet juice of the Popsicles spilling over the cracked cement. She says, in a lowered voice, "But why didn't any-one tell me? Why didn't you tell me?"

Patty Ann stares at her and again shrugs.

"Oh, for God's sake. Why didn't Francis tell me, then? That's awful. *Awful.*" Eugene? The story seems too strange to be possible. Granted, she hasn't seen him in five—no, maybe six years; by Luke's funeral, Eugene'd already been called up. There was a time he was almost her fourth son. But when kids move outside their family's sphere, their friends move even further.

Still, Eugene was always the very spirit of optimism. What could possibly make a person change that much? "Maybe it was an ac-cident. It must have been an accident. Was he drinking? Was he hunting? People said his dad used to go into the hills with a shotgun when they didn't have anything for dinner."

"He was sitting in his parents' backyard. Maybe he used his father's old gun. I don't think anyone knows exactly why, except maybe Francis. But Francis isn't telling anyone anything. After the funeral, he took off."

She's been trying to reach Francis ever since she got Patty Ann's phone call, without success. This explains why. It hadn't seemed strange; frustrating but not unusual. Francis is often difficult to get hold of. "You went to the funeral?"

"Yeah. Eugene's father called me."

"Eugene's father? Not Francis?"

Eugene's parents! His hapless father with the missing finger. His worried, bedraggled mother. How could Eugene do such a thing to them? And not just to them—to Francis?

Could *this* be why Patty Ann asked her to come?

She sits down and stares at her two grandsons, so young, so innocent, bent over the swarm of ants, oblivious to the grown-ups, to the world around them.

"I don't get it," she says softly. "Eugene makes it safely all the way through Vietnam, and then he comes back and kills himself? It just doesn't make sense."

"Maybe he *didn't* make it safe through Vietnam."

She sets her lemonade down. "Kenny, go in and change your pajamas. It's your bedtime."

"We don't have a bedtime," he says, looking up.

"That's ridiculous. All little boys have bedtimes."

"We don't. Mommy says they aren't natural. Mommy says when we are tired we will sleep."

"That's not exactly what I said, Kenny." Patty Ann extends her hands toward her sons. "Both of you. Come on. I'll read you a story."

Soon the sound of Patty Ann's voice, low and rhythmic, wafts out from the boys' bedroom. With a wet paper towel, she wipes up any trace of the Popsicles. Then she extracts the hidden vodka from its cabinet and sprinkles it over the ants. She splashes some vodka into her lemonade, too.

Michael. Luke. Now Eugene.

———

"So, boys," she says the next morning, shaking off the night's restlessness, once they've finished their second round of pancakes. She'll pay her respects to Eugene's parents this evening or tomorrow. They'll tell her where Eugene has been laid to rest so she can visit him before she heads back to Phoenix.

But right now, her job is her grandsons. "What shall we do on my last day here?"

"Are you leaving?" Kenny says. "Don't go yet."

His little brother shakes his head in agreement, rattling the G.I. Joe he still hasn't let go of. The kid doesn't talk. Before, he was small enough to pass for a late bloomer. Or for someone who is just very quiet, like Francis. But really, something is wrong. Something is very wrong.

"Why are you leaving already, Mom?" While she feels somewhat worse for wear this morning, Patty Ann looks better: her shoulder-length hair freshly washed and tied up in a high ponytail like a teenager's, her jeans switched for a rumpled but clean sundress.

"Well, it's been nice to visit," she says. "But I'm not sure why I'm here."

"Isn't visiting enough?"

"Visiting is great, Patty Ann. But I have my own home to look after."

In fact, with Sissy almost eerily self-sufficient, plus the hired girl

119

in to help, there's nothing keeping her from staying a little longer. Francis clearly hasn't headed back to Phoenix and there's no use trying to track down *where* he's gone, not if he doesn't want to be found. She isn't due at the library until next Wednesday, and that's the only volunteer work she's involved in other than the odd cake or costume to be made for Sissy's school. She hasn't been able to step back into their church—or any church—since Luke's funeral mass.

Still, if Patty Ann doesn't want to come out and say what's on her mind, she knows how to call her bluff.

"I think the zoo today," she tells the boys.

"I'm staying home with the baby," Patty Ann says, making a vain effort to hide her irritation. The zoo must be another thing Patty Ann doesn't approve of. No wonder the boys were so fascinated by the ants last night—probably the only wildlife, other than terns and seagulls, they've ever seen. "I have work."

"Work?"

"I've been making jewelry." Patty Ann leaves the room for a moment, then comes back with a big wooden box in her hands. "I comb the beach for shells, paint them, then string them alongside beads on necklaces. The boys help me. When I can get the car from Lee, we drive down to Laguna Beach and look for the shells together, and sometimes they paint them."

She lifts a knobby twist of macramé and shell up to the light. It spins in space like unspoken memories of summer days at the beach. The kind she spent with the kids when they were still small and living together in Los Angeles, everyone still alive, everything still ahead of them. She drops the necklace back into the box. "That's pretty, Patty Ann. Do people buy them?"

"Some. Sometimes."

The two boys pour into the front passenger seat of her car. "You're fun, Grandma," Kenny says. "It's fun when you visit."

She flips on her sunglasses. A tire drops into a pothole, jerking the little boys forward. "Hold on to your hats, boys," she says gaily. Even the streets are disintegrating in this hellhole. Was Eugene living in poverty like this? Did he, like his parents, feel doomed to a life of scraping by? Boys can't marry their way out of their pasts so easily. Still, Eugene was bursting with ideas and energy. And he had an honorable discharge from the army. Last time Francis mentioned him he had a job somewhere—a lumberyard?

"Daddy says the zoo reminds him of high school," Kenny remarks.

Her grandkids. This is her last day with them. "Right," she says. "And your dad and his friends were the monkey exhibit."

Kenny hesitates, unsure whether he should laugh. "No—because of the cages. Mommy says the animals are all stolen from their mothers and sad."

Patty Ann thinks *she* spoils every treat? "There aren't real cages at this zoo, Kenny. The animals are lucky to be here. They always have food, and they live much longer than if they were out in the wild." He's such a sweet boy, so naturally diplomatic. She doesn't want to push him to betray his parents. "Anyhow, they are living here now. So we might as well enjoy them."

And they do. Once they've arrived, the boys run from exhibit to exhibit. They want to see everything. The big cats, the bears, the reptiles. They spend an especially long time in front of the enclosure of Methuselah, the alligator.

"I have a purse that looks just like his backside," she tells the boys, and Kenny makes a face. "It's true. Step-grandpa Ronnie brought it back for me from one of his business trips."

"Grandma."

They munch on the bologna sandwiches she packed for them,

and then, with the sun heating the day up, she buys them all slushes. Slurping happily on their straws, they move on to the zebras when the G.I. Joe somehow manages to fall inside the animals' enclosure.

The panic in Sean's eyes is something terrible to see. He grabs onto her arm.

"Wah!" he says, almost moved to speech.

The old man standing beside her sees and intervenes. "Don't worry!"

He stretches his cane between the bars and deftly hooks the doll under its arm. Slowly, gently, the old man lifts G.I. Joe out.

Everyone around them claps.

"No big deal," the old man says. "I'm a lifetime fisherman."

"You and my father," she tells him, and then tells the boys: "Your great-grandpa would take you fishing if you went up to see him." Even when no one had anything, when whole families appeared on street corners in San Francisco, their faces caved in with hunger and despair, her mother kept the family larder stacked with mason jars of tomatoes and beans and peppers grown in window boxes, and her father would take her and her brother down to the new pier every day before school and not leave until they caught something. To this day, she can't stand the smell of walleye or sole or perch. Actually, the only fish she can bear is canned tuna.

But Patty Ann has never taken the boys up to San Francisco to see their great-grandfather and never will. In truth, he probably couldn't take the boys fishing now, anyhow. With his emphysema, he's not likely to last much longer. After her mom died, she and Ronnie invited him to stay in Phoenix with them, but he has his group of fellow Czechs, the same ones he's worked alongside, played fiddle with, and drunk beer with for the last three-quarters of a century. Why would he leave it now to live in a strange place, with virtual strangers, at the end of his life?

"Let's go see Twinkletoes," she says. "And then we'll have seen everything there is to see, I think."

"Who's Twinkletoes?"

"A black rhinoceros. They are rare."

Kenny whistles, a little-boy whistle without much sound. "Groovy!"

On the way home, no one speaks. The boys are hungry, but she doesn't stop. There are still the steaks and some potatoes in the fridge for dinner. Maybe she'll go to the shop one more time before she leaves, buy some more meat, some more iceberg lettuce. Or maybe she'll just have to give Patty Ann some money—though how can she be sure it'll go for groceries?

Patty Ann and the baby are sitting on the living room floor, surrounded by cord and shells and large beads. It's difficult to tell which are finished and which are still works in progress. The baby is sucking on a scrap of blanket. Patty Ann is smoking a cigarette. How she'd love to smoke a cigarette herself! She sends the boys to the bathroom to wash their hands and busies herself in the kitchen, putting the potatoes in the oven, tenderizing the steak with the back of a spoon, rubbing it with salt and pepper, then pouring a little splash of the vodka mixed with Aunt Jemima syrup over it. There doesn't seem to be any other type of seasoning in the kitchen. She sets tall glasses of milk on the kitchen table for the boys to have while they are waiting for dinner. Then she picks the baby up from the living room floor beside Patty Ann and settles into the old armchair Michael favored, passed on when Ronnie moved in. She fingers the scars in its fabric: this is where Luke spilled cola; this is where Luke left a pen on the seat. She cradles the baby and kisses his head.

"How about Lee?" she says.

"Lee's gone."

"I see that. Until when?"

Patty Ann stubs out her smoke. "Until never."

She sighs. "But seriously. Until when?"

"But seriously. Until *never*. I'm going to get a divorce."

She stands back up, shifting the baby onto her hip. "Come on, boys," she calls. "I've set glasses of milk out for you."

The boys rush through, the heat of their young bodies pressing past her. She follows them into the kitchen. The potatoes in the oven bring the smell of hominess with them. She prods them with a fork.

Patty Ann comes in and stands by her.

"He's your husband, Patty Ann," she says, setting the fork on a piece of paper towel so as not to dirty the counter. "For good or for bad. You married him."

"Mom," Patty Ann says, leaning in close, as though waiting for her to fix a hair barrette before church on Sundays, as she used to do when Patty Ann was little. "Mom, I want to ask you something."

She doesn't want Patty Ann married to Lee, but marriage is not like a house you outgrow and put on the market. Doesn't Patty Ann know how difficult it is to erase the touch of a first husband? Ronnie has never tried to replace Michael, and she doesn't want him to. Part of the reason she agreed to marry Ronnie was she knew he never would.

"Mom," Patty Ann says, very, very softly. "I'm all alone here now. Entirely alone. Lee is gone. I'm not having him back. And Francis is gone. He's not coming back."

Francis is not coming back? How can Patty Ann know this?

But, of course, Francis is not coming back. He's been waiting to leave since the day his father died. With Eugene gone, what would there be to hold him?

"Mom," Patty Ann says, "I want you to take Kenny."

And, now, she understands. This time it is Patty Ann who has called *her* bluff.

BOOK THREE

1984

You think to possess for long the vanities of this world, but you are deceived.

—Saint Francis of Assisi, in "Letter to All the
Faithful," 1215

The Inner Hebrides / June 2–8, 1984

FRANCIS

HE PULLS ON HIS jacket, already forgetting the woman he's just left behind. They've begun to blur, the two on Iona, nice women but with the same infrequent hearty laugh, prematurely worn skin, and strong torsos. Even their names slip haphazardly around in his mouth: Moira and Muira. He's taken to calling both of them Lady.

You cannae call me Lady, Moira or maybe Muira said. *The most title I have is Postmistress.*

I'm American, and yes, I can, he said, unbuckling his belt. And he does.

A five-pound note lies under a wineglass on the kitchen table. He shoves it into his front jeans pocket: a meal at the restaurant, a pint of bitter he can pay for himself. The women are only being friendly; it's not as though they are a job. By the time he's outdoors, he'll have forgotten the little gift. At thirty-one, he's never had a bank account. He couldn't even say how much cash he has in his wallet.

He can make it another day. By how much doesn't matter. There are benefits to being no one and nowhere.

The North Atlantic morning air is damp, bracing, but sharp June sunlight is chasing the night's dew. Today makes five weeks on the tiny isle of Iona, longer than he would have expected to stay if he'd made a plan before arriving. Iona's a good place, an oasis among the battling gray, aqua, white, and green waves of the open ocean off the western coast of Scotland, buffeted interchangeably by untempered wind, lashing rain, misty still, and blunt sunshine. There's an uncanny peace in being naked in the eye of nature. He's parked his pack in a lot of places since leaving America. But nowhere has felt quite so separate, so otherworldly. On Iona, he feels closer to having escaped than anywhere else he's been in ten years of traipsing around Europe. Not just from crazy, needy Georgina. From all the ghosts chasing him.

He pulls up the collar on his jacket and starts down the road past Martyr's Bay toward the harbor. He's missed the first thread of locals heading out to check on their sheep or fishing boats or to the neighboring isle of Mull. The next ferry doesn't reach the dock until 8:55 a.m.

When he arrived on that ferry five weeks ago, pushing his way against the wind, past the crumbling rosy-gray stone of a long-ago nunnery, wondering where the hell he'd ended up, he fell in step with a short, stocky man with a white beard, a heavy Celtic cross swinging around his neck.

The man glanced at him sideways, lingering over his guitar and worn cowboy boots. *Are you looking for a place to sleep? We need a young set of arms up at the Community and could make you up a bed somewhere.*

The strange calm of the island drew an honest answer from him. *I don't mind hard work, but I'm not among the faithful.*

Do you believe in the existence of God?

It wasn't an issue of whether or not to lie. He wasn't sure of the truth. How could he feel so let down by something if it didn't exist?

I guess so.

That's enough, then.

They gave him a solitary cot in a small office inside a thousand-year-old stone shed by the water that once served as the abbey's infirmary and offered him a regular seat at the communal dining table. In exchange, he does the odd job around the abbey: rebuilding a wall ravaged by winter snow, patching a roof, turning the half-frozen May soil for the kitchen garden, lending a hand to the ongoing reconstruction. Now a beacon for believers all over the world, the abbey was founded by an exiled Irish monk named Columba back in the sixth century. There's plenty of upkeep to be done. Yesterday he cleared spring weeds from around the graveyard and Saint Oran's Chapel, final resting places for a gallery of early Scottish kings, among them Macbeth of Shakespeare fame. Luke would have liked that.

The Community doesn't give him cash, though. He has to get that however he might if he's going to purchase a ferry ticket back off the island. Or just to buy this morning's cup of coffee at the general store, down by the dock. Thus, the gifts of the ladies. The generosity of its women has been the one familiarity on Iona.

He pushes open the general store's door. The ginger-haired girl who runs the shop looks very young, fourteen or fifteen, but the coffee she brews is as black as the most starless night and as stern as the stiffest island wind. Maybe the best coffee he's ever had, even better than any he drank during the months he spent picking olives in Italy or the spring he passed busking on the Karlsplatz in Vienna. The girl's father must be gone to work on the mainland, and the mother must be sick or tending a newborn. She's dropped out of school to pull on her mother's apron, a girl who is fifteen going on forty.

But that doesn't make her not jailbait. He had a couple of run-ins of that sort early on in Europe; young girls still have hopeful imaginations. They blur the lines. They romanticize the lives of wanderers like him.

He nods at her curtly, careful not to appear too friendly.

The coffeepot on the shop counter feels heavy, like it's just been filled. He pours a cup and takes a sip. Not a twinge on the end of the girl's long nose, not a blink of her ginger-lashed eyelids. It's like a dance they are doing together. He throws some coins on the counter, more brusquely than he intended.

There's that old feeling of being watched, of being followed, like the way he started to feel even with Georgina. It's not that he didn't like Georgina. That was, in a way, the problem. From the first time they spoke it was as though they'd known each other always. Georgina once remarked, *The thing about Francis and me is we're both so serious we can't take anything seriously.* It felt, when she said that, as though she'd seared a hole right into his heart.

She got under his skin. She made him feel too much. Georgina, stretched flat on a chaise longue in a black leather miniskirt and black lace shirt with no bra under it, her delicate chin tipped back, her caramel-colored hair sprayed out over the cushions, laughing and adjusting a leg to let him see that she had no panties on, either.

A track mark in the crook of her knee catching his eye instead.

He doesn't have the stuff to help someone like Georgina. And he doesn't need another lost life on his conscience.

The general-store girl drops the coins in a small chipped cup with a couple of lonely clinks.

He tries not to feel ashamed of himself for being so rude to her, throwing those coins down like that. As though it were her fault he's been stupid enough in the past to sleep with too-young girls like her. The people on Iona are nice. They deserve better than a person like him on their little island.

He was at a bar in Manchester, a scatter of empty beers in front of him, no idea where to go next or how he'd get there except that it had to be someplace where Georgina wouldn't find him and try to drag him back into their sick life together in London. The idea of making it east to India and Nepal had come up over the years, but all that love and lies, dregs from a decade earlier—the very thought depressed him. Anyhow, the hippie trail pretty much closed down with the Soviets in Afghanistan and the shah out of Iran.

Up to Oban the morra, the guy on the neighboring bar stool said. *My sister makes cheese there, sells it to a wee island, Iona. Crazy wee place. Hae to tae the ferry fae the mainland to the island of Mull, cross all of Mull, and then tae a second ferry just to get to it. A dot in the middle of nowhere.*

Hey, man, he said. *Can I hitch a ride with you?*

In the middle of nowhere, and yet *there.* Not in the middle at all: the end of the earth, or maybe the beginning. Iona is solid. Iona is timeless. If he stayed longer, he might even find that elusive holy trinity or at least get closer to it: Peace. Freedom. Absolution.

With summer coming, though, other young men and women will start stepping off the ferry with strong arms and backs and considerably more commitment to the Community's mission of seeking new ways of "living the Gospel in today's world." Locals say the island swells with visitors over the warmer months, the population exploding along with purple-blossoming wild thyme. The Community won't need to turn to a prodigal son for its heavy work.

Men will be returning, too, from winter jobs on the mainland. Back to their women.

Time to move on.

"You know, miss," he says to the girl, "you make a killer cup of coffee."

An ugly wash of red creeps across the girl's round face.

He carries his mug down to the dock. The morning sky is clear enough for him, with his prodigious eyesight, to see the captain stepping in and out of the small cabana on top of the ferry, the mile away to Mull. Of course, the correct word can't be *cabana*. The bridge? Wheelhouse? Boats never have held any appeal for him.

Three last passengers stride onto the ferry, all wearing red jackets. Two men, one taller than the other, and a woman. Already the island's population of ninety has begun to grow in number daily, along with the meadowsweet and Scottish bluebells bursting forth in the fallow fields. Some of the new arrivals come toting heavy duffels or suitcases and letters of introduction to the island hotel or the Community, ready to settle in for the summer. Some come, as he had, just for a day and find themselves unable to leave. The peace of Iona.

Georgina, spilling her pill case onto her naked lap, a cascade of light blue and pink and yellow polka dots against her pale pubic hair. *Francis, darling, I had a looooong talk today with Daddy.*

Are you really going to take that shit?

Her laughter, hiccuping up through her lank hair as she bent over, picking the pills out of herself. *Well, I'm not going to fuck it.*

You know, Georgina. You go alone. We'll dance another night.

Her pale fingers, waving this away, then selecting a light blue pill. *Oh, don't be such a bore. It'll be a loooovely party. It'll be an ecstatic party.* She popped the pill on her tongue and stuck it out at him. *The point is, Daddy says we can get married.*

He stopped strumming his guitar. *Married?*

He quite fancies the idea. He says it'll be good to add some fresh American blood to the family. He says you're sure to give him attractive grandchildren.

Down went the pill, her lovely swanlike throat rippling slightly.

As wasted and useless as his life might be, he doesn't have a death wish. He doesn't need to be around anyone else who might, either. Done that. Not doing that again.

The ferry separates from the pier, lurching its way into deep water. Once clear of the dock, it moves slowly but smoothly through the water toward him. It will take ten minutes to cross, the wind warming and sweetening.

Time to get a start on his day also.

Back in the store, he sets his cup on the counter and flashes the girl a smile. Red rushes again across her smooth young face, spilling into the roots of her carroty hair. She hurriedly begins counting up the change in the register, and he looks away. It's been good on Iona; he doesn't want to leave anything bad behind him. At least Georgina was twenty-two, or almost twenty-two, old enough to be held responsible for bringing him to the British Isles and settling him into her fancy Belgravia apartment.

Who'd ever have guessed her father would decide they should get married, him a shiftless, penniless SOB from America? What kind of parenting was that? Fuck, Georgina must have been in even more desperate shape than he thought.

People are out in the village now, a few tending gardens beside their low-roofed, whitewashed stone homes, a woman bicycling down the road lined with golden yarrow. He nods at each islander as he passes. Some greet him by name; five weeks now, and it is such a small island.

Around back of the abbey, his makeshift bedroom is still chilly from the night. He lifts his guitar case onto his cot and pops it open, checking the instrument for damage from the cold. He adjusts the tuning, then picks out a few bars of "Roxanne" by the Police. "Roxanne" was playing the first time he saw Georgina, in a club in Palma de Mallorca, leggy in a pair of yellow silk shorts, dancing with three Spanish boys wearing sorbet-colored Lacoste shirts with the collars turned up. Smooth, handsome, dark boys, a striking contrast to fair-haired Georgina, creating a tableau watched by everyone around them.

Don't put on that red light, she mouthed in his direction, abandoning her dance partners to pull him onto the floor.

Someone had brought him over to Palma from Barcelona on a long white yacht with two levels and teak trim, although who it was and how it came to pass he can't remember. He had his own room for the week they floated around on that boat, with its own little bar and a double-size bed that he wasn't alone in for long, then they docked on Mallorca and everyone on the yacht spilled out into the breezy Mediterranean night. He took up with Georgina and, once he'd fetched his guitar and pack from the yacht, never saw those people again. Instead he and Georgina spent a couple of sangria-soaked weeks hopscotching around the clubs of Palma, fucking like rabbits and laughing. Suddenly, she had bought him a ticket to come back to London with her. They were still having fun, and winter was coming. There was no reason to say no. The minute they disembarked at Heathrow, however, rain slapping down around them, Georgina wasted from downing four Bloody Marys during the two-hour flight, everything felt different. Everything felt rotten. He should have split right then.

I don't normally live like this, he told her after she'd thrown open the door to her posh apartment.

She dumped her ankle-length leather coat on the floor and sank onto a massive chintz-covered sofa. *I don't imagine you do, darling.*

Georgina's father had bought the flat, and her mother had gotten it put together, lavishing it with flowery prints in silk. Georgina joked that the only thing she did herself was change the locks, so they couldn't sneak in and lift her stash.

He's not one to judge others' lifestyles, but how Georgina

managed to hold so many drugs in that slight body mystifies him. In London, it no longer seemed like holiday fun. She was still lively and wry and, of course, pretty, but she became something else, too. Dangerous. The smooth walls of the room where he sleeps on Iona, the tiny square window facing onto the sea and the stone fragments of ancient grave markers stored under the gables; if he's going to thank God for anything, it's that he managed to get out before there was real trouble.

Tomorrow, however, he'll bundle up his things and say good-bye to Iona. Better to leave before the Community has run out of need or space for him, struggling to tell him to go, with a lot of coughing behind fists and embarrassed glances. He'll ride the ferry back to Mull, hitch across it to the larger ferry for the mainland. From Oban, he'll hitch again or hop on a train. He is sure to have enough money in his pockets to pay for a ticket and a couple of weeks in a room somewhere until he picks up another job or meets a nice lady. Maybe he'll go to Glasgow—it's supposed to be a scruffy town with a decent music scene. So far, Scotland has been good to him.

He digs his shaving kit out from his duffel and, pouring water from a pitcher into a porcelain-covered bowl, mows the stubble from his face, nicking the slight cleft in his chin in the process. He dabs at the blood with a towel, slaps on some oil to guard against midges, and slides into a clean shirt. He's been shaving since he was sixteen but for some reason has never grown hair on his chest. Some women ask whether he shaves it; at least one asked whether he waxes it. *Like a swimmer? Nah. Then I'd have to shave my head, too.* Of course, she took it as an invitation to run her fingers through his wavy shoulder-length hair. Well, fair enough. Although he didn't enjoy her calling him Goldilocks.

Maybe he should head north when he leaves instead of east to

Glasgow, up to the Isle of Skye. According to legend, selkies guard the Isle of Skye's shores. Jethro Tull has moved up there. Or was it just Ian Anderson? He slides his canteen into his jacket pocket and picks up his guitar.

He stops in at the abbey kitchen. He tucks a fistful of warm oatcakes and a scrap of cheddar cheese into a paper bag and fills his canteen up at the tap, the clear, cold water spilling onto his fingers. He writes a swift note for the cook: *I won't be eating at the abbey tonight, thank you. Francis.* If he eats with the Community, the groundskeeper may mention a task for tomorrow or the day after, and then he'll have to say he's leaving, and then there will be the need for good-byes. Better to leave quietly.

And then he'll be gone, and they will swiftly forget him. Someone who actually belongs here, someone of faith, will take his place. He made his peace with not being at peace with God or even knowing whether there is a God years ago, maybe when, as a nine-year-old boy, he saw his father die right before his eyes. Certainly when he watched his brother's coffin being lowered into the ground beside the mound over his father's body.

And then Eugene's, two years later, in unconsecrated ground because the son-of-a-bitch priest at the Catholic cemetery said they couldn't take him.

One thing is certain. If there *is* a God, he wouldn't turn Eugene away. Not any God he could ever believe in.

———

A soft northeasterly wind is blowing, rustling the new wildflowers in the machair. White-bellied, long-beaked oystercatchers and flocks of small black starlings pass overhead, as though leading the way to Saint Columba's Bay. He hasn't taken the long hike down to the southern tip of the island since shortly after he arrived, although some in the Community make the hour-and-a-half pilgrimage over rocky hill and sheep-strewn meadow every Sunday afternoon, regardless of the weather. After rowing across the open sea from northern Ireland, with the help of his twelve acolytes, Columba pulled his wooden currach up onto the shore here in the sixth century and effectively established Christianity in Scotland. Spiritual seekers on the island consider the bay sacred.

No one much walks down to the bay during the week, however. Maybe in the summer, when the number of overnight visitors with more time to spend on the island picks up, but today the bay should be a good place to play music and enjoy some sunshine undisturbed and disturbing no one, a good way to spend his last day on the island. He hasn't brought his guitar outside much here for fear of it being damaged by rain or the heavy mist that often veils Iona. Other than the guitar, the sum total of his possessions is the shaving kit, a wallet, a US passport, a knife, his boots, the leather jacket Georgina gave him, a rugged sweater a Norwegian girl made for him, a few changes of clothes, a bandanna, a belt, the two books he always carries, and the canteen. Georgina gave him stuff during the five months they were together, but he left everything except the jacket behind. He had to take that because she'd ruined the one he had, throwing up on its shoulder outside the Wag on a cold January morning. This new jacket—warmer and softer leather than any he's ever owned—appeared two days later, with a note saying: *So I don't have to lean my head against my own sick. Your G.*

Ah, lovely Georgina.

He likes his guitar, though. *Don't get some dumb, lousy one,* Eugene said after they'd fried enough fish sticks and poured enough sodas for him to afford it. *Get one you'll want forever. Cause you are going to want it forever.* Well, Eugene is gone, but he still has the guitar. He'll busk on the street in decent weather, but he'd go hungry before exposing its rosewood curves to snow or rain.

There've been some hard times in Paris, one very difficult winter in Amsterdam. But something or someone has always come through. When not caught up in wars, the world is a pretty hospitable place.

By the far end of the machair, the relentless beadlike rattle of the corncrake call is almost deafening. He heads up over the hillock, past the tiny heather-ringed loch, and down toward the bay, almost stepping on a nest containing four large eider eggs. The sea opens up before him, a deep blue seething expanse ringed by an orange-, green-, and black-pebble beach divided in half by a large rocky outcrop jutting into the sea. He settles into a nook on the eastern side of the outcrop, out of the wind and not too far from the water's edge, knocking a couple of carrot stubs out of the way with his boot. The remains of someone's picnic, maybe the rest carried off by the seabirds swooping overhead. Maybe the picnicker was carried off by the birds as well. Or a mermaid or a selkie. It feels wild enough here for that.

There's a song one of his Iona ladies was singing the other night. He asked her to repeat it, slowly, committing to memory the words and melody.

> *An earthly nourris sits and sings,*
> *And aye she sings, "Ba, lily wean!*
> *Little ken I my bairn's father,*
> *Far less the land that he staps in."*

He figures out the chords as he goes: G F . . .

Then in arose he at her bed fit—
    And a grumly guest I'm sure was he—
    "Here am I, thy bairn's father
    Although I be not comely.
"I am a man upo' the land
    An' I am a silkie in the sea
    And when I'm far and far frae land
    My dwelling is in Sule Skerry."
Now he has ta'en a purse of gold
    And he has put it upo' her knee
    Sayin', "Gi'e to me, my little young son
    An' take thee up thy nouriss-fee.
"And it shall come on a summer's day
    When the sun shines het on evera stone
    That I will take my little young son
    And teach him for to swim the foam.
"And thou shall marry a proud gunner
    An' a proud gunner I'm sure he'll be
    An' the very first shot that e'er he shoots
    he'll shoot both my young son and me."

A cormorant pedals the sky directly overhead, throwing a flitting shadow over his face and guitar. The song itself is a darkness, rumbling with the waves of the sea, skirting its frothy surface, sinking into its opaque depths, at odds with the brilliance of the morning: the seal-like sea creature who can only mate when transformed into human form, the unsuspecting maiden who gives birth to his son, fated to be taken back to the sea by his father, then felled by his mother's new husband, the maritime gunner. The truth of fairy tales is, they rarely have happy endings.

Something dim and spectral has sunk into his heart. Another old ballad he's learned since arriving on the island comes to mind, about a Molly. Not his sweet, funny cousin—wherever she is and whatever she may be doing. It's been years since he's spoken with anyone in his family. About a Molly Bawn, who, shielding herself from the rainfall with a white apron, is taken for a swan by her lover, shot, and killed.

> *I shot my own true lover—alas! I'm undone*
> *While she was in the shade by the setting of the sun . . .*

The sea seems to be listening to him. He lays his guitar down on his knees and listens back.

"Well!" a voice says.

A young guy, with a rush of shiny dark curls framing rosy cheeks, is suddenly right there, almost at his side. "The obvious moral being never to play fast and easy with the gun."

The guy's accent is as posh as Georgina's. Not many people speak like that on Iona. He clasps the neck of his guitar. "I never play with guns, period."

"No?" The guy drops onto his haunches and sticks a hand out. "Rufus."

Could Georgina—or her father—actually have sent someone after him? He has to have been as expendable to her as any of the beautiful objects decorating her flat. People like him and Georgina, what could they ever really know about love? After he took off, she undoubtedly spent a few nights in histrionics, drinking to excess, fucking everyone in sight, calling him names they hadn't taught her in her string of fancy schools. But she did that most nights anyway.

Thick blue-jeaned legs tucked into galoshes. A sturdy neck and back, sporting a white scarf and a bright red Windbreaker. So healthy looking. None of Georgina's crowd would look this square.

"No. I'm a pacifist, man," he says, reluctantly putting his own hand out.

Rufus pumps it. "Conscientious objector?"

Here it's not like in the US, where some people consider conscientious objectors to have been traitors and others consider them to be heroes. Few older Brits get far away from their experiences in World War II, but no Brit his age or younger could care less who fought or not in Vietnam. There's no reason to lie. "No. Never got called up."

"But you *are* American. I thought for certain from the song you'd be Irish."

"I learned that song here, in Scotland."

"Well, it's originally Irish."

He shrugs. "My father's ancestors were Irish."

"You look like your dad, then." The guy picks up a stone and dances it one, two, three times across the surface of the sea. "What are you? About six foot one? One hundred and eighty pounds?"

The questions are weird, but there's something curiously appealing about this Rufus, something strangely familiar. "My dad's dead," he says. "Twenty-two years."

"Whew, young. Cancer?"

"He was a POW in the Pacific during World War II. Got to him eventually."

Rufus hops another stone across the face of the water, bestowing tiny kisses. "My regrets, man. War is hell."

"Yes."

"You get seasick?"

Where is this leading? He shakes his head.

Rufus jumps to his feet and claps him on the shoulder. "Ghislaine! Eamon! We've found our man."

He turns his head to discover a young man and woman, also wearing bright red jackets, standing a little ways down on the edge of the beach, tossing pebbles into the sea.

The trio from the ferry in Mull this morning.

"Hey, wait a minute—"

"We're staying at the inn, the Argyll," Rufus says. "Meet us in the dining room at seven p.m."

"Right," he says, picking up his guitar. People don't decide things for him. That's the one thing he has in his life.

Rufus laughs and twirls a dark curl. "Seven p.m. Dinner is on me."

They don't look anything alike, other than the dark curls. Rufus is the picture of health, the glowing pink cheeks, the shining eyes.

It's that same boundless enthusiasm.

Eugene was the most cheerful son of a bitch on the planet.

He looks out to the sea, out over that huge body of water, spanning his today and his yesterday. Eugene was cheerful, that is, until that gentle evening when, with a full moon rising, having plowed through three six-packs, Eugene shot himself in the head. He himself having gone off to meet some girl.

If he could cram the memory into a bottle and throw it far out into the waves, send it back to America.

Remember when we were kids? Eugene said. They were sitting in his parents' backyard, drinking Buds. Eugene had just gotten off from work at the lumberyard and was still wearing navy blue coveralls with GENE written in red script over his heart. *And I never got picked for any teams because I had asthma?*

He wasn't wearing work coveralls. He'd just graduated from college, had a little cash in his pocket from his new job stringing guitars in a music shop and a little more from his stepfather stuffed in an envelope by his bed—*It's high time you open an account, Francis,*

Ronnie had said—and there was a pretty girl waiting to meet up with him. It was a fine August evening. He laughed. *Back in grade school? Before smoking weed cured your asthma?*

Eugene laughed, too, a bitter, dry laugh. No one knew what made Eugene's asthma go away so suddenly at puberty, but it wasn't smoking weed. The big joke was that it cleared up just in time for him to pass the army physical. *Yeah, exactly. Well, those days when I never got picked for teams were the good days.*

He popped the tab on another Bud and watched the evening star grow in the waning light, lay back to soak in the warm Southern California nightfall. Only later did he hear what Eugene was really saying: *And I never got picked for any teams.*

It really wasn't a joke that asthma had kept Eugene off every team when they were growing up but not out of Vietnam. It turned out not to be funny in the slightest. The army in Vietnam: the worst team of all.

What happened? people asked afterward. *Why? Why'd he* do *it?* Eugene's mother clung to his arm, her worn face swollen from crying: *Eugene must have said something to you. You were best friends since forever. You were like brothers.*

Eugene did say something to him, something else earlier that same last evening. But not until it was too late did he hear him.

After the funeral, he borrowed a girl's car and drove to Patty Ann's. It was a terrible place, where she and her kids were living. They didn't talk about his plans or about Eugene; she talked about music, about some jewelry she was making, about her sons. They shared a joint and a bottle of cheap wine. But she knew he'd come to say good-bye. *I'll always be your big sister. I'll always be here,* she said when he left. He went from there to the TWA ticket office and bought a round-trip ticket to Paris, because it was the cheapest flight for Europe available and round-trip cost less than one way.

The return half of the ticket, long expired, sits at the bottom of his pack.

Over here no one asks him, *What happened?* He's almost learned how not to ask himself.

"Sure. Dinner at seven," he says, although he has no intention of going.

———

The sun is still high when he heads back toward the abbey, but a hazy pink film hugs the dark blue edge of the horizon. In June, the sun sets late up here. He passes the four pale green eider eggs, still unguarded. Perhaps a gull caught their mother.

Back in his makeshift bedroom, he lies down and closes his eyes, drawing in the day's tender, salty scent of sea, the flinty embrace of the June sun, the hours of solitude. He falls in and out of sleep, but as peace grows within him so does a hollow feeling. He has no oatcakes left and no food in his room, and he's told the Community he won't be eating with them tonight. Neither of the women he's befriended on the island has invited him around this evening.

On Iona, that doesn't leave many options. There's the Argyll and then there's . . . the Argyll.

Fuck it.

He draws himself up from his cot and pulls his jacket on.

The air is silvery with the sound of singing from within the abbey. A lone cow lopes its way down craggy Cnoc Mor, the hill behind the tiny island school. He makes his way down and around the short row of waterfront houses. Inside the Argyll, Rufus and the two others are installed around a wooden table.

"Hello!" Rufus says, waving to him. "Sit down! I've already ordered for everyone."

He slips into a chair at the table, checking to see who else is in the tranquil dining room, evening sun streaking its windows. No one tonight. A plate of mutton pie appears before him.

"What's your name?" The girl in Rufus's group has a slight accent he can't place. She's dark-haired, sleek, and good-looking in an unfrivolous way. "I am Ghislaine."

She doesn't offer her hand. He likes her matter-of-fact manner. "Francis."

"Ah, Francis! And this," Rufus says, introducing the thick-necked, flat-headed boy who completes their trio, "is Eamon. Eamon from Belfast."

Eamon nods at him.

"So, Francis," Rufus says, "you are wondering what we are doing on Iona."

"No, not really," he says, cutting into his pie. "Lots of people come to Iona."

"Last December," Rufus says, "right after the Harrods bombings, I woke up, made a cup of coffee, and thought: this is madness. We need to reach out across the water."

Rufus stops and looks at him expectantly.

He swallows a forkful of warm, savory pie. It's good—better than good. Surely worth having to sit through this.

"*Across the water!* We're going on a mission of conciliation," Rufus says, "one that we hope will be heard by both Protestants and Catholics, by both Ireland and the UK—by the world, even. Next weekend is the anniversary celebration of Columba's arrival in Scotland. We're going to undertake his two-hundred-kilometer journey *in reverse,* from Iona to Northern Ireland. The twist is that half of *our* crew will be Catholic and the other half Protestant. You see the symbolism, I'm sure. We're pulling *together.* I've had an old currach shipped, refitted, and kitted out here on Iona, and we've been training in another one off the coast of Devon. And—very important—I've reached out to as many newspapers and television stations as possible. Maybe you've even heard about us."

He's seen a currach. It stuck with him because it seemed such an unlikely sea vessel—something between a rowboat, sailboat, and canoe. These three red-jacketed knuckleheads are going to row all the way from Iona to Northern Ireland, over open sea, in a boat that's little more than a wooden butter dish?

He shakes his head. "No. I haven't heard anything."

"The thing is," Rufus says, unfazed—it's hard to imagine what would faze Rufus—"we have a little problem."

"Not so little," Ghislaine says.

"We've lost one of our crew members," Rufus says. "Our Irish Catholic."

He lays his fork down.

"It was a bit of a freak accident. We were training in a borrowed boat in Oban yesterday. He slipped on a mound of harvested seaweed and knocked his head against a pier. He's laid up in a hospital bed for the foreseeable future."

Rufus stops again to look expectantly at him.

He picks his fork back up. "Must have been a nasty fall."

Ghislaine frowns. "Rufus insisted we continue on to Iona. He said he was sure something would come up."

"And by God, it has!" Rufus says. "Will you believe this, Francis? Our lost crew member is six foot one and weighs one hundred and eighty pounds. Exactly. You'll fit his kit perfectly."

He wipes his mouth with his napkin. As he inclines his head, he catches sight of Moira—or Muira?—walking into the kitchen. The one who isn't a postmistress. She flashes him a glance before disappearing behind the kitchen door.

"*You're* Irish-American," Rufus says. "It isn't Irish-Irish, but it's close. You look very fit. You obviously have no commitments to keep you from stepping into the boat when we push off tomorrow morning—you wouldn't have been sitting out there in the middle of the day playing your guitar if there was someplace you had to be."

He takes a last bite of the mutton pie. The meat falls apart on his fork, soft and tender. He tears off a piece of bread and mops up the remains of the cheddar–mashed potato topping, gravy squeaking up over the all of it. Perhaps Moira/Muira is waiting in the kitchen, hoping he'll leave with her. Suddenly, there isn't anything he wants less. What's more, for reasons he can't quite put his finger on, the idea of Rufus seeing him leave with her turns his stomach.

"Well, that was good," he says. "Thanks for the meal. Best of luck on your journey." He squeezes his napkin into a ball and drops it on the table. Maybe he can sneak out before she comes back.

"I do not think he is interested," Ghislaine says.

"Where are you from?" he asks her.

"Bordeaux, in western France," she says. "My family has owned vineyards there for centuries. We're Huguenot," she adds. "That means I am Protestant. That's how I can add the second Protestant to the crew."

"You are a sailor?"

She smiles, catlike. "I have a wall of trophies at home."

"Of course he'll do it," Rufus says. "We'd have to cancel otherwise. And look at him. Not just the right size, the right religion, and available, but *beautiful*. It's like a gift dropped right down from the skies. They'll put him on the front page of the *Times,* the *Guardian,* and the *Daily Mirror.* He looks like a rock star."

"I don't want my photo on the front page of the *Times,*" he says. Georgina doesn't read the *Times* or the *Guardian* and certainly not the *Daily Mirror,* and no one reads any of them in the United States.

But someone who does might recognize him. Not that he's an out-law. He just likes to live under the radar. That's his way.

Ghislaine tilts her heart-shaped face to one side. Her hair, black and straight, cut along the length of her jaw, swings against her pointy chin. "No. Not a rock star. Jesus, maybe."

"Well, isn't that what the handsome rock stars look like? Jesus Christ with a hard-on?" Rufus says.

"You're an ass," he says.

"Come on, man. Don't be offended. It's a good thing."

"Oh, for Christ's sake, show some fucking class."

At this, Rufus and Ghislaine burst out laughing. Eamon says nothing. God only knows how Rufus bullied *him* into being part of this venture.

Through the kitchen door, Moira/Muira reappears. As far as he's heard, she doesn't work in the restaurant, but she fiddles with the salt and pepper on an empty table until she catches his eye. He shakes his head. She returns the salt and pepper to their places and slips back into the kitchen.

"Nice people on this island," Rufus says, watching. "Friendly."

"Nice enough." He can't leave, with Moira/Muira hovering. How the hell can he not even remember which one was named what? The two of them weren't *that* much alike. Truth is, he decided he couldn't be bothered and never even tried. "You know, I saw the three of you boarding in Mull this morning. I thought you were Jesus freaks."

"You saw us all the way from Iona? You could make us out?"

He shrugs. "Yeah."

Rufus and Ghislaine exchange looks.

"Francis," Rufus says, "I thought you're a pacifist. Isn't that what you told me down at the seashore this morning? You would never hold a gun because you are a pacifist?"

Moira/Muira on one side. Rufus on the other. Eugene would have had a field day with a predicament like this. So would Georgina, for that matter—she's the only other person he's ever known with an equal appreciation for irony. Maybe Molly.

"And what of it?" he says. "I don't need to prove it to you."

"No. Not to us. But how about to the world? Or prove it to yourself. Or don't prove it to anyone and just come along for the hell of it. Come along because it will be a great story to tell your children someday. We're going to do something really important together, something you'll remember all your life."

"Maybe I don't need to do something important I'll remember all my life. Maybe I'm not looking for that. Anyhow, I don't know anything about the sea. I've probably never even rowed a boat." He looks at his hands, tries to remember if they've touched oars. "This is just stupid."

"You look strong," Ghislaine says. "You work in manual labor?"

"Trust me, man," Rufus says. "We know what we're doing, and we will carry you. You just give us your body and your looks."

It's like being punched in the gut. When he first discovered girls and what he could do for them, he felt like a wizard. Every encounter felt like a little miracle, an escape to a place where no one could catch him. He was set free and, at the same time, made powerful. Almost like a hero. That was a long time ago now, though.

The emptiness of his life hits him with the force of a heavy wave. Here he is, in his thirties, tossed about like dreck on the sea, sleeping wherever he can find a welcome pillow, fucking women whose names he can't even keep straight. What the hell does that make him? Whom is he kidding? No one would recognize him. He's not anyone's memory.

Rufus's and Ghislaine's faces look so hopeful. If he's nothing more than a body, maybe it is time to find a better use for it.

Except—they'll end up in Northern Ireland, where they pop bombs off like they're lighting candles on a birthday cake. They killed fifteen in one day three weeks ago.

If he's going to be flotsam, at least he doesn't need to wash up on *those* shores.

He rises. "Sorry, man. The world needs people like you. Sincerely. People ready to get involved. It's just not my bag."

Rufus stands up, too. "Are you scared?"

From behind the kitchen door, Muira/Moira reappears. Their waitress follows close behind her. They pretend to fuss over the salt shakers again, but the waitress is a bad actress. He can feel her give him a careful once-over.

"Okay," he says, because fucking fuck. *Fuck.* "When and where?"

———

At 2:50 a.m., the water is shiny and black, and the white trim along the boat's top edge reflects the rays of the moon. There is no sound apart from the voices of Rufus and the man who refitted the boat, come down to see them off, and the rippling of water. They need to depart just before high tide at 3:29 a.m.; his pack was bundled, his sailing attire in order, and his guitar enveloped in a plastic sleeve within a large plastic barrel before he had time to think twice about having agreed to the journey.

I won't get to tell the groundskeeper at the Community I'm off.

They'll be following you via the news, Rufus said. *They'll be cheering for you.*

You can send them a postcard from Northern Ireland, Ghislaine added, with an edge that lets him know she realizes he's not the type to send postcards.

The boat is about twenty-five feet long and narrow, with high sides and one blunt and one upturned pointy end. It slides sideways in the water while Ghislaine restrains it with a rope and Eamon trundles small plastic barrels containing their clothes, rain gear, and sleeping bags out of a cart, setting one under each of four wooden benches. Another, medium-sized barrel, with food, tools, and cooking supplies, goes in the blunt end of the boat, by a fifth bench without a foot brace. A larger barrel holding his guitar is tied down in the other, pointy end of the boat. The mast for the sail, plus what looks like a spare oar, lies lengthwise atop the benches, along one side.

There are no permanent fixtures within the boat's shell apart from the benches and foot braces. No wheelhouse or shed or equipment box or anything. The floor is an open plaid of long, thin, light-colored wooden slats and curved-rib frames. More than anything, the currach looks like an oversize wooden bassinet.

"We're going to cross open sea in this?" he says.

"We are," Rufus says.

He doesn't bother telling Rufus how crazy he is. "Who's the last bench for?"

"My daughter," the boat refitter says, pointing. "She's your spare man."

He turns to look. The moonlight shines on her long nose, round face, and frizzy red hair as she lumbers down to the dock, waddling from the weight of a fifth small plastic barrel. She stops a few feet from them.

Holy fuck.

"She's a *kid,*" he says.

"You need someone fae the island," she says, avoiding his eyes in the same way she used to in the shop. "You need someone to represent Iona."

"Katie isn't regular crew," Rufus says. "She's our escort, a set of hands should someone need a break or have an accident, and she knows how to handle a steering oar. It's brilliant she's offered to join us."

He's spent five weeks minimizing contact with this underage girl, and now he'll spend at least five days trapped on a boat face-to-face with her. If he weren't half asleep, he'd fall down laughing. As though this trip weren't fucked enough already. He looks in Ghislaine's direction, but she's busy with the boat. Where is Georgina when he needs her—she'd die laughing. Well, Eamon can't be more than twenty. Maybe the girl will fix her attention on him. As for how the boat refitter can let his daughter go on such a journey or how Rufus can be ready to accept the responsibility, it's not his problem. *He's* not responsible for her. He's not responsible for anyone on this journey. As Rufus said, he's *just a body*. As far as he's concerned, his guitar's the *only* thing on the voyage he has to look out for.

Still, she's a kid. He has a red-haired little sister somewhere. Sissy is a lot older now than this girl is, of course, but it's hard for him to think of her as more than eleven or twelve—her age when he last saw her. There aren't many ways to keep track of people, people like little sisters, without being seen.

"We'll take care of her," he says to the boat refitter, because it feels as though someone should.

"Oh, she's Rufus's now. He can do what he wants with her," the refitter says, stroking the side of the boat. "Though I'm lookin' forward to hearin' how the new paint works out. It was Rufus what told me to try it. He read they were trying the bitumen on roofs in England."

"If it can handle the weather in England, it can handle the sea," Rufus says.

It sounds like a jingle, in a way that bothers him. "I meant your daughter," he tells the refitter. "Not the boat."

"Who, me?" Katie helps Eamon lift their water supply into the boat, then turns to stare him down, as though he's a crab nipping at her rubber boots. This time she looks right at him. "I know the sea here like I was born right in it. Take care of *you* is more like it."

———

At 3:00 a.m., Rufus takes one last look at his watch and compass, and they set out. Ghislaine, Eamon, Rufus, and he, with their backs toward the open sea and their hands, in fingerless gloves, gripping the boat's long, slender oars. Fifteen-year-old Katie on the bench at the back of the boat facing them and the great expanse of the Atlantic ahead. Her expression holds the sternness of an ancient grandmother.

Eight long pale oars, their tips painted red, dip into the black sea like drunken, uncoordinated spider legs. The boat swivels over the sea's calm surface in an ungainly fashion, spinning slightly east, then west.

"Francis," Rufus says, "the trick to rowing a currach is to go deep into the water, as much as five feet. You saw how the oars have almost no paddle? That's because the currach is designed for rough seas, and in rough seas a large paddle can get tripped up on the waves. The trade is that you need to get further down in the water."

He doesn't need anyone to tell him he is the problem. He's off stroke from the others and can't seem to find their rhythm. It feels like the story of his life. He's sleepy and a little cold and would be glad to be still in his bed. He doesn't particularly appreciate hearing that the boat is designed for rough seas, either.

The impulse to get up and walk away comes over him like a

terrible itch, but the deep, dark Atlantic surrounds them. He is stuck in this damned boat.

Georgina used to say, *Love, you got a song going through your veins instead of blood.* He sets up a tune in his head to the rhythm of the oars and lets it take over his body, digging into the sea with each stroke until he can find unison with the others.

"That's my man," Rufus says. "We'll make a sailor of you yet."

"Rufus," he says. "In the interest of peace, I shall not knock you into the sea."

Within little time, Iona is swallowed up by the darkness. All that is left is the light of the lamp hanging over the dock. After a while, that, too, disappears. Occasionally, to the east—on his right—he can make out a flicker of light or shadow of shore. The coastline of Mull.

"This will be our longest day," Rufus says. "Our longest cross-ing."

"We're heading straight for Colonsay? We're not going to hug Mull?" Katie asks. They are seated single file, Ghislaine directly face-to-face with Katie, he behind Ghislaine, then Eamon behind him. Rufus claimed the bench after Eamon, in the front of the boat but behind all the other rowers, undoubtedly to keep an eye on and be heard by all of them. Rufus is just the sort of assertive nut whom people either adore or run from.

Born into a different family, a different circumstance, Eugene might have been like that. Wiry-haired, wiry-bodied Eugene in his silver-rimmed glasses, waiting in grade school to be picked by the boys, then waiting in high school to be picked by the girls. In the end, being picked by Uncle Sam.

He digs his oars into the water. He pulls. He circles. A seabird flies overhead, its underside huge and white; probably a gannet awakened by their passage.

"We can stop somewhere among the Torran Rocks, catch our breath while we're still warming up," Rufus says, "if we need to."

Katie clicks her tongue. "You cannae do that."

"Can't do what? Tie up along the Rocks?"

"You don't know the Rocks."

"It'll be day by then. We'll see anything in our way."

The frizzy red tendrils of hair around Katie's round face shake. "There are smaller rocks," she says, "stickin' up the surface o' the water, like the stones on a dragon's tail. One minute they're there, and another they are under water. Meanwhile, the sea churns up around them like a washin' machine. Haven't you ever read *Kidnapped,* man?"

His body tilts forward and back, forward and back, forward and back. He wants to ask Katie what Robert Louis Stevenson's novel has to do with her argument, but he can't bring himself to address her directly. Wasn't there a shipwreck in *Kidnapped*? He should have read the stupid book back in school instead of relying on Eugene.

"Try tae keep starboard," Katie says. "Just pass 'em by."

"Look," Rufus says. "The sun is rising."

To the east, the island of Mull is a blackened but discernible silhouette. Dark, waterbound rocks lie like flat, benign sleepers. To the west, dusky orange glows in an ever-growing band where the deep violet sky plunges into the sea. Pulling hard on her oars, Ghislaine glances over her left shoulder, and he follows suit. A landmass, not large enough to be inhabited but large enough to be called an island, has materialized in the distance ahead.

"Are those the Torran Rocks?" Ghislaine asks. "It seems calm enough."

"We're not halfway to the Rocks yet," Katie says. "That's Soa. My da sometimes takes lobsters from there. The Rocks are more like chips. Not the tattie kind. You'll see. You'll be sorry if you don't listen to me, Rufus. We'll all be sorry."

Where is Katie's mother when her father's out trapping lobsters or laying boats together? Could she be dead? He's seen the father on the island but never at the shop; the shop is clearly left up to Katie, and so, apparently, is her life. No mother would agree to let her fifteen-year-old girl go off on a journey like this.

"Katie," Rufus says, "the sea is calm, the sky is clear, the forecast is mild. It should take us about eight hours to get to Colonsay. If everyone is holding up fine once we get to the Torran Rocks or we can't find an anchorage, we won't stop. But we're on a mission of peace. It won't do to have discord on our vessel."

Eight hours. In the rush of getting ready, it hadn't occurred to him to ask how long they'd row each day. In the gathering light, Ghislaine's back, arms, and shoulders slide effortlessly. *A wall of trophies,* she told him. Under the loose sweater she wore to dinner, her body remained a secret to him. The life preserver she now wears over a ribbed long-sleeved shirt still keeps him from seeing much, but her upper arms are full and hard, and so is her ass, on the bench in front of him. She's bigger than he initially thought, but tight. A slender woman who has packed on lots of muscle. She must be very strong.

Normally, the gamines like Georgina are the ones who catch his attention, but what would it be like in bed with Ghislaine? Is she tight everywhere? Would they row along under sheets, finding the same sort of rhythm as they do in the boat?

"If you kept your eyes on your rowing and off my body," Ghislaine says over her shoulder in a low voice, "you might not create such a drag on the boat."

He laughs, hoping Katie won't have heard. "You have eyes in the back of your head, Ghislaine?"

But she's right. He's fallen off unison again.

Dawn opens up the sea around them, moving through deep blues to a sweet dusky azure. There's comfort in being able to see land out there. It helps him to gauge the steady pace they are keeping, with the low northwesterly wind and tide in their favor. His hands already feel stiff, but his arms and shoulders are moving better than during the first hour.

"We got lucky with the weather," Ghislaine says.

"God is on our side," Rufus says. "Or at least the weather god. Remember that time down in Devon, and big pieces of hail started to fall from the sky?"

"Pouah," Ghislaine says. "Don't remind me. That wasn't hail. They were like frozen lemons."

"I wouldn't mind a lemon right now," Rufus says. "Or, more precisely, a tall glass of lemonade."

"Bah, lemonade. A nice cup o' tea," Katie says.

"We know that's what Eamon's dreaming about. Aren't you, man?" Rufus says.

Eamon grunts.

"What about you, Francis? A cup of tea or a glass of lemonade?"

They were drinking lemonade when his father dropped to his knees, crumpled like a doll, nothing like the tall, steady hero who was his real father. The taste of lemons always used to bring that moment back to him, that slice in the wall of time between before and after, when his cheerful mother suddenly shouted *Stay with us!* But his father didn't.

"Water," he says.

But then, one night in Mallorca, he and Georgina ended up squeezing lemons over each other, licking the juice, laughing. They'd begun by slipping raw oysters into each other's mouths preceded by gulps of cava and followed by squeezes of lemon. *You* have *to have the lemon,* Georgina said. *You need the bitter to make the sweet taste so good.*

After they ran out of oysters, they just kept going. Lemon juice in each other's hair, on their shoulders, down his smooth chest.

A few years ago, I spent two months in Greece picking lemons, he told her, dripping beads of lemon juice the length of her leg. Her ankle, her shin, her knee, her thigh. *Seven days a week, ten hours a day: pull, twist, pull, twist. Finally, I caught a ride north through Yugoslavia and Italy into France. The driver stopped in Menton. Nice town, he said. You'll find something here. So I got out, so happy to be done with all that. It was March. Turns out that's Menton's lemon-picking season.*

Sounds like sour luck to me, Georgina said, laughing hard, drawing her leg up and around him.

That night, lemon juice didn't taste so bad to him.

There are moments when he wishes things could have been different. That he could have been the kind of man who would have stayed and helped Georgina. That he could have been the kind of man who was able to help her.

He leans on the oars, stroking away the rush of loneliness that overcomes him, beating it out of his body. His tongue sticks a little in his mouth. His lips feel swollen. A tall glass of water or lemonade or anything would be nice. At the same time, his lower abdomen has slowly been tightening. The piss bucket is in the front of the boat behind Rufus. He doesn't want to pull his dick out in full sight of Katie.

The sea tugs on his oars. He glances over his shoulders: up ahead is a scattering of dark rocks, some almost large enough to be called islands or at least skerries, others more like giant teeth jutting out of the sea. The boat is suddenly moving faster, almost, than they are rowing.

"The start of the ebb tide," Rufus says. "On its way out from Mull it splits up on the Rocks and doubles its strength. You'd best get hold of the steering oar, Katie."

The once placid sea is now rumbling, splashing against the rocks. The boat is moving at twice the speed it was ten minutes earlier, as though it has been lifted onto a liquid conveyor belt, almost beyond their control. They pass a first skerry where three seals, their mottled gray backs shiny with water, raise their heads to look at them. A fourth seal, a large shapeless body reclining on an adjacent rock, shakes a flipper.

"Friendly," Ghislaine says, puffing a little as she wields her oars in the current.

The seal slips off his rock to swim up beside the boat. He stares down into the animal's soft black eyes.

"Can see," he says, "why people—"

"Starboard!" Rufus shouts.

Which is starboard? Ghislaine is pulling with her left arm. He'll pull with his left too, then.

"—made up selkies," he finishes, once they are safely away from the rock. "Those eyes, those little hands."

"Made up?" Katie says.

"Do you believe in selkies, Katie?" Rufus says in between pants.

The seal slips away. Katie harrumphs. It's impossible to tell whether it's a sign of assent or disgust.

"Watch out for that rock," she shouts. "There. Leeward."

They row as hard as they can, washing up and down in the break of the water. Another skerry, thick with nesting birds, comes up fast. They pull around it.

Once the tide is no longer aiming them against rocks, they take a collective breath. In unspoken agreement, they lighten up on their oars.

"Do you like fairy tales, Francis?" Ghislaine says.

He wipes his forehead against his forearm. "They're okay."

In his plastic barrel is the book of mythology his aunt sent them for Christmas many years ago. All these years, he's carried it around with him. He's not even sure why. When he left Phoenix for LA, he put it in his trunk. When he left LA for Europe, he stuck it in his pack. Every once in a while, he opens it up, reads about another long-ago hero.

The sun has fully risen. They've been rowing for over an hour, maybe two. His back and underarms feel hot and damp beneath his life preserver, and he *really* wants a drink of water now, even more than he needs to relieve himself. But a shout from Katie lets them know new rocks are sticking up ahead. They're a team. He can't just stop because he wants to.

"Let's move westward," Rufus calls out.

"See that?" Katie points to an ugly round black rock with a lighthouse perched on top of it about a mile off in the direction of the horizon. "They built that one hundred years ago efter twenty-four boats went doon in the course of twenty-four hours in the waters here. Stop alang the Torran Rocks, my arse."

They row until the Torran Rocks are finally safely and entirely behind them, and Katie can put the steering oar away. The sea becomes smooth and oily again, and, to his relief, drinking water gets passed around.

"Who has to use the bucket?" Rufus says. "Come on. Just get up and do it."

Once everyone has both drunk and peed, they return to rowing. Hours of open sea still lie between them and the Isle of Colonsay. "Perfect conditions!" Rufus exclaims from time to time. Small islands, long and low in the water like the backs of submerged cattle, dot the sea. A little farther, the bigger islands—Mull to the north, Jura to the southeast, and Colonsay directly south—shimmer. The sky becomes brighter as the sun climbs higher.

More drinking water gets passed around. They grab egg sandwiches from their plastic barrels and wolf them down between strokes. They row.

His arms become machines. His body hums alongside the others. Toward late morning, the wind picks up. Low, white rolls of wave skate toward them over the sea's surface, rocking the boat in a constant urgent rhythm. The egg sandwich in his stomach starts to turn on itself. He wills himself to ignore it.

The wind dies down again.

Still, they row.

The morning grows long. Katie switches places for a time with Ghislaine. The sight of her thick back in front of him throws him off, and he has to recall the song that gave him the rowing rhythm.

Still, they row.

Hours upon hours later, tired, salty, sweaty, they round the northern tip of Colonsay.

———

Terra firma beneath his feet, he strips off all his clothes but his briefs and throws himself back into the water. Kittiwakes circle above in a needling chorus of protest. The others watch him from the empty white-sand beach, looking half bemused and half amused. He turns away. He doesn't care if he's showing off his naked skin, that smooth hairless chest that has over the years drawn so much comment. He doesn't care, either, that the water is so cold it burns. This was the longest day of rowing, and he made it through as though he were one of them. Something opens up inside him. Maybe Rufus isn't so crazy. Maybe this journey is doable. And he will be able to see it through.

"What a great first day!" Rufus shouts happily, over the cry of the kittiwakes. "We've got a nice stretch of sea behind us now."

A farmer appears on top of the dune, edging the beach. While Rufus and Ghislaine climb up to greet him, he stands spread-armed by the shore under the June sun, his face tipped toward its rays. It's still early afternoon. Although the air isn't warm, he feels barely chilled.

"Put yer pants on, man," Eamon says, betraying a heavy Northern Irish staccato.

It may be the first time he has heard Eamon speak.

"What's your story, Eamon?" he says.

But Eamon has turned away, busying himself with the oars. Katie is settled on a boulder nearby, her face back to being as inscrutable as it was in the shop.

He grabs his pants and pulls them on over his damp legs. He can hear snippets of Rufus up above, explaining their mission, while the farmer nods his head and fingers the collar of a thick gray wool sweater. By the time he's dressed again, Rufus has won an invitation for them to spend the night in an empty byre beside the farmer's house; it turns out, with all his planning, Rufus didn't arrange a place for them to sleep at each stop.

The farmhouse lies about a quarter mile up over the rocky, eruptive hillside. After they've met the farmer's pretty young wife and parked their gear in the small stone shed, Rufus says, "If the plan is to spread the word, it's time to start talking. How far is the walk to the village?"

"I'll take you," the farmer says.

"You go ahead," he says. "I'm going to hang out."

Rufus glances at the farmer's wife. "Not a chance, my man. You are coming also."

"What's that supposed to mean?"

"You're part of the team, Francis. We stick together."

For fuck's sake. Just because he's popular with the ladies doesn't make him some sort of predator. "I'm not part of anything," he says. "I'm just along for the ride."

He turns to the farmer. "Do you have a bicycle I can borrow?"

He rides across wide green fields. Fulmars and guillemots fly overhead. Cicadas buzz and saw. At the top of a hill, he leans the bike against a mossy cairn. It's an old bike, two-speed, with no kickstand, curiously similar to the one he had as a kid: green, with a curved upper crossbar, like the lid of an almond-shaped eye. A hand-me-down from Luke, one of the last hand-me-downs he ever had from his older brothers. By the time he was thirteen, he was as tall as Mike and Luke; in retrospect, it's nothing less than a miracle that his mom managed to keep him in shoes and pants and a decent bicycle. Eugene's was a one-speed, with a rusty chain that kept slipping off. *It don't matter. With your asthma, you can't go pedaling fast anyhow,* Eugene's mom said.

The wind has risen, bringing the smell of algae and salt, and fat drops of rain begin to fall. Two black cows amble down the hill below him to another large and sandy beach. Even in the clouding air, with his remarkable eyesight—*Don't tell anyone about that, buddy,* Luke warned him before he was shipped out, *or when your time comes up they'll have you on the first plane out*—he can make out seals on this beach, one flipping a fish back and forth in its mouth. He's pretty sure he sees an otter.

He stands the bike upright and starts pedaling.

———

After an early dinner of nettle soup, oysters, soft crowdie cheese, warm brown bread, and a slice of sponge cake with marmalade, washed down with ale, he falls asleep as soon as he's pulled the zipper up on his sleeping bag. He wakes a few hours later, his body heavy and a little sore, to find another bag pushed up beside his—he can't tell whose. With the door to the byre closed, it's pitch-black.

His first thought is of Katie. He gives the bag a shove.

"Mais quoi . . ." comes Ghislaine's sleepy voice.

He rolls over and tumbles back into sleep.

He wakes next to the sound of Rufus's tiny portable alarm clock. Eamon, closest to the door, pushes it open. A gust of wind, dense with raindrops, blows in over them. Eamon pulls the door shut again.

There'll be no getting back on the sea today.

"It's okay. We'll make use of the delay to visit Colonsay's school," Rufus says. "And there's a radio broadcast from the island. We'll make an announcement."

He hangs out on the farm, lending a hand as he can, until the others return. Toward evening the clouds open, leaving a violet wash above the fields. Rufus studies his tidal charts. "Good news for you lazy buggers. No hurry heading out tomorrow morning. We'll hit the northern end of the Sound of Islay, then wait until the day after tomorrow to catch the ebb tide to move on to Port Ellen, at the bottom of Islay."

"Is Islay close?" he asks.

"Closer than Iona was. It'll be an easy row."

With Rufus, that could mean anything.

Sleeping is more difficult this night. He is less tired, and at the same time his body feels stiffer. The floor of the byre is unforgiving. The breaths of the others fill the small, darkened space and trap him in their dreams. He's almost glad when Rufus's alarm goes off at 6:30 a.m.

The rain has ended, but the sea remains heavy. They zip up their rain gear, tie on their life preservers, and drag the boat out into the waves. The air is a veil of mist; the wet is everywhere, not falling but floating. Underneath his fingerless gloves, his chafed hands grip the oars uncomfortably.

They navigate out of the shallow bay, down past the main port of Scalasaig. Two men and a woman standing on the dock, waiting for the ferry or mail boat, wave. They reach the bottom of Oronsay, cut off from Colonsay by the tide.

Ghislaine points at the dark sky. "When clouds look like black smoke, a wise man will put on his cloak," she says.

"That's all right, then. We're all wearing our cloaks already," Rufus says.

Rufus's endless cheer is maddening. "Ghislaine," he says, "how come you speak English so well?"

"My mother is from Dorset. That's why I went to school in London."

He knows nothing about these people he's been sitting in a boat with for hours, sleeping alongside in a barn. "You went to school in London?"

"Of course. That's how Rufus and I met."

"You were in class together?"

Ghislaine laughs. "No. I read psychology. Rufus read economics. We were both in the rowing club."

"At Oxford?"

"Didn't I just say in London?"

"Imperial College London," Rufus says. "Best rowing club in the country."

"I used to get up at five thirty, five days a week to train," Ghislaine says.

"Only five days?" Rufus says. "When I was captain, we were on the water six days a week."

"We weren't there at the same time," Ghislaine explains. "We met through the club after we'd both graduated. Which it sounds as though might have been lucky for me."

Rufus laughs. "Oh, you would have gotten used to it. There still was a day off."

"I wouldnae want to live in London," Katie says.

Ghislaine's oars send a tiny flash of water against his cheek. "No?" she says. "It's fun for a young girl. I had fun."

Katie looks markedly worse for wear, her broad, fair face stained from the sun and wind of being on an open boat, her hair matted from the salt. "I wouldnae have fun. Too many cars. Too many people. Everyone tryin' to steal somethin' from everyone else. Boys who are liars."

"It's not like that," Rufus says, laughing. "When we're done, if your father agrees, you can come down to visit. My mother will show you around."

"Look," Eamon says.

A minke whale loops through the dark gray-blue water, his back an almost matching color. The beast glides beside them, his dorsal fin slicing the sea, disappears, then rises again, creating another loop through the water.

"He wouldn't go under the boat?" he says.

Everyone laughs at him, but good-naturedly. There's a good feeling in the boat this morning.

"You want to start a song for us, Francis?" Ghislaine says.

The wind is growing stronger.

"I've done a bit of singing in my time," Rufus says. "I even was a choirboy."

"Start us off, then," he says.

Rufus launches into the Eddy Grant hit "Electric Avenue," affecting a reggae-style accent so confident that everyone loses his or her stroke. He joins the laughter. And then they get their oars going again and all sing along. Even Eamon hums. The wind carries their voices away, across the sea. They share a few more songs as the water swells beneath them but eventually fall into silence, focused on the dancing waters. The boat bobs, slapped by the sea. It rocks them from side to side.

He pulls his oars in, leans out of the boat, and throws up.

"See, that's one of the beauties of the currach," Rufus says. "No matter how heavy the seas, the waves rarely get in. The sides are too high, and the currach rides too high on top of the sea. She just bounces along on top of the waves. It's almost impossible to knock her over."

He wipes his mouth and takes a drink of water before picking up his oars again. "What's that for, then?" he says, nodding at the plastic jug tied to Katie's bench.

"No boat, not even a whaler, can resist everything the sea has to offer," Rufus says. "This is just a little swell. It's a nice breeze, though. Time to put the sail up."

He and Eamon stroke, with Eamon moving into Rufus's place, while the others work together to set the currach up for sailing. Putting the mast up, getting the sail ready, and attaching the ropes proves no easy feat with the boat in a continuous rocking motion. No sooner do they have it up and the sail fills, however, then the currach takes off at a clip. They tuck the oars away.

"If the wind keeps up like this, we'll make it to Islay in no time," Rufus says, reclaiming his bench. "We can just sit back and enjoy it."

He is ashamed by the relief he feels when Eamon grabs the side of the boat and also retches into the ocean.

———

Once they reach Islay, they again have to figure out where they'll spend the night.

"If you want to look for another byre, fine," he says. "But then we're parting ways for the night. Sorry, man. Too claustrophobic."

Rufus points toward a small stone structure, not much bigger than the byre was but with a window and door, on a low, square-topped grassy bluff. "There's a bothy. Maybe it's empty."

They tramp up to look. The bothy is clean and dry with a steeply pitched tin roof. A faded poster for a church Christmas sale back in 1978 is taped to one interior wall. There's no other trace of human habitation.

Rufus steps back out onto the road to survey their surroundings. "All right. It's close by the boat, too. Ready for tomorrow morning's departure. Let's bring our stuff up."

While the others go looking for civilization, he settles against an exterior wall of the shepherd's hut. The wind has calmed, and the sea grass stirs gently. Seabirds fill the air with cries and shouts that become a kaleidoscopic shanty. He falls fast asleep.

A shoe kicks his boot. Rufus looks, if possible, even more ebullient than usual.

"You should have come with us, man! We got a ride into Port Askaig, and everyone promised to spread the word. Letters, phone calls to the mainland. Someone knew someone working for the *Campbeltown Courier.*"

"If you want to get the word out, you're going to need more than some small local newspapers," he says, standing up, stretching. The others gather around them.

"Of course! But I've already written to the bigger newspapers. Ghislaine even translated a letter into French for *Le Monde, Le Figaro,* and"—Rufus turns to Ghislaine—"what's that Jean-Paul Sartre one?"

"*Libération,*" she says.

"*Libération.* I knocked on some doors and took some reporters to lunch also. But it's great to get these local newspapers. Grass roots, Francis. People power!"

He laughs. When it's not annoying, Rufus's enthusiasm is infectious.

"You belong back in the sixties, Rufus. Power to the people. Peace, love, and harmony."

"Well," Rufus says with a smile, "peace, love, harmony . . . and money." It's no secret Rufus has bankrolled this endeavor. He wouldn't be surprised to find Rufus has cleared out his bank account to do it.

"Some people hae some words fer the English," Katie mutters. "Bloody English."

"I'm English," Rufus says. "Ghislaine's half English."

Katie kicks the ground. "Sorry."

"It becomes a habit, you see," Rufus says, "passed from one person to another. That's just what we're trying to break out of."

Katie flushes.

"Are we going to catch some fish?" he says. Katie's just a kid. And probably some of the islanders the others spoke with today did have some choice things to say about the English.

"You just play your guitar," Ghislaine says. "I have *le menu* taken care of."

The evening sun throws brilliant ribbons of orange and yellow across the horizon. They're all too spent from rowing to argue, anyhow. He unwraps his guitar from its folds of plastic and settles down by Ghislaine's side, not playing anything in particular, just strumming. Although he wouldn't want to admit it, his hands are too sore to pick the strings. Katie and Eamon search the beach for driftwood, and Rufus collects rocks from the road to make a fire ring. There's a fireplace inside the bothy, but Rufus points out they've no way to know the state of the chimney. They don't want to get smoked out.

From the supplies barrel, Ghislaine takes out a pan, flatbread, cheese, a package of smoked fish, an onion, a square of foil containing dried oregano, and several tins of baked beans. "There," she says, tapping the top of a tin. "Proof I am half English."

"Au contraire, ma belle," he says. He learned a few crucial words during his stays in France. "No Brit would have thought to bring the herbs or the onion."

Rufus looks up from his fire-ring construction. "I brought the herbs and onions."

Katie reappears with an armful of branches. She dumps them onto the ground next to Rufus. Little twigs stick in her jacket and hair. Eamon follows close behind and, adding his branches to her pile, starts snapping them in half, carefully laying them in an intricate pattern within the stone circle.

He plucks alternating G and C chords, willing his sore fingers to work:

Across the rolling sea,
Pulling as one,
Across the rolling sea
Day not yet done . . .

"What's that?" Ghislaine says.

"Just something I was thinking."

"You write your own songs?"

He shrugs.

Katie sits down on her life preserver on the opposite side of the circle of rocks from him and Ghislaine. She studies Ghislaine.

"How do you get yer hair so straight?" she says.

Ghislaine starts opening a tin. "How do you get yours so beautifully curly?"

"It isnae beautiful," Katie says. "It's awful."

"Perms are very popular. Lots of girls are getting them in London. They'll pay fifty quid to get hair like yours."

"An' then yer arse fell aff." Katie tears the band out of her hair, scrabbles the whole mess up in a hand, and reties it, generally making things worse, not better. "Maybe I *should* come down to London."

Everyone, even Eamon, laughs.

"Do *you* like London?" he asks Eamon.

Eamon shrugs.

"Do you live there?"

"Nay," Eamon says. "Kent."

"Eamon works on my parents' estate," Rufus says. "He's on the garden staff."

"But your family's back in Northern Ireland?" he asks.

"Aye." Eamon shrugs and stands up. "Gotta take a slash."

"Eamon's father is UVF," Rufus says once Eamon has lumbered down the road, looking for a shielded spot to pee. "In the Maze, doing a seven-year sentence."

"UVF?"

Ghislaine and Katie look at each other.

"Ulster Volunteer Force. It's a loyalist paramilitary group in the north." Rufus strikes a match and holds it against the driftwood. "Eamon's father blew up a car driven by a Catholic bringing her kid to visit her granny."

"Holy shit." He stares down the road. "Why's he here, then?"

"Because his father blew up a car with a Catholic and her kid in it."

The flames grow steadily. Rufus's red cheeks shine even brighter in its light. Katie's hair glints even more copper. A piece of driftwood explodes, and he pulls his guitar back. "I thought Eamon was your second Catholic," he says. "Ghislaine's not Catholic. Katie's too young to be an official crew member. Anyhow, she's representing Iona, not a denomination. Who's the other so-called Catholic on the boat?"

"I am," Rufus says.

"How can you be Catholic?"

"What's that supposed to mean?"

"Never mind."

"There *are* some of us, Francis. Cromwell didn't get us all."

"I didn't mean that. Just that . . . you know, nothing."

"Right. Nothing."

Ghislaine settles next to him. "Where is your family, Francis?"

It's not as though he's some sort of idiot. Anyone would agree it's confusing: Ghislaine is French but Protestant; Rufus is a British posh but Catholic. Eamon is Irish but Protestant. At least Katie is what one would expect. She's sitting on the other side of the fire, chewing off a fingernail, scowling at him. She took offense at his calling her too young to be official, undoubtedly.

"The States," he tells Ghislaine.

"Do you see them often?"

Six years ago, a girl he was crashing with in Paris suggested they busk in front of the Louvre. *C'est parfait. All the world goes there.*

She was right. Even his oldest brother.

Mike was on his honeymoon. *I didn't know we had family in Europe,* his bride said with a heavy Texas accent, looking confused, glancing at his open guitar case with its smattering of francs and the raccoon-eyed girl beside him.

I didn't know, either, Mike said. *What the hell, Francis? Mom has been going nuts.*

Language, honey, Mike's bride said.

Her name was Holly, and she was an army brat, met while Mike was finishing his medical training in Texas after his last tour in Southeast Asia. *My daddy was part of the liberation of Paris in 1944,* Holly said, babbling, while he and Mike sized each other up. Who knew what she'd been told about him. *I grew up looking at the pictures—the big stone arch, all the men spilling over that big avenue. My dad was one of them, told me Paris was so beautiful even after being through the war that someday I needed to go see for myself. I'll go for my honeymoon, I always said. So here we are!*

Mike folded his arms over his chest. *Mom and I thought Canada—with the draft dodgers. Patty Ann said Thailand. Only Sissy thought Europe.*

I didn't dodge the draft. Remember? I didn't get called up.

Exactly. Don't you think Mom has lost enough family already? Couldn't you have at least let her know where you were? That you're alive?

You're right, he said, hoping this would be enough, knowing it wouldn't. *Yeah, I should have let her know.*

All she's got left are me and Sissy.

This frightened him. *What about Patty Ann? What about Ronnie?*

Okay, and Ronnie. God knows what Mom would do without Ronnie. But Patty Ann—forget it. At least she got rid of that bastard. Mike squints and places his hands on either hip. *Did you even know she's divorced again? And had a fourth kid? Hang on. Did you even know she remarried? Goddamn, Francis. Your own sister.*

It was like being buried alive in sand. All this . . . *life,* suddenly dumped on top of him.

Look, let me go put my guitar away and get cleaned up. We'll talk over dinner.

Mike unfolded his arms and grabbed his wrist. *No fucking way. I'm not letting you out of my sight.*

He couldn't remember having ever heard Mike curse before. Luke, yes. Patty Ann, always. This was a new, tougher Mike, one whose staid determination had morphed into something steel-like and enduring. Or maybe it was a reflection of just how angry Mike was. His bride's hands fluttered nervously at her blond ponytail, touched the little gold cross on a chain around her neck, like this was an unknown Mike to her also.

Dinner—oh, we've eaten some strange things since we got here. But the pastries! Holly said to no one in particular.

He stared down at Mike's strong hand, wrapped tightly around his arm, stared at it until Mike let go.

Don't be ridiculous, he said. *I'm a grown man now. You can't pick me up and carry me home if I don't want. Why would I run off?*

They made a plan to meet at 8:00 p.m.—*They eat so late here!* his new sister-in-law said, *but it's okay . . . y'all know, the jet lag—* and in the back of his new sister-in-law's guidebook he wrote out detailed instructions on how to get from Mike's hotel to a nice but not too snails-and-frog-legs restaurant he felt sure they would like. Then he kissed the raccoon-eyed girl good-bye and hitched a ride to Spain.

Ghislaine has piled flatbread on a plate. He helps himself. "Not much," he says. "I haven't seen my family in a while. Haven't those beans jumped around enough in that pot? I'm starving."

"*Voyez?* He can't wait for that French haute cuisine." She slaps his hand.

Rufus pitches a stump at the fire. "Watch out you don't burn yourself."

"You're going to get ash in our beautiful dinner," Ghislaine says.

Rufus sits down on the other side of Ghislaine, a small bottle of whiskey in his hand. Katie looks on with interest as he reaches over Ghislaine for it and takes a sip.

"Don't even think about it," he says to her.

"What a spoilsport," Katie says. "You of all people."

"What's that supposed to mean?"

Rufus waves a hand. "Peace, everyone. Francis, you've never said how old you are."

"Thirty-one. Almost thirty-two." His birthday will be in less than two weeks.

"So you were about twelve? Thirteen? When you lost your father, I mean."

He takes a second tug from the bottle and hands it back. "I was nine."

Ghislaine stops spooning beans onto tin plates. "I'm sorry. That's young."

He shrugs. "I lost a brother, too. In Vietnam. And a friend. My best friend."

Rufus nods sympathetically. Ghislaine rests her hand on his shoulder and gently rubs it.

Here he is on some island off the coast of Scotland—he can't even remember which one right now—with these people he barely knows, and he's telling them all this stuff he never tells anyone. He, of all people, doesn't deserve anyone's sympathy. Especially not if they knew *how* he lost his best friend, that he was with him that very night. That maybe, if he were stronger, if he were better, if he had only been *listening,* he might not have lost his best friend at all.

"Isn't anyone else hungry?" he says, moving his shoulder out from under Ghislaine's hand.

They gobble down Ghislaine's meal and brush their teeth at the side of the road. "Right," Rufus says. "We have another early start tomorrow."

The others withdraw into the bothy. But the sky is still light, he had that nap earlier, and talking about his family—just thinking about them—has awakened something long dormant in him that doesn't want to lie down again. He stays outside, staring at the sea, the rolling waves, the swallowing expanse. Birds fly off into that void, some alone, some in pairs. The odd thing about the sea is, its huge expanse means freedom to some and emptiness to others.

He extracts the book of Greek mythology from his plastic barrel and opens it to the words his brother Luke penned once, years ago, on the back flap.

Good luck to you, father stranger; if anything has been said amiss may the winds blow it away with them, and may heaven grant you a safe return . . .

Ghislaine appears in the doorway of the bothy. "What are you reading?" She sits down beside him.

He closes the book. "Nothing."

The sun is finally setting, falling over the line of the Atlantic. There are haddock and mackerel and even whales out there, some heading west toward America.

"I was telling you about my family earlier," he says.

"Yes."

"Well, my father died of a heart condition from being a prisoner of war during World War II. And my brother—he was killed in Vietnam."

"That's terrible. War is terrible."

"But my friend. He killed himself. After he got back from Vietnam."

He waits for her to ask why. She doesn't. Instead she takes his hand. The skin on her fingers is hard and calloused but warm.

"He said something to me. Before." He pauses, remembering that gentle late August night, the full moon rising. Eugene in his stupid blue coveralls with GENE written on them when no one had ever called him Gene in his life. "He said: *I knew I was going to get called up. And you wouldn't be. I knew I'd be the one to get a low number.*"

And he recognized, when Eugene said it, that he also had always known this was how it would happen, just like all the good luck that had come his way but not Eugene's. But he brushed the thought right out of his head. Instead, he said: *That's just stupid, man. You're just talking bullshit.*

Eugene had lost his one special gift. Hope.

He lets go of Ghislaine's hand. "We should get some sleep."

He unrolls his sleeping bag inside the bothy and slips inside. The late night sun, the currach, the moon rising over the Hebrides.

"Bonne nuit," Ghislaine says softly, sliding into her own bag.

He pulls the flap of his sleeping bag over his head.

———

Rufus's alarm rings before the moon has gone to sleep and the sun has awakened. It's cold, and in the damp and insinuating air, last night feels like a nasty dream physically stuck to him. His legs itch; the space between them and his crotch, the front of his thighs, his ankles, the back of his neck and hollow of his back. Maybe it's the salt from his brief swim two days earlier or from the sweat of rowing or the combination. He hasn't bathed since leaving Iona. No one has. They take their places in the currach under the moon, pick up their oars, and head into the sound. Once so shiny, Ghislaine's straight hair, in front of him, has self-sectioned into clumps.

"Don't get too close to me," she says from her bench.

"You're going to keep your arms down when you row?"

"Nice."

They slip through silky black water. At least it is calm; yesterday's tempestuous sea is as hard to imagine as winter's cold is during the summer. An otter paddles by, the struggling fish in its mouth catching silver in the moonshine. They pass an entire colony of seals lined up along a strip of sand, one slick fat body squeezed next to another. Two pups thump their way down into the water.

"Did you know, Francis," Rufus says, "that the male Atlantic seal mates with up to ten different females during their mating season?"

"Oh, for Christ's sake."

"You think you might be a selkie?"

"Shut up, Rufus."

If Rufus keeps this up, their next stop may be his last. Leaving is one of his best-honed skills, after all. They're supposed to berth in Port Ellen, at the bottom of Islay. There's bound to be a ferry from there to somewhere. Katie can make the final stretch in his place.

The sun begins to rise. They enter the Sound of Islay and let the tidal race take hold of the boat. Suddenly, they are moving so quickly the currach is nearly slipping out from under them. The compulsion is strangely exhilarating, half frightening and half thrilling. They speed by the island of Jura on one side and Islay on the other, passing a handful of larger boats whose captains toot their horns.

The sound throws them out into the sea, and they have to start working again. It's becoming a fine day; once they are out of the tidal race, the sea is royal blue and slack. Any bad feeling he may have had evaporates with their mutual strokes. *Dig and pull, dig and pull.* For the moment, there's only rowing across the water. He unwraps sandwiches with the others, joins Rufus in a string of weirdly chosen songs. They pass Ghislaine's tube of ChapStick around, smearing it over their burned, broken lips. A pod of dolphins follows them for a while, and Rufus points out an eagle soaring over the water in the distance.

"You're dreamin', man," Katie says. "That's a skua."

"Come on, Francis," Rufus says. "You have the eyesight. You tell her."

"Tell her what? I wouldn't know a skua or an eagle if I saw one."

"Are its wings straight across and thick like a glider plane or curved?"

"I dunno. Straight, I guess."

"Ha!" Rufus says.

"He doesn't know his arse from his elbow," Katie says. "He wouldna know if it were a sheep flyin'."

"I'd know if it were a sheep. It's not a sheep or a cow. It's not a goat, either."

Slowly the day has become beautiful. His hands are raw, but his body feels awake in a way it hasn't since longer ago than he can remember.

His mind feels awake also. He feels strangely, inexplicably free. Inexplicably, because here he is, tied, almost literally, to these others. *Dig, pull, dig, pull.*

They reach Port Ellen five hours later in a stream of sunshine. The harbor comes into view, low-lying and flat, rimmed with a string of white and gray peaked houses.

As soon as they hit the shallows, Katie jumps out of the boat. "I'm away for a bath." She grabs her small barrel and sloshes onto the beach. A border collie runs up to greet her.

"Where?" Ghislaine calls, tucking her oars along the floor of the currach, grabbing her own barrel and taking off after Katie.

The rest of them climb out of the currach also. Eamon drags the boat to the edge of the sand and ties it to a low pier. Rufus sorts out the oars, then faces back out over the sea and hoots. "Just one more leg. We're going to make it by Columba's Day."

"Rufus," he says.

"Yes."

"Can I ask you something, man?"

"Fire away."

"Why is this so important to you? I mean, why *this?*"

Rufus crouches down on his haunches and, removing his rowing gloves, runs his hand over the black coating on the boat's bottom. "Any war affects all of us. We're the common family of man." His short, strong fingers crawl over the bitumen, inspecting its surface, pushing, poking, prodding.

If it can handle the weather in England, it can handle the sea. Like an advertising slogan.

"Holy shit," he says. "The material you got Katie's father to use on the boat—the bitumen. Are you making money off it? Is this, like, one big advertisement we're risking our fucking lives for?"

Rufus continues to explore the state of the bitumen, showing no sign of having heard. "She's doing just fine, she is."

He kicks the side of the boat. "Do you have shares in the company? Are they paying you something to use it?"

"Francis," Rufus says, standing, turning now to face him. "What are you going to do with your life to make up for those who have lost theirs? Like your father, your brother, your friend?"

"Fuck," he says. "Fuck."

The high of the morning comes crashing down on him. Has Rufus been *lying* to him this whole time? Is he the only one of the others to realize it? Just how much is one person supposed to take? Measure it out, toss the moon, the earth, the sun up in the air and juggle them, throw this person together with that—his whole life has been spent trying to catch balls someone else tossed up when they came tumbling down again. Did he ever say he knew how to catch? Did anyone ever ask him? Why does everyone always expect so much from him?

He shoves Rufus's barrel-like chest with both his palms. Rufus flies backwards onto the sand, narrowly missing the side of the boat.

Eamon's broad arms swiftly wrap around him. "Enough of that, ye."

He shakes Eamon off. "What are you? His fucking bodyguard?"

Rufus rights himself, gets back onto his feet, brushes the sand from his pants. "Pacifist, eh?" And then, laughing, "Let's go find the girls."

"Fer feck's sake," Eamon says before joining Rufus in walking toward the white houses, "get yerself together."

He feels sluggish, almost drunk with his sudden outburst. As an adult he's thrown a punch a few times—at one girl's boyfriend, at another's brother. The time Georgina got into a fight with a dealer in a club. But never to inflict damage, only to deflect it. And, yet, he's felt the urge to punch Rufus pretty much ever since they met. Why? He likes Rufus. He *admires* Rufus.

The truth is that Rufus is a beautiful person, everything they all tried to be back in the days of Woodstock and the Summer of Love. If Rufus *is* getting money for testing out the bitumen, it's just to fund this project. Rufus hasn't lost hope. Rufus is a true believer. Rufus is everything he isn't.

He leans down and scoops some pebbly sand into his hand. He throws it at the air, feeling like a five-year-old boy again.

———

The border collie belongs to an ample, good-natured woman named Fiona. Her two sons have left home, freeing up a bedroom for the two girls. He, Rufus, and Eamon will get the floor of the sitting room. They all can have a swift shower. And then they'll eat.

"Ah've nothing in," Fiona says. "A'll have tae away to the shap."

"Do you understand anything she's saying?" he whispers to Ghislaine. She stifles a laugh and inclines her head once: no.

Rufus gives them a look. "We'll bring some things from the shop for dinner, ma'am. We have to set out anyhow to talk to people before evening comes, share with them what we're doing."

"Aye," Fiona says. "But furst you best all wash. You smell like the bottom of a fishing boatie. With the fish still innit."

This he understands.

To everything Fiona says, Rufus nods, adding a word here or there. The bastard probably even studied up on Scots these past six months, preparing for the journey. Rufus really is about the most amazing guy he's ever met. And it rubs off—he's felt better these last days than he has in years. Ever, maybe. It's almost as though he's courageous, too. At the very least, he's useful.

"Listen, man. I'm sorry about back there on the beach," he whispers, after the girls and Eamon have withdrawn to get cleaned up.

"Ah've never met an American afore," Fiona says, putting the kettle on.

"Don't look at him for an example, ma'am," Rufus says. "They kicked him out."

"Did they? Whit fer?"

"Threat to the ladies," Rufus says and claps him on the back.

It's good between them.

Rufus picks up a well-worn copy of *The Daughter of Time* by Josephine Tey from the kitchen table and begins to thumb through it, wrinkling his brow in concentration.

He leans back in his chair and stretches his legs. "Rufus," he says, "why didn't you go to Oxford? You look like an Oxford man to me."

Rufus puts the book down. "My father thought so, too. But none of the colleges at Oxford agreed."

"Oh, shit." He looks at Fiona. "Excuse me."

"I'm glad I went to Imperial," Rufus says. "First of all, it's a great uni. Secondly, I'd never have met Ghislaine if I hadn't."

"Oh, right. I'm sorry about that, too, man." Really, there's nothing going on between him and Ghislaine. But she is a tonic. It's hard to ignore.

"Sorry about what?"

"Here you go." Fiona sets the teapot on the table and herself on a chair. "Ghislaine—that's a different name. Welsh, is it?"

"I don't think so," Rufus says, laughing. "Ghislaine is from France. But this journey would never have happened without her. We met at a dinner for the rowing club at Imperial. She was telling a group of us about a French windsurfer, Arnaud de Rosnay. Do you know what I'm talking about?" He and Fiona shake their heads. Rufus adds, "Sort of a cross between sailing and surfing—one person on a board with a sail."

"I've heard of windsurfing," he says. "I meant the guy."

"De Rosnay? A Frenchman. Ghislaine's family is friendly with his family. She's been sailing with him. He took this mad ride alone over a great stretch of sea—he has the idea of windsurfing between hostile countries as a symbolic bridge between them. Sport, the arts—ways to find connections between people. I hear he's planning to take on China and Korea next autumn. Ghislaine was explaining this, and I thought: Why not rowing?"

"But you said the idea came to you over breakfast this past December."

"That's when I figured out how precisely to use it. I was searching for Ghislaine's number before my coffee was cold."

Eamon appears in the doorway, filling it with his large frame. Drops of wet from his hair trickle down his neck.

"Your turn," Rufus says. "Get in there and scrub."

He pushes his chair back. Sports, the arts. Music, for example. Yes, a little bit of him is starting to feel proud to be part of this. Not just a body.

———

They wake later than usual the next day, sun filtering through the windows. This last stretch is one of the longest and most difficult, but after talking with locals and consulting his tide charts, Rufus had decided they wouldn't leave until 8:00 a.m.

"We'll be halfway into the ebb tide," Rufus explains as they begin the now-familiar tasks of fastening their life jackets, settling onto their benches. "We'd have just tired ourselves out trying to fight our way across if we'd left earlier."

He takes his accustomed place behind Ghislaine. His hands are still raw, and he fondles the end of his oar tenderly before committing himself to gripping.

They row in silence but for the sound of their oars dipping into the waters. The morning sun is soft, almost hazy. An inshore trawler passes them on its way back to the docks, its sides decorated with faded red buoys of different sizes. On its deck, a fisherman bends over nets full of prawn. Behind the helm, a second fisherman cups his hands and calls something out to them, but the words are lost between the cries of the seabirds. They raise their hands and wave.

"Are we goin' to stop at Rathlin?" Katie asks.

"Do you know Rathlin?" Rufus says. "Have you been there?"

"No," Katie says. "Just wonderin'."

They row out of the trawler's wake. "We're going to keep to the west as much as possible, with Rathlin Island to our port side, to avoid the worst of the MacDonnell tidal race," Rufus says. "Once we get past Rathlin, a flood stream will bring us back east, down into Ballycastle. We'll cross those last six miles in a heartbeat."

Before long, they've left the coast of Islay behind. Low-lying clouds have moved in, and the sky has darkened so much that even he, with his sharpshooter eyesight, has trouble making out anything beyond the shape of the island.

"Looks stormy," Ghislaine says, her voice sounding tight.

Katie studies the sky. "Weather changes more quickly on the

islands than a baby's temperament." She looks down at her hands. "This will be the first time for me." Their oars trip-trip-trip through the water. "Where'er we land now, be it Rathlin or Bally-castle. That will be ma first time out of Scotland."

"You've never even been to England?" Ghislaine says.

"I don't know what's so 'even' about it. You'd ne'er been to Iona, had you?"

"The Northern Irish are good people," Rufus says, "when they aren't killing each other. They aren't so different from the people you'd meet in Scotland."

"Not to the eyes of an Englishman," Eamon mutters.

"They do talk quite a bit," Rufus says. "Our friend Eamon here being something of an exception."

A fine rain has begun to fall, a delicate whisper across his face. It feels fresh. He's worked up a sweat, pulling against the sea. The water seems unusually heavy this morning, like a swirling, viscous pot of heated tar—something he once spent some time on a job stirring. At least the sea smells better, salty and green.

"Ma ma's family," Katie says, "were Irish Scots. Her grandfaither come to Glasgow, and met ma grandmaither while she was boardin' for school."

"Where's your mother now?" he says. "Is she in Glasgow?" Katie's situation has bothered him since the start of their trip. In a way, it's been bothering him since he first saw her standing behind the counter in the general store, that stern round face, the strong black coffee in a pot before her. Maybe this crazy journey looks dif-ferent to a seafarer like her father. But that doesn't explain her being left to run the store.

Katie stares into the water. "On the island."

Could he have met her mom? He thought he knew pretty much everyone out and about on the island. Or is she truly bedridden, as he initially thought? It's hard to think of any other explanation for Katie's independence. "What's her name?"

"Muira," she says moodily.

If he could just shove the question right back into his mouth.

Worse, he can't even remember which one is Muira. He *never* could remember which one is Muira.

"She and ma da are taking a bit of a break, what's all," Katie says. "They had me when ma ma was barely seventeen. He says she's going through a midlife crisis already now, cause she started grown-up life younger." She sticks her chin out. "They'll be back together, and she'll be back at the shop. It's just one of those stupid things grown-ups get up to."

The clouds have gathered darker and deeper, like gray cotton batting in a giant's hand. He scans the sea for anything. A bird, a shoreline. There's nothing to be seen but shades of gray to one side and what looks like a curtain of black to the other.

"I'm sorry," he says.

Katie doesn't answer.

The first drops fall, small and uneven. The wind begins to pick up.

"Dirty weather," Eamon says.

"This doesn't look good," Ghislaine says. She stops rowing long enough to pull the hood of her rain jacket over her hair. "Maybe we should head for the Kintyre peninsula. That's the mainland over there, isn't it?"

"Rathlin is equally close," Rufus says. "Or at least it should be. It's hard to see anything in this weather. Can you, Francis?"

He pulls his oars out of the water and this time takes a good look in every direction. In the distance, a bolt of lightning lights up a shadowless expanse of sea just for an instant, but nothing else. "No."

"Okay. The compass says we're headed straight for the western tip of Rathlin. We'll miss the worst of the MacDonnell tidal race and find someplace to land there."

It's disconcerting rowing through the heavy mist, unable to see the various shorelines that have accompanied them at a distance throughout the journey. At least the rain remains tentative. Maybe the worst of the storm won't pass by their corner of the Atlantic.

"Francis," Rufus says. "You never told us where in America you grew up."

He understands Rufus is trying to distract them from the possibility of being caught in the worst of the storm before they can get to Rathlin, but he can't offer up his past for the purpose. "You never told us anything about your family."

"That's true. But Eamon knows them. Ghislaine has met them."

"They're very nice," Ghislaine says.

Rufus laughs. "*You're* very nice." After a few more strokes, Rufus adds, "My grandfather was in the trenches in France during the Great War. He came home with only one hand and half a heart."

"Jesus," Katie says. "How can you live with only half a heart?"

"He doesn't mean literally," Ghislaine says.

"I can't tell you how it happened. He never said one word about his experience," Rufus says. "But I can say, Katie, that you can't live very well."

"He died three years ago, right about when you met Ghislaine," he guesses. So this was the catalyst that made Rufus hook onto Ghislaine's talk of the peace-seeking French windsurfer.

"Yes," Rufus says. "Two weeks before, actually."

"And your father fought in World War II?" he says.

"Everyone in Great Britain fought during World War II. London, Birmingham, Bristol, Plymouth, Southampton. We were bombed, after all. Glasgow, too."

"The Huguenots protected the Jews in France when no one else did," Ghislaine says. "My father was part of the Resistance."

He thinks of the tin canteen his mother gave him, the one he still carries, the only thing he has of his father. And his mother handing it over to him, that indefatigable determination she had. That faith that somehow he could grow up to be as good a man. "Everyone everywhere was involved, I guess."

And then the black curtain is upon them. There's so much water he can barely open his eyes. His ears flood, the space down his neck into his jacket. He grabs his hood, pulls it tight. He opens his mouth for just a moment, and it fills with water. It slides down his jaw onto his chest despite his rain jacket. It batters his back and shoulders. It pounds his half-gloved hands, making the oars slippery. The sea swells, molten, almost as confused as they. It plays with them, throwing the boat up and down.

"Row," Rufus yells over the din of the rain. "Row."

He pulls as hard as he can, trying to keep his grip in the torrent. The rain is so heavy it's hard to find the edge of the sea, to tell where the surface starts. *"Fuck."*

He can't seem to find purchase with his oars. The water starts to break up into smaller pieces; waves toss the boat, a toy between their white-capped fingers, roiling his stomach. He doesn't have time to lean over the boat to vomit and throws up onto his own knees, still pushing, still trying to fight back the ocean. In the madness of the deluge, its thickness, all he can make out is the shine of Ghislaine's slicker and the white of Katie's forehead as she leans forward and back, forward and back, bailing bucket after bucket of water, not even attempting to wield the steering oar.

It's not wind. It is Rufus shouting: "Can you see it? Katie, can you see it? Can you see Rathlin?"

But Katie either can't or won't stop to answer. Or doesn't hear

Rufus over the noise. She is nearly out of her seat, bailing as fast as her arms allow her. The water is rising at their feet, and most of it is coming straight from the sky and not over the sides of the boat. He has never felt rain like this. It's like being beaten not with pebbles or stones but with metal bars. It slams down on his neck and back and arms, choking him, beating at his face and arms and shoulders.

A huge jolt, and suddenly he is in the sea.

The cold shock of the water knocks his breath away. And the pressure is enormous, the weight of his boots, his pants, the water, everything pulling him down. He flails against the ocean. He pumps his arms, grabs on to the only solid object around him, squeezes as hard as his gloved hands allow him.

"Grab the boat!" Ghislaine shrieks. "Not me! The boat!"

The currach is there, in front of them, about three feet away, bobbing in the torment. It's right side up, not capsized, solitary and empty as though laden now with ghostly passengers. Why isn't he in it? Why isn't Ghislaine? A wave wallops him, blinding him again. Ghislaine is moving through the water, away from him, toward the currach, and he fights his way forward after her, reaching the currach, grabbing for the rim of the boat. Water pours down his face; he peers through it into Ghislaine's face. Each with a hand on the edge, wordless, they spin their heads around in the chaos to find the others.

Water slaps him against the boat. He clutches on.

There is Eamon.

Just behind Eamon, Rufus.

A swell slams Eamon and Rufus against him and Ghislaine. His head hits hard, by the prow. He shakes it back and forth, clearing his ears. Somehow, Eamon manages to get hold of the boat's rope.

"Are you all right?" Rufus shouts. "Are you hurt?"

Another swell pushes them together. They are debris, tiny specks in a cold, angry ocean. The rain is still coming down in torrents; there is water everywhere, above his body and below, in his eyes, his ears, his clothing. Grabbing on to the cord and then pulling his way to the prow of the boat for ballast, he kicks off his rubber boots. They sink below him, into the void. His body is already starting to go numb; he can hardly feel his freed toes.

Ghislaine pushes past him and takes hold of Rufus. *"Je t'aime!"* she shouts, panting. Even drenched, her eyes are visibly filled with tears.

Rufus reaches for her through the water. "We're going to be okay! We're going to be okay! As long as we don't lose the boat and don't lose each other."

Through the seething water, the four of them look at each other.

Rufus swirls around, shouting. "Katie!"

He has already pushed off from the boat. Treading water, he scans the horizon. A mountain of swell lifts him up and then down; at the peak, he catches a flash of white, a flash of gold. He fights his way through the undersea world, giving in to being tossed over and under. Again he sees the white. The rain is still blinding, as confusing as the sea. His mouth fills with water, and his throat. He chokes, coughs, spits, forcing the sea out of his body. Another swell, and there she is, her arms grappling with the heave of the sea, her back to him, her head turning desperately left and right, away from the currach, searching.

"This way!" he shouts.

It's a miracle, but Katie hears him. They crawl through the water toward each other until their bodies collide. He wraps an arm around her torso, paddling with the other just enough to keep his nose above the water.

"I lost the fuckin' boat," she gasps.

He straps her in close to him, hugging her against the sea, a misplaced convulsive desire to laugh rocking his body. "It's behind us," he says. He swivels them to face the direction he's come from. But there is nothing but water and gray. Rain pummels the sea's surface, creating a viscous screen. He squints, lets one hand free of Katie long enough to wipe his eyes. He scans in every direction. Water.

"It's gone."

Swells lift them up and drop them. "Don't let go," he shouts. He can no longer feel his legs in the freezing water. He wraps both his arms around Katie, pumping with unfelt limbs. Together, they form an egg in the sea, their humanness the embryo, lost amidst the waves.

"*Find* it," she says, grasping his shoulders, squinting into the miasma.

He squints, too; first here, then there, then there. The rain is still heavy, flooding his face; the sea choppy now, large, spiky peaks. His eyes are leaking water, his own or the sea's—there is so much salt they sting. The only sure thing he can make out is Katie's face, even whiter, now bluer.

"For Christ's sake," she shouts. "Find it! Do you want to die?"

His body is becoming less and less his body by the instant. Is this what death is like? Is this it? Soon his arms will no longer belong to him. His hands will have stiffened. He will let go of Katie, let go of the waves, let go of his fight. He will float, carried along by his life jacket, until he feels nothing at all, swept farther and farther out into the Atlantic, becoming nothing, finally, definitively, nothing at all.

Katie kicks him.

He kicks back hard. Not against her but against his weakness. He has no idea what the right way is, but any direction is better than no direction. He releases Katie's waist and grabs hold of a strap of her life jacket. Still pumping against the sea with his legs, he ties it to his own strap. The sea is shaking them around, knocking them against each other, pulling them apart, but he will not let go of her. He will not let her get lost. The boat has to be somewhere, and he is going to get her to it.

They swim awkwardly, he dragging, she bumping against him. The rain slows, more a downpour than a torrent. He stops and looks again.

"There!" he says, catching a glimpse of hard against the liquid.

They begin their fight again, clinging to the hope of his miraculous eyesight. That God-given eyesight, which Luke said would get him killed in Vietnam if he let on he had it. Now it will keep him alive, him and Katie both. There's that flash of something concrete again. They struggle on, and suddenly he sees the prow pointed directly at him, Katie, Eamon, and Ghislaine on one side of the boat, Rufus on the other, creating ballast.

"I cannae breathe," Katie gasps.

They stop for one moment, floating in place, expending only one or two kicks as necessary. Another fifty feet and he and Katie will be with the boat. They will get Katie in first, then Ghislaine, then Rufus. He and Eamon are the largest. They'll have to pull themselves in at the same time from either side of the currach. It has to be soon, though. The feeling is beginning to go in his arms now.

"Almost there," he says.

Katie's cold fingers press into his neck. "I, I . . ." she whispers, her voice fainter. Her lips have turned blue. Her kicking is slowing.

"Here," he says, doing his best to support her. "Kick off your boots."

"Uh-uh."

"Do it!"

"Okay. Okay." Boots off, she throws herself forward. They swim again, battling the disheveled sea. It sweeps them past Ghislaine and Eamon. They paddle and turn. From the other direction, a huge swell, a mountainous swell, lifts the empty currach right out of the water. The currach comes down with a violent punch. Ghislaine is chucked in their direction. Eamon, holding on to the boat by its cord, is thrown backwards and submerged.

He wills Katie the last several feet forward. She grabs for the side of the boat.

Ghislaine splashes up beside her. "Katie!" she shouts. "Katie!"

Ghislaine's lips are purple. Eamon resurfaces, the rope still wrapped around his wrist, his face strange. They need to get back into that boat fast to survive.

"I'm going around the other side," he says to Ghislaine. "Rufus and I will hold it down, while you and Eamon help Katie in."

An odd sensation of calm slips over him. Is this hypothermia? The waves are still heavy, the air viscous, but the rain has stopped, and he no longer feels as though he is drowning above water. Rathlin has come into focus, too, not so far off. The storm is ending. As long as they have even one set of oars left, and don't freeze first, they can make it.

He works his way around the bottom of the boat, keeping a careful distance. Without their weight inside, the boat is dancing on top of the sea, bobbing up and down. If another swell hits, he doesn't want the boat to come down on him. He swims hard, and with his last strokes gets around to the other side.

There is no one there.

Damn Rufus! "Rufus," he yells, "come back 'round this side!"

But he's heavy enough to hold this side of the boat down while the girls climb in the other, even without Rufus's weight to help him. He can do it. He *can*. He lurches out of the water and grabs on to the edge. "Now!" he shouts, putting dead-man weight on his side, pulling down with whatever strength is left in him. He feels a countertug from the other side but holds his own.

Katie's white face flashes in front of him as she flops into the boat. She immediately turns to pull Ghislaine up. All he can see is the broad of her back.

The boat swings precariously back and forth, up and down; it wrenches his arms. Still he holds on tight. Ghislaine's face appears over the side.

She looks down toward him. Her mouth opens in horror.

"Rufus," she whispers.

He whips his head around. But Rufus hasn't come back to his side.

"Rufus! Rufus! Rufus!" Ghislaine screams.

She stands up in the boat and trips. Grabbing for her, Katie looks over the side of the boat, too. Her broad face crumples. Her mouth forms a wide O.

"Rufus!" Ghislaine screams again, drawing herself back up. "Rufus!"

And, in that instant, he understands.

"Oh, my fucking God." Still holding on to the boat, he turns southward to scan the horizon. The sky has cleared, and the sea has flattened. He can see cliffs, can make out a white-and-blue striped lighthouse. To the north is Islay. He can't quite settle it in his vision, but he can distinguish the Mull of Kintyre peninsula to his right. And there to his left is the open sea.

He can see everything now. Everything but Rufus.

"He's on the other side," he says to Ghislaine, as though saying it will make it true. "He's with Eamon."

Ghislaine shakes her head. She is shaking all over, her teeth chattering convulsively.

Katie's face reappears. "Eamon's arm snapped when the boat jumped. The rope snapped it."

Rufus is gone. Floating away, swept out toward the open ocean. Had he only arrived on that side of the boat a few moments earlier, maybe he would have been able to grab Rufus and save him. Or maybe it would have been he whose head was smashed when the boat flew up over the enormous swell. Or maybe both of them.

"We have to get Eamon into the boat," Katie says, pulling on Ghislaine. "Now."

"Pull Eamon up," he says. "Ghislaine! You're strong. You can do it."

Ghislaine nods, sobbing. His own face is soaked. This fucking life. This fucking life. He keeps holding on to the boat, feeling the tug and the jerk, hearing Eamon grunt with pain, until he's the only one left in the sea beside the boat.

Katie and Ghislaine reach their arms down for him.

———

There are no oars left. They float, helpless, huddled together for warmth, he and Ghislaine on one bench, Eamon and Katie on another, the island within sight but not within reach. All the barrels are gone except for the one containing his guitar, which was strapped down. They are shivering so violently that their bodies sway the currach. He searches the sea for any sign of Rufus, but even if he caught sight of a fleck on the horizon there's no way he could reach it. There's nothing he could do.

Eamon loses consciousness, and he and Ghislaine lurch forward to grab him. "He's gone into shock," she says.

"Katie," he says. "Use your body to warm him. Wrap yourself around him."

He and Ghislaine put their arms around each other as well. Still, he keeps looking. The sea is vast; man is small. But the waves are gone, and the sky has cleared. If Rufus were floating anywhere within sight, he would see him.

"He had his life preserver on," he says.

"I think he swam for shore," Katie says. "He went to get help for us."

He looks toward the shore, hoping to see an orange dot walking along the coastline. Would Rufus have been able to swim all that way? Would Rufus have taken off for help without saying so? Is it possible no one heard him saying so?

He doesn't see Rufus, but he does see a trawler heading toward them.

"Someone's on the way," he says. "Help."

Katie nods through her shivering. "See? He's sent someone."

Their bodies racked with shakes, he and Ghislaine nod back. He pulls her tighter to him, tries to get his arms to work, rubbing hers.

There's no way Rufus would make it to shore without freezing first. There is no way possible.

"He's somewhere bundled up," Katie says. Clack-clack go her teeth. "They've got him safely."

The trawler grows larger and larger, pulling up beside them. "That were a storm," a man shouts, throwing a rope down. "You're lucky to come out of it alive."

Katie tries to grab for the rope, but her hands are too unsteady, her fingers too stiff. The rope falls into the water.

"Not that you don't look hauf dead," the man says, throwing the rope again. "Tie your craft up with the rope. I'll bring you into the harbor."

Katie manages to grab hold. "No, wait!" she shouts, but the man is gone.

"Get your clothes off," the man says, reappearing long enough to throw down four thick wool blankets before disappearing again.

"We have a man lost!" he shouts, but the man doesn't hear him, doesn't turn.

The trawler's motor revs. The currach tugs back, then starts sliding behind the trawler toward the island.

The sudden fast-forward motion creates a breeze. He lets go of Ghislaine, and together they tug at Eamon's pants while Katie tries to remove his jacket. Once they have him swaddled in a blanket, they strip to their underwear and wrap themselves up. It's not warm, but it's better.

"If anyone could do it, Rufus could," Katie says.

No one answers. A brittle silence cloaks them.

The trawler brings them around the island to its south shore. Once it's berthed in the Rathlin harbor, the captain reappears from the wheelhouse to throw the rope tied to the currach to a second man on the dock, who pulls them into the shallows. Two more men splash into the water to drag the currach onto the sand.

"Did someone else come onshore?" Katie cries to them, trying to stand up, grabbing the side of the currach to keep from spilling again into the water.

The men stop short. "Wha' you mean, lass? Fra your party?"

She nods, wavering, a tangle of wet blanket. The two men exchange glances. One lifts her up and out of the boat, cradling her as though she were a baby. "These are rough waters, lassie."

The other pulls the currach the rest of the way onto the shore.

He and Ghislaine help each other out of the boat, clutching their blankets around themselves, while a man wearing a rain jacket bearing the insignia COMMISSIONER OF IRISH LIGHTS leans over Eamon's ruined arm, examining it.

"I was inspecting the light at the far end of the island when the storm hit," the man says, trying to lift Eamon up. Eamon leans forward, unable to find his balance.

"More proof why they shouldn't have got rid of the keeper last year," the captain of the boat says, coming over to help. "This one goes straight to the pub. Doctor's thare. We'll get the others wairmed fest."

On his feet now, Eamon looks around, confused. "Have to go for Rufus."

"There's nothin' you can do the shape you're in," the captain says. "None of you are fit fer helpin' anyone but yourselves right now."

"You'll look fer him, though?" Katie says, trembling. "You'll tell the coast guard?"

She looks at Ghislaine, then at him. In her face, he sees what they've left behind: the long days on the boat, the sudden rain, that final swell.

The captain sighs. "Who'll I be looking fer?"

"I'll come with you," he says, trying to will his rigid limbs forward, to push his breath through them.

"I will come, too," Ghislaine says between clenched teeth.

"And die in my boat of hypothermia? No. You hae to get wairm noo."

They all turn toward the sea. Puffins dot the shore, their gay orange feet and beaks, their dandy white chests and cheeks. Guillemots and razorbills sweep overhead, filling the air with the sound of their squeaks. The water is a deep gray-blue, just slightly choppy. An iridescent rainbow lights up the sky in a pastel arc.

He puts an arm around Katie. "Rufus Richardson," he says. "Twenty-seven. About five foot nine, a hundred and sixty pounds, black hair. British national. Leader of our expedition."

How ridiculous to try to sum a person up in a name, an age, a nationality. As though the shell of an egg could tell anything about the bird inside it. As though any of those things could come anywhere near to explaining Rufus.

———

He's led alone to the boat captain's house, a whitewashed cottage with blue shutters and a thatched roof, just off the harbor. "You have a good soak," the captain's wife, Jane, says, hurrying him into the kitchen, where she has filled a metal tub. "Come out when you kin feel your digits agin. Dinnae worry about the girls."

The warm water soaks into his limbs. Slowly his body stops fighting. His feet and fingers, his ears, his arms swell, then burn, then tingle. Every few minutes, Jane raps once, hard, on the door to the kitchen and calls, "Are you all right, then?" to make sure he doesn't fall into a stupor. It's dark in the room, despite the late afternoon light slanting through the windows. The only lamp is not lit.

When his body is loose enough, he dries off, drags on some borrowed clothes, and heads for the pub.

Eamon is sitting next to a roaring fire on a chair packed with hot water bottles. A makeshift cast supports one arm, darkening colors spreading up toward his neck. His eyes are normal again, though—quiet and watching.

He touches Eamon's arm gently then gestures toward a half-empty bottle of whiskey. "They got you fixed up?"

The bartender leans over the wooden bar. "We'll send you all to the mainland tomorrow, and they'll take him into the surgery. I did what I can meanwhile."

"Did someone call the coast guard?" Eamon says.

The bartender nods. "Radioed."

"They could send a helicopter," he says.

"They're doing the best they can out there," the bartender says.

He accepts a glass of whiskey and drinks slowly, letting the Scotch burn through him, down his esophagus, through his shoulders and chest, out to his hands, down to his knees. Georgina called that first rush "pouring boiled blood into the body." If the force of the sea could do this to Eamon's thick arm, it must have killed Rufus instantly. Maybe it's best they don't find what's left of him. Maybe Rufus would prefer that, floating off among the sea creatures.

"Thank you, man," Eamon says to him in a low voice.

"For what?"

"I'd be dead without you, wouldna? All of us. The girls are strong, but they could never have done it without ye. And Katie'd be gone."

The shock of cold, the splashing, the confusion. The strange beauty.

"I had a little sister," he says. "Have, somewhere."

Eamon nods. "Still."

"Let's call it even," he says. "We all helped each other."

The girls have apparently been given sedatives and sent straight to sleep. He and Eamon sit before the fire drinking Scotch, saying nothing but thinking about the same thing, until Eamon's eyelids begin to dip, then shut.

"I'll get him into a bed when I close," the bartender says.

Back in the captain's house, he takes to bed also, listening to the sound of a motor in the sky, propeller wings slicing through the air over the sea. This is the first night he's spent without the others since they left Iona. A lifetime ago—in Rufus's case, literally. After dark finally falls, he sleeps fitfully, tossed between the trench of exhaustion and the discomfit of grief. Several times he jolts awake, thinking himself back in the sea, feeling the pressure of a mountain of water coming down on him. He's glad enough when morning light starts sneaking through the windows.

"John McCurdy will ferry you over to Ballycastle soon as tide's in," the captain says over coffee, eggs, and brown bread with black currant preserves.

He shakes his head. "We're going to do it in the currach."

The captain shakes his head also. "No."

"Yes."

If there's one thing he knows, it is that nothing will keep him from completing Rufus's journey.

Katie and Ghislaine are already down by the currach. All that is left inside are the benches, the sail, and his guitar, still lashed in its plastic barrel behind Katie's bench. The other barrels and the oars are gone. Still, there's nothing to make the currach unseaworthy. A few dents is all.

They're in Northern Ireland now. Some suitable oars should be easy enough to find.

"It's only six miles from here to the mainland," he says. "Remember? Rufus said so. I checked the captain's charts this morning. If we hug the coast of Rathlin until we get to the end of its southernmost peninsula, we'll avoid most of the Slough-na-more tidal race, and what we do catch will shoot us right into Ballycastle."

"You sound like Rufus," Ghislaine says, looking away.

"He was an excellent teacher."

"He was."

They have moved into the past tense now. When they arrive in Ballycastle, there will be forms to fill out, police reports to complete. Rufus's family, or some emissary from it, will probably be waiting to speak with them.

"How about Eamon?" Katie says.

He thinks. "You're going to row, Katie?"

"Of course. What do you think?"

"Well, he can sit in your seat, in the back of the boat."

No one is going to sit in Rufus's seat.

They find Eamon awake and dressed.

"How fucked up are you?" he asks Eamon.

"Pretty fecked," Eamon says. "They gave me some painkillers... but I won't fall out the boat."

"Okay, then."

They set out under a perfect sky, the sun burning through the thick, long, low-lying clouds ringing its edges. The sea is a royal blue, as still as he has seen it since arriving in this part of the world. Harbor seals with mottled, prehistoric faces flop in the sun; eiders laze on the stone walls edging the marina. Auks and gannets and gulls fly overhead, filling the air with a flurry of white and black and shrill cries. The light wind ruffles his hair. They glide past a long beach, then a stretch of high cliffs, the sea crashing against their base, the water becoming a turbulent green-and-white fluff.

"What happened yesterday?" Katie says, looking around at the calm.

"I think a wave," he says. "Or maybe a whale under us."

"I think we hit something," Ghislaine says. "A rock sticking up."

"Then why wasn't the boat shattered?" Katie says.

"I don't know. Maybe the bitumen," Ghislaine says.

Eamon leans to look at him over Katie's and Ghislaine's shoulders. "Ye thought he was using the journey to sell the bitumen. But he was using the bitumen to sell the journey."

He dips his oars into the sea, watching the sun turn the drops of water into diamonds. So beautiful, the sea. How different it looks to him from the way it did a week ago. How different everything looks to him. "I know that."

"I think Francis is right. It was a wave," Katie says. "A big, huge wave."

"We had just hit the tidal race," Eamon says. "It can do strange things to ye. Toss ye up, play with ye like a beach ball. And at the same time the storm hit. It was a million-in-one chance. Of bad luck."

Everyone is quiet, probably—as he is—remembering that moment when the currach suddenly evaporated from under them, replaced by walls of moving sea, the confusion, the shouting.

"I don't even know whether the boat rolled three hundred and sixty degrees or just flew up in the air," he says. "But something knocked every one of us out of it."

"I went flying," Katie says. "It was like being a bird."

"You weren't facing the same way as we were, with your feet against the foot braces. You weren't even sitting when it happened, were you?"

Katie shakes her head. "I went far."

They lapse back into silence, rowing.

After a while, Ghislaine asks, "Are you okay, Katie? Not getting tired?"

Katie doesn't answer this. Instead she says, "I think he wouldn't have felt anything. If the force of the boat didn't get him instantly, he would have drowned before he woke up."

Ghislaine stops rowing. "How can you know that? How could he have just disappeared, anyhow? He couldn't have sunk. He had his life jacket."

"Katie's right," he says.

"Ye, she is," Eamon says.

They reach the end of the Rathlin peninsula. The water, still calm on its surface, tugs slightly on the boat, propelling them forward.

"You're a prostitute, aren't you?" Katie says to him. "That's what you do. We all saw how it was with you on the island. I knew how you paid for your coffee."

The word is so ugly, so harsh, a slashing. He thinks about her mother, or the woman who he thinks is her mother, unless it was the other. The hearty laughter, the quiet mornings. He thinks about

205

Georgina, too, and his panic when she tried to elevate their time together into something more than partying and pulling down his zipper. When he had to face whether he had it in him to stay and help someone he could love. How he ran, the farthest distance he could find. How he ran to Iona.

But that was before. *I am someone else now. I will be someone else now.*

"Yes," he says softly. "I suppose you could call me that."

They enter the sound between Rathlin and the northern tip of the Irish mainland. In the distance, large tankers plow the sea between Northern Ireland and Scotland. The sun shines off their railings and sterns and smokestacks. A converted fishing boat trails not far behind them; this must be the so-called ferry they'd declined passage on. His father's canteen must be floating somewhere out in the ocean, or maybe sunk to the bottom. It feels oddly freeing to be rid of it. Once he needed it. He won't need it anymore.

"Did Rufus know?" he says.

"Yes," Ghislaine says. "Rufus knew everything."

A school of porpoises swims up beside them. They jump through the air, creating graceful half circles. How easy they look in that deep, unknowable water.

"I *hope* he knew everything," Ghislaine adds.

"He did," he says.

Tears fall freely down her cheeks. "Do you think he would have loved me?"

"He already loved you."

Katie nods, shaking her brilliant curls. "Of course, he did. I'd already decided you'd be the godparents of my kid one day."

Ghislaine gives a short laugh, more like a hiccup. She stops rowing for a second and wipes her face. "I was just cozying up to you, Francis, so you wouldn't leave the expedition. I knew it would keep you."

He pulls on his oars, guiding the boat through the water. "Okay."
She picks up her oars again.

The porpoises gather, then divide, then regather, disappearing under the water only to pop up again. Eamon uses his good hand to touch the plastic mound tied to the bottom of the boat behind him. "Yer guitar all right?"

"I haven't looked," he says. "But Rufus said the plastic would protect it, even if it were dunked directly into the water."

"It was dunked."

"It sure was. But it'll be okay."

"Are you going to use it to write a song for him?"

"Yes," he says. The shore of Northern Ireland is directly ahead of them now. Soon they'll pull the currach up onto land for one last time. "I'm going to write a song for all of us."

BOOK FOUR

1987–1996

You will not fear the terror of night,
nor the arrow that flies by day,
nor the pestilence that stalks in the darkness,
nor the plague that destroys at midday.

—Psalm 91:5–6

Los Angeles / September 30–October 1, 1987

Barbara

They reach the outskirts of Los Angeles after midnight, the sky darkened, the city a hum of disembodied lights ahead of them. Lit highway signs, a garish green and white, appear with increasing frequency.

Soon the signs are coming every few yards.

ALAMEDA ST. CENTRAL AVE.

Her heart pumps a little harder.

In the ghoulish light of the dashboard, the silhouette of Ronnie's face looks sharper than usual, his hair even whiter. "Hanging in there?" she asks.

"I'm okay." He snaps the door locks down and adds gently, "But next time we really should fly."

It was she who insisted they drive. But it was Ronnie who said they had to wait until 4:00 p.m. to leave Scottsdale, not so he could get a full day's work in but because the desert can still be broiling hot in autumn.

Somehow the drive across the desert seems to have gotten longer.

"I offered to drive after we stopped for dinner."

"I'm okay," Ronnie repeats. "Anyhow, we're almost there now."

"Yes," she says. "We're almost there."

When they get to Santa Monica, they'll tumble into bed. She'll close her eyes, and next thing it will be tomorrow.

NORMANDIE AVE. WESTERN AVE.

"I feel silly," she says. "I feel like a kid the day before her birthday."

Ronnie laughs. He reaches over and pats her shoulder.

ROBERTSON BLVD.

"I called the hotel this morning," she says. "I told them we wouldn't be checking in until very late."

Of course, she told him this already: before they left, when they stopped for dinner. It's just something to say.

"It's supposed to be a very nice restaurant, where we're meeting them for lunch tomorrow. It's hard even to get a reservation there."

She's probably said that twice already also.

The cars on the highway have thinned out. Nearly all the trucks are gone. The brightest lights are gone, too. They are nearing Santa Monica. She rolls down her window. Warm, moist air whooshes in.

"Smelling the ocean?" Ronnie says.

"More like asphalt and car exhaust." She rolls her window up. "I swear, Los Angeles just gets more and more polluted. When we first moved here, it was different. After San Francisco, it felt like one long beach vacation."

"It was different when I first moved here, too," Ronnie says.

"*We* were different," she says.

CALIFORNIA 1. LINCOLN BLVD.

Ronnie puts his blinker on. "We sure were," he says. "What's the number of the hotel again? It's at Ocean Avenue and Wilshire? Or California?"

—

She's startled awake. A strange room, a strange bed. Morning—there's light behind the drawn curtains. The hotel in Santa Monica.

That's it: the sound of sirens is rolling in toward the hotel, scores of successive car alarms. And then the deep rumbling, soon more like a roar.

"Ronnie!" she says, throwing back the top sheet on their hotel bed, grabbing her bathrobe. "Get up! It's an earthquake!"

Ronnie turns his sleepy face toward her, and the pallor under his tanned skin stops her for a half second. But only a half second. The floor has begun to move. "Come on," she says, grabbing one of his hands and tugging. "Come on!"

He stumbles out of bed after her, fumbling with the front of his pajama shirt, almost falling as a land wave knocks him against a chair. The glass of water on the night table by his side of the bed topples and crashes onto the carpeting. She struggles with the door; he slides the lock and pushes it open. They huddle under the door-jamb while the earth shudders beneath their feet.

Ronnie draws her to him. "We should get out of the building."

"Too far," she says, glancing down the hallway toward the fire stairs.

Along the corridor, other hotel guests, some dressed and some also in their nightclothes, crowd together in their own doorways. Many, by the looks on their faces, have never been in an earthquake before. Somewhere someone is screaming. Others grit their teeth and grab on to their companions or whatever is closest to them, like the lap bar on a roller-coaster ride.

A woman one room down throws up her hands in front of her face, says something in a foreign language, and starts to weep.

"Shh, shh," she says. "We'll be fine. This is a good building."

And then it stops. The noise of the alarms is still there, but the earth is silent.

"What do we do now?" one of the hotel guests asks, running a hand through uncombed hair. "Is it over?"

The woman one door down has dropped to her knees. Whether to pray or be sick is unclear.

"You're supposed to go outside," Ronnie says. "In case there's structural damage. Or a gas main has broken. Just a precaution."

A guest takes the arm of the kneeling woman, helps her to her feet. The floor's occupants troop toward the fire stairs, a parade of jittery half-clad strangers. "This is why I brought my bathrobe," she whispers to Ronnie, attempting a smile. This isn't the first quake she's been through. No one lives forty-three years in California without getting bounced around some. Still, she's shaken. Maybe because she's grown out of the habit, living in Arizona for so long now.

Or maybe because her heart has peeled back its skin already in making this trip to LA. Just a few hours now, and she'll see Francis and meet his girlfriend.

"Do you want to slip some clothes on quickly before we go downstairs?"

"No. I'm okay."

"I'm just going to grab my pants." Ronnie pops back into the room, shutting the door behind him. In a few seconds he emerges still in his pajama top but wearing slacks. "Sorry about that, sweetheart. Let's go down."

They join the hotel guests filing down the stairs and through the lobby. A few paintings are askew; some lamps seem to have fallen. In general, the hotel looks pretty good. On the lawn out front, the Pacific Ocean stretching wide before them, a hotel employee is wandering among the guests, assuring them that everything is fine and that they will be able to go back to their rooms momentarily. Another is handing out blankets. Although it's already a hot and muggy day, a number of guests accept, swaddling themselves for comfort.

"That was a big one," Ronnie says, rubbing his lower back.

"Is your back hurting again?"

Ronnie shrugs. "The driving. I'm sure it'll go away."

There always seems to be some reason. Really, he should get that checked out. But she told him so already weeks ago.

"That place where Patty Ann is living now," she says. "It looks like the big bad wolf would have an easy time blowing it down."

Ronnie shakes his head. "It's made of wood. It's brick you have to look out for during an earthquake. Or adobe. Wood is flexible."

With the morning sun on his face, Ronnie looks unusually tired, still handsome but older than his sixty-four years. When did that happen? He's made plans to retire on his next birthday, to hand the day-to-day management of the company over to his vice president. Not a moment too soon, in her opinion. He's become thinner also. His collarbones jut out under his twisted pajama top.

She straightens his collar. "I hope there hasn't been too much damage anywhere."

"It was a big one," he says again. He sniffs the air. "Smog but no gas. I'm sure we can go back in soon. I'll get us cups of coffee." The hotel has set up a little station on a folding table.

"Better make that a double," she tells him, retying her bathrobe.

The plan is to meet for lunch today after Francis's morning meeting. Francis has written a bunch of songs. A record label in Los Angeles wants to produce them.

Three years ago, on a quiet Monday morning, the phone rang. *Mom,* Francis said on the other end of the line, as though he hadn't dropped off the face of the earth for ten years. As though she hadn't even known most of those years whether he was alive or dead. *We've just gotten a phone hooked up. I'm glad you are still at the same number. How are you?*

215

She didn't drop the phone. She didn't cry out: *Francis! Francis! Francis!*

Francis, she said, as calmly as she could, as though the past ten years weren't rushing in a torrent through her head and heart. *Where are you?*

I'm in County Clare, Ireland, he said. *In a little stone cottage.*

Are you living there? she asked.

He didn't answer for a moment. *Yes. I'm living here now.*

And then there was a silence.

It was like being in the room with a mouse: any sudden movement, any sharp sound, and it might bolt. She racked her brains for what she could safely say next.

Sissy just graduated from college, and Kenny has just begun. And Ronnie is traveling.

So you are alone.

Oh, no, she said, although she did feel very alone suddenly. *Ronnie will be back soon. It's just a short business trip.*

Ronnie hands her a Styrofoam cup. The coffee is lukewarm, hurriedly made by some poor soul frightened to be in the kitchen but even more scared of losing his or her job. Someone has brought out a transistor radio, and guests are gathering in a tight cluster to listen, bare shoulder to bathrobe, the sudden intimacy of disaster.

"We could just drive over to Venice and check," she says. "Patty Ann's."

A hotel employee approaches the group around the radio, saying something slowly and earnestly. Their circle breaks open, and guests begin to reenter the hotel. She discreetly pours the remainder of her coffee on the lawn.

Ronnie sighs. "Let's get some clothes on first, okay?"

It's an even shorter drive than usual from Santa Monica down to Venice Beach. Although now nominally rush hour, the traffic on both Ocean Avenue and Main Street is light. The world feels strangely still. They find Patty Ann out on the porch of her rickety wooden house, a stone's throw from the water. Her latest husband, Glenn, sits on a step beside her in a sleeveless undershirt, the tattoo on his upper right arm a flat bluish green in the morning sun: LO QUE SEA NECESARIO.

Sean sits on a crate by the door. He gets up and goes into the house.

"Sean, come back out and say hello to your grandma," Patty Ann calls. She reaches for Glenn's cigarette, takes a drag. "Hi, Mom. You all shook up?"

Glenn stands up and extends his hand. "Good morning, Mrs. McC., Mr. McC."

"Good morning, Glenn."

Glenn is three and a half years younger than Patty Ann, and Patty Ann met him at an AA meeting. But he, at least, seems to have stuck by the program. Most important, he treats Patty Ann decently. In comparison to Lee and certainly to Patty Ann's last husband, Troy, Glenn is a prince.

Troy was the worst of the worst. He left Patty Ann with two broken ribs.

She only wishes Glenn had a steady income. Patty Ann says he's begun training to be a stonemason, that being a sculptor makes him a natural for the work and soon he'll be "making a mint." But who trains to be a stonemason at thirty-seven? That's the one—and only—thing anyone could say for Troy. He did pay the bills.

"Where are the other boys? Did the schools open?" she says, stooping to kiss Patty Ann on the cheek. Up close, Patty Ann smells stale and sweet and smoky, like last evening spilled over into this morning.

"Isaiah's with the SOB this week." That's Patty Ann's code name for Troy. No one is allowed to speak his real name. In front of Patty Ann and Troy's one son, it's "your dad"—which makes her feel bad

for Isaiah, as though somehow he's at fault for how awful his father was. *What's the hurry?* she told Patty Ann, but Patty Ann could
hardly wait for her divorce from Lee to come through to get hitched
to Troy, scared to be on her own with two small children and no
job. Or maybe just angry—after all, Patty Ann gave up her future
so Lee wouldn't be drafted.

It took less than three years for Patty Ann to get a divorce this
second time. Troy told the judge that Patty Ann got those broken
ribs falling down drunk. For whatever reason, the judge believed
him, and though Isaiah was barely more than a baby, the court
granted him joint custody. She knows Patty Ann was telling the
truth, though.

At least Patty Ann waited another eight years before getting married a third time.

"And Lucas?"

Patty Ann shrugs. "Around."

"How was it over in Santa Monica?" Glenn asks.

Ronnie shakes his head. "It was a big one."

"But we're fine," she says. "Less tossed than salad. We didn't see
any damage on our way over here, either."

"There was smoke rising downtown," Ronnie says.

Glenn nods. "Fires."

Ronnie looks the house over. "Did you close the gas main?" It's
one of those wooden homes from the beginning of the century,
three stories but with a low roof and fronted by a brick, wood, and
paving-stone porch, shadowed by an overgrown sapote tree on one
side and a coral tree on the other. The first time they visited, an
evening shortly after Patty Ann and Glenn moved in, they heard
what sounded frighteningly like gunshots down the road.

Oh, there's the gangs in Venice Beach, Patty Ann said. *But we don't
bother them, and they don't bother us.*

"Of course we turned it off," Patty Ann says now, sharply.

She can see Sean inside the living room. She steps around Patty Ann and Glenn and goes inside. She and Sean get along fine—it just takes him a while to get used to seeing her again. At nineteen, he's full-grown—dark-haired, round-faced, and freckled, like her side of the family—but in many ways still a little boy. For years, she tried to get Patty Ann to let her take him to see a specialist. *For what?* Patty Ann would say. *So they can treat him like the counselor did at school? Sean's fine. Sean's just Sean.* Secretly, she wonders whether Patty Ann refused to let her pursue it out of fear it would give her cause to take Sean, as she took Kenny.

Except she didn't *take* Kenny. That's just a myth Patty Ann has tried to introduce into the family history. Patty Ann gave Kenny to her.

She wouldn't mind taking Lucas now, though. Even with Ronnie's retirement coming up. She's been thinking she and Ronnie might start traveling together—all these years he's gone off on business trips on his own while she stayed back in Scottsdale—but family is family, and Lucas is her grandson. Not only does he look just like Lee, at fourteen he's also showing signs of having inherited his father's slippery personality. No good can come from the way Patty Ann lets him wander.

A purple bedspread covers Michael's old armchair, but when she sits down in it, the sensation is still familiar. Many a night after she lost him she would sit in it, once all the kids were in bed, trying to feel him. She fell asleep in it more than once, exhausted from the weight of it all.

She'll visit Luke and Michael tomorrow. Maybe Francis will want to come with her. She won't propose it, though. She'll let him bring it up.

"So, Sean, how's work?"

Sean has been working at a nearby gym, Gold's, since leaving school, maintaining the equipment, wiping down the exercise mats. He may not be like other kids, but—unlike his too-smart-for-her-own-good mom—he has been able to hold down a job.

"Mmm."

"I can't offer you coffee," Patty Ann says, walking through the room, her bare feet echoing on the wooden floor, toward the kitchen. "The electricity's out. And the gas is off—as you know. We've got orange juice, though."

"That's okay, dear. We just came by to check you were okay."

"We should drink the OJ before it goes bad," Patty Ann calls from the kitchen. "Here, Sean, I'll pour you a glass. We can walk up to the Rose Café after and get scones."

Patty Ann's living room is large and low-ceilinged, with white-painted wooden beams and wooden built-ins lining three of the walls. Bearing only a jumble of worn paperbacks, a collection of shells, and what look like crystal rocks, the shelving just adds to the house's abandoned feeling. In addition to Michael's armchair and the matching sofa she gave Patty Ann years ago, the only furniture are two oak rockers with lattice backs and torn leather seats that were in the house when Patty Ann moved in and a strange stone object with a wooden base that is either one of Glenn's sculptures or a coffee table. Or both.

Indian-print cloths are draped over the sofa and pinned above the windows in lieu of curtains. A few large, fluorescent canvases have been nailed directly into the walls. One is of a big peace sign. Dust and pollen lie in clumps on the floor. Patty Ann has never been much of a housekeeper. Her daughter also doesn't seem to have noticed the hippie era is over.

At least there isn't much to fall down on anyone during an earthquake.

"Ronnie needs to have *two* scones. Why's he losing weight?"

Patty Ann says, coming into the room with two glasses of OJ, handing her one. "He's not fat."

She takes a little sip of the OJ and sets it down on the marble object. Then, just in case it *is* one of Glenn's sculptures, she picks the glass back up and sets it down on the floor. How pale Ronnie looked, jerked awake this morning. "I think it's good he's retiring. You know. We're not that young anymore."

"You look good, Mom. You always look good."

Suddenly, the earth bounces. She reaches out automatically to grab the glass. It's just a small aftershock. Sean, drinking his orange juice, doesn't budge.

"Don't worry, Mom," Patty Ann says. "This is a good house. A really solid house."

"I don't know, Patty Ann. The roof... have you had it checked?"

Patty Ann frowns. "The roof is *fine*. The owner, he had everything checked before he bought it. *Everything* is fine. It just needs a little paint."

"It does have nice woodwork," she says, looking around, trying to find something positive to say about the big beaten-down shell.

"You'll see. A little work and this house will be worth a mint."

Last visit, Patty Ann told her the scuffed oak table and chairs in the dining room, also left in the house by the owner, are by the same furniture maker—Stickley, Patty Ann called it—as the two rockers in the living room. *A little work and they'll be worth a mint,* Patty Ann insisted. Patty Ann is always saying with a little work something will be worth a mint.

If only Patty Ann would realize that with a little work Patty Ann could be worth a mint.

"But what worries me, is it *safe?* I don't mean the house. I mean the street. The neighborhood."

Patty Ann laughs. "Well, that's one good thing about being married to a guy like Glenn. Nobody fuc—I mean, bothers you."

She won't ask why. Glenn's mom is American, but his father's family is Mexican, and for some reason he landed below the border with an aunt and uncle for a few years while he was a teenager. There's a story behind that she's never asked about. Everyone has some kind of past, whether good or bad. Nowadays Glenn is sober, on the right side of the law, and committed to her daughter. He doesn't mistreat her grandkids. That's all she needs to know.

"What's a scone?" she asks.

"Sean!" Patty Ann says. "Grandma doesn't know what a scone is!"

At the Rose Café, Patty Ann brings up her house again. "It's so large! Big enough to take in a boarder. Or make the top-floor bedroom into a B and B for weekly guests. I told Francis he and his girlfriend would be welcome to stay with us."

She'd like to call Francis, but neither Patty Ann's phone nor the pay phone at the Rose Café is working. Will he still be able to join them for lunch at 1:00 p.m.?

Another aftershock rolls through. Ronnie grasps her arm. Her heart leaps. Life has so much uncertainty.

"I think I wouldn't mind a nap before lunch," Ronnie says, climbing carefully down from his high stool. This café is a funny place. A huge wall painting of a rose almost swallows the front door. "All this excitement. It's taken the life out of me."

"Great idea." The phones at the hotel will be good. She's sure of it.

In fact, there's already a message at the hotel reception: *Lunch will have to be dinner, 6:30 p.m. Same restaurant. Francis says sorry.*

"Just as long as he shows up," she says, drawing back their room's curtains, opening the window. Amazing that the cleaning service has managed to pass through already, while elsewhere in LA some people are undoubtedly battling fires, rummaging through rubble. If not for the aftershocks, she could pretend there's no disturbance anywhere but the one inside her.

She lost one son already during the Vietnam War. It would have been too much to lose another. But she knew Francis would return someday. She never gave up hope.

The Pacific looks so blue and calm. The beach stretches long and flat and brown. A strip of white licks the shore where the waves hit. It seems so long ago and yet just yesterday when she and Michael would bring the kids down to the beach here to play. Francis was, already, a beautiful baby. She'd unlock the bassinet from the baby carriage, set it in the sand, prop an umbrella up overhead, and turn away to play with the bigger kids. When she turned back, there'd be some woman or girl cooing over him.

"What'd you say?" Ronnie asks, slipping his shoes off, stretching out on the bed.

"Nothing. Just talking to myself."

When she flew to Dublin to see Francis six months after he called, the only time she's seen him since he resurfaced, she refused to think about the possibility he might not be there waiting as promised. *Shall we lay bets on whether he'll show up?* Patty Ann said during the flight over. She'd brought Patty Ann along, partly because she didn't want her to be the only one of the kids—now that Sissy had spent her junior year of college in Paris—never to have been outside of America and partly because that was before Glenn, and she didn't know what Patty Ann might get up to with her out of the country. Kenny went to stay with the younger boys, and Patty Ann came to Ireland with her.

It was her first time across the Atlantic also.

Don't be ridiculous, Patty Ann, she said, looking out the plane window, down below at the vast gray nothingness of sky and ocean. *Even Francis wouldn't have me fly all the way over here and not show up.*

She turns away from the hotel window and sits down on the other side of the bed from Ronnie. Francis was right there in the airport when she and Patty Ann disembarked. The rest of the week was perfect also. Even Patty Ann behaved well. They went around, eating smoked salmon and brown bread, visiting music halls and old town houses, laughing at how she kept forgetting to look right when she stepped off the curb. Being together. She didn't ask questions. She didn't ask whether he would ever come back to America, even to visit. Now, finally, he has.

"Glenn told me, while you were inside, that he and Patty Ann have a chance at buying their house," Ronnie says.

"That old wreck?"

"The owner's going into foreclosure. They could get it for a song. One hundred and forty thousand dollars, Glenn says."

"You'd have to *pay* me more than that to live there. I think there are drug dealers on that street. Anyhow, where would Glenn and Patty Ann come up with one hundred and forty thousand dollars? Who would give them a loan?"

"Well," Ronnie says.

She takes in his profile. Ronnie is lying on his back, staring at the hotel bedroom's ceiling.

"Ronnie. You are so good to Patty Ann. But you don't have to do this. She's got a husband again now. She turned forty in July."

"The owner said they can keep the furniture he left behind. Maybe Patty Ann is right. Maybe that Stickley stuff is worth something. And it is only a block from the beach. Four bedrooms."

"That's not the point."

"It wouldn't really require that much money. We can afford it."

"That's not the point, either."

"Look, I know Patty Ann has never taken to me like the other kids did. We've never had such an easy time together. But she's a good person, deep inside. She means well. And she's smart, she's strong. She's like her mother." Suddenly, he sits up on the bed and takes her hand. He looks her in the eyes. "I love you, Barbara."

What in the world has gotten into Ronnie? He's affectionate, but he never says stuff like this. She squeezes his hand. "I love you too, dear. But that doesn't mean you have to buy my oldest daughter a house."

He keeps hold of her hand, keeps looking straight at her, so serious. "I'd insist the title goes under her name. I won't be here forever, and I want to be sure she has something solid for her future."

"Good grief. You are talking like you're one hundred years old! And if we did help her to buy a home, why not a cute little two-bedroom condo in Marina del Rey, at least? Or, if that's too much, in Culver City? Someplace clean and new and safe."

"Barbara. This house in Venice is what Patty Ann wants. It's who she is."

The homemade wind chimes fluttering on the porch. The mysterious muddle of books and shells on the shelves. The scrappy neighborhood.

She sighs. He is right. This *is* Patty Ann.

"You'll tell her she has to pay it back? To be fair to the others?"

"I'll guarantee the loan and give her the down payment as a gift. We paid for everyone else's college tuition but Mike's. I know I've helped her out more than the others over the years, but I think it still works out fair. Mike worries about her. He'd give her the money himself if he could. If she'd even take it from him."

"You have this all figured out."

Ronnie lets go of her hand and lies back down. He closes his eyes. "Yes. I do."

He folds his hands over his chest. She rolls onto her side and lays her head by his shoulder. Not on it but touching.

"Well, who knows?" she says. "Maybe Patty Ann's right. Maybe it'll turn out to be worth a mint."

Ronnie laughs softly.

She closes her eyes also.

After their nap, they use the hotel phone to call Patty Ann, whose home phone is working again, and let her know lunch has been moved to dinner, in case Francis hasn't gotten through to her. Neither of them is feeling very hungry, so they share a club sandwich in the hotel's restaurant. Then they venture out and walk north through Palisades Park, stopping to rest under the shade of the palm, pine, and fig trees. Even here by the beach, the day weighs heavily, hot and soupy. A few Rollerbladers have come out, and bike riders. When another aftershock occurs, everyone freezes, re-living the morning. Then they pick themselves back up and keep at whatever they were doing.

The same sudden quiet occurs again that evening when they are in the restaurant, waiting with Patty Ann, Glenn, and Sean for Francis and his girlfriend to arrive. But this time it's not from an-other aftershock. It's *Francis*. When he walks through the front door, the other diners clearly think because of his looks that he must be a famous actor.

Has life always been like this for poor, shy Francis? The other diners all swiftly return to their grilled chicken with sun-dried tomatoes and their blackened ahi. This is Los Angeles.

"Hello, Mom," he says carefully. He kisses her on the cheek and greets everyone else slowly, individually, politely shaking hands with Glenn, whom he's never met before. Then he introduces his girlfriend, standing a few steps away and looking around the nautical-themed whitewashed walls of the restaurant with an amused expression.

"This is Georgina," he says. "I should tell you. We were married three weeks ago."

Francis has gotten married? Without telling any of them? Will she never be part of her youngest son's life again? *Was* she ever?

Francis's new bride seems to notice them for the first time. There's something curiously disconnected about the girl—and *girl* is really the word for her. Younger than Sissy, willowy, with straight blond hair and a fragile face. Very pretty, of course. "I told Francis we had to if I was going to move to the United States with him," Georgina says with a laugh that sounds like running water.

"Well, that's quite the news!" she says. "Welcome, Georgina! Welcome to America!" She doesn't know whether to embrace her new daughter-in-law; something tells her no. She shakes her hand instead, then sits down at the table, watching everyone else do the same. And then, because she doesn't even know where to start, she turns to what sparks hope in her heart. "So you are moving home?"

Francis frowns. "It depends on what you mean by 'home.' We're going to try out living in America, yes. But not California. Not the West."

Patty Ann shoots her a warning look—has she already been too intrusive?—before exclaiming, "All these years, all these brothers and all these sons, I always had only one sister. Now I have *two*. This is a reason to celebrate!"

"Oh, isn't that sweet." Georgina's smooth English accent makes it hard to tell whether the words are meant to be sincere or sarcastic.

"What about Mike's wife?" she says. All she did was ask whether he was moving back. He brought it up first. Or, really, his surprise *bride* did.

"Ha!" Patty Ann says. "Right. *Holly.*"

"Holly is Mike's wife," she says to Francis and Georgina. It's hard to know what Francis is up to date on. He may have resurfaced, but it's not like he's suddenly become anyone's pen pal, and this is—at least as far as she knows—his first visit back to the United States. Although maybe he has been back without telling her. He stopped in New York City on the way here, but even that much she only knows from Jeanne, who heard it from Molly. Molly apparently neglected to mention he brought along a wife. They always were thick as thieves, Francis and Molly.

Patty Ann drinks from her wineglass. "Holly is *very* enthusiastic."

"I've met Holly," Francis says, looking uncomfortable, as though it's cost him to say it. And then she remembers. Holly was with Mike in Paris when Mike caught and then lost Francis. Mike blamed himself so terribly for that, afterward. *I should have known better than to let him out of my sight. I mean, this was Francis.*

She waves her hand. "Well, congratulations."

"We didn't want to make a fuss," Francis says. "It was very last-minute. I'm sorry I didn't get a chance to tell you."

Apologizing seems to be part of the new Francis. Please, God, don't let him be in a twelve-step program. One in the family is more than enough.

"Shall we order a bottle of Champagne?" Ronnie says.

Again, that silvery laugh. "Always," says Georgina.

Patty Ann raises her glass. "We should go out after dinner to some places I know, Georgina. I'll show you Los Angeles."

"No," Francis says swiftly.

Patty Ann takes a slug of her wine and sets it down heavily on the table. "What do you mean 'no'? I wasn't talking to you, Francis, anyhow. I was talking to your bride. My new *sister.*"

"No," Francis says again, quietly. He puts his arm around Georgina. "Hello, Sean. You've become a man since I last saw you."

"What do you mean, *no?*" Patty Ann stands up and throws her napkin down on the table. "I'm going out for a smoke."

"She's excited to see you," Glenn says to Francis, shrugging. "She's excited to have you here in Los Angeles. Family is everything to Patty Ann."

"Waiter?" Ronnie says, lifting a hand, looking around to find one.

"Never mind us," she tells Georgina. "We're all mixed up because of the earthquake this morning. I'm sorry you had to experience that."

Georgina claps her slim pale hands together. Yes, there's the wedding band. A single band, but studded with diamonds. Where would Francis get the money for something like that? He couldn't have gotten it from the record company; he's signing a contract this visit. In Ireland, he said he was supporting himself by working in construction. "The earthquake? Oh, that was so fabulous!"

"Georgina, some people died," Francis says. "There was a lot of damage."

"Oh, darling. Of course, it's awful people were hurt. But it's good to be reminded about the power of the earth, isn't it?"

"That's what sunrises and sunsets are for."

"No, darling, that's the power of the *sun*."

"Okay. Then gravity."

"Speaking of *which*," Georgina says, frowning. "*Someone* is acting a little heavy."

"Speaking of which," Glenn says, setting his glass of Coca-Cola down. "The David fell over again."

She and Ronnie look at him, grateful. "Who's that?" Ronnie asks.

"The *David* in Forest Lawn cemetery. The replica of Michelangelo's statue. It fell over during the 1971 earthquake also, smashed to pieces. Or maybe that was in a different Forest Lawn cemetery. Anyhow, this one fell on grass, which cushioned the fall, so just a few pieces. It's made from Carrara marble, brought from Italy."

"Glenn is training to be a stonemason," she tells Francis and Georgina.

"I'm a sculptor," Glenn says, smiling.

"And he's a sculptor," she says.

"This quake wasn't like other ones, you know? It felt like being on a boat in a terrible storm," Glenn says. "I used to go out fishing with my *abuelo* in Tecuala? It felt like that. Not a rocking back and forth, like most earthquakes. More like a bouncing up and down."

Patty Ann apparently hasn't told Glenn much about Francis, or else Glenn has forgotten. One night during her and Patty Ann's stay in Dublin, a bunch of locals in a pub started singing a sea ballad, and Francis said something about writing a few of his own, about an experience he had had on the sea between Ireland and Scotland. There was something in his face when he said it, something that stuck with her. After she got back to Scottsdale, she searched through the news microfilm at the central library and found the whole terrible story.

"Oh," she says quickly, "let's—"

"Yes," Francis says evenly. "It felt like that."

Ronnie lays his hand on hers under the table. "Did you know," he says, "some biblical scholars argue that David wasn't really the one who slew Goliath? I read all about it in *National Geographic*. Or maybe it was *USA Today*."

"David now?" Patty Ann says, plopping down in her seat again, bringing the scent of cigarette smoke to the table. "Can't we have any heroes?"

"That doesn't take any hero away. It just means we called one by the wrong name. And anyhow, David was still a hero. You know what for first?" Ronnie smiles. He's looking better since their walk this afternoon. "As a musician."

"I thought he was a shepherd. Remember catechism class?" Patty

Ann says, turning to Francis. "What was that awful woman's name? I'm sure you had her also. *Everyone* had her."

Francis makes a face. "I remember."

"Mrs. Dawson," Patty Ann says. "Her name was Mrs. Dawson."

"David could soothe King Saul with his lyre," Ronnie says. "That's how he got his start. It was an important talent."

"Well, here's to all of us," she says, lifting her glass, trying not to watch Patty Ann refilling hers again. "Musicians and not. Here's to being together. My cup runneth over."

Everyone looks at her. Georgina starts to laugh, that tinkling laugh, then Patty Ann starts to laugh, and then they all are laughing.

"Good grief," she says. "Let's order."

After their food comes, things improve. It turns out Georgina is funny and, despite the accent, not nearly as snobby as first impressions suggested. And it's nice to see how comfortable Francis is with her. It's hard to remember Francis ever seeming so at ease with anyone outside the family or even in the family, other than maybe Molly. Anyone, of course, other than Eugene.

And then it hits her. There's something about Georgina that reminds her of Eugene. Not just the way Georgina doesn't seem in thrall to Francis's beauty. Georgina has the same odd combination of optimism and cynicism as that funny, wiry kid always had.

She won't say so, though. Eugene might belong on the list of topics that can't be mentioned, and things are going so well—she doesn't want to say or do anything that might scare Francis away again. After dinner, he even agrees to come over to Patty Ann's house to meet Lucas, who, Patty Ann says, should be home now.

"Plus you can tell Mom to stop worrying that the house might fall down around my ears," Patty Ann says to Francis once they're all outside the restaurant. "You worked in construction, right? You can tell us whether it's solid."

Francis laughs. "Am I getting in between something?"

Patty Ann makes an innocent face. "Not at all, not at all..."

"You kids," she says, and for a second it almost feels like years ago.

"Want to come with me, Georgina?" Ronnie jangles the keys to his car. "Let Francis go with his mother?"

Georgina slips her arm into his. "Delighted."

Francis's rental car is parked a block away, a yellow convertible with the top rolled down. "She's nice. Your Georgina," she says, sliding into the passenger seat.

Francis fits the key in the ignition. "Do you want me to put the top up? Georgina saw it in the rental lot. She insisted."

"No. I'm all right."

They pull onto the street. The evening air feels warm and thick. It's odd sitting next to her youngest son while he drives—last time they sat like this he was still a kid, probably not even twenty-one. Now he's a man. His cheekbones are sharper now, his skin no longer so fine. His blond hair has darkened. He still looks like his father, but mostly he looks like himself.

"Did you have your meeting after all? About the record?"

"We did."

She cups her hand over her hair against the wind, looks out over the streets of Santa Monica. "You always loved that guitar of yours. I remember when you went out and bought it with Eugene." When he doesn't say anything, she adds. "Well, I think it's great. Good for you, Francis."

Francis is silent. They drive several more blocks, the dark running through her hair. She can't smell the sea, but she can feel it is close. They come to a crossroads, and Francis slows to a stop.

He turns to look at her.

"I was a disappointment," he says. "Mike was strong and steady.

Luke was smart and funny. Patty Ann was...like an arrow. And Sissy was *Sissy*. I was just, you know, pretty. I could never live up to any of you."

It takes her breath away. "Is that how you think?"

Francis just looks at her. Even in the night, his eyes are so clear and blue—even more Michael's eyes now than they were when he was still a boy. Her youngest son has seen things. Like Michael, he has stories he may never tell.

"You are so stupid, Francis," she says.

He laughs softly. "That doesn't help."

"That's not how it is when you have children. To me, each and every one of you was—*is*—perfect. Even Patty Ann, who has given me a headache for, well, basically since the day your father died, is still utterly perfect to me. You were, all of you, the *best* kids in the entire world. That's what it means to be a mother. You'll see when you and your girl start having children."

Behind them, a car honks.

"I may be perfect, but I don't think I can ever be a mother," Francis says, putting the convertible back in motion.

"You know what I mean. You were all perfect to your father also. We didn't say this one is *a* and that one is *b*. We said this one *wants* that and that one *wants* this. That's how parents think about their children. You'll see."

They drive again in silence until they reach Patty Ann's desolate street. Shadows have fallen over the overgrown trees, the yard, the boarded-up houses around it. The Pacific whispers gently in the viscous night air. Ronnie has taken the space behind Patty Ann's in the driveway. Francis pulls up next to the sidewalk.

"I don't know about having children," Francis says.

"Oh, you'll have kids," she says. "Georgina is too pretty not to have a child. *You're* too pretty not to have a child."

He looks at her. She smiles at him, and he smiles back. They both laugh.

"I'm proud of you, Francis," she says. "Always proud of you."

"Hey, you two! Are you coming in?" Patty Ann calls from the porch.

Another aftershock hits, bouncing the convertible just a little. They wait to be sure it's not the big one, then walk toward the porch together. She slips her hand through his arm. It feels like something she's been waiting to do since forever.

Graduation Day / May 15, 1996

BARBARA

EVERYONE'S ELBOWING SOMEONE FOR something in New York City. Two women in skintight jogging clothes, pushing three-wheeled strollers down West 81st Street, practically knock her over. A cluster of fat-bodied pigeons fights over a scrap of pizza. And there's that woman standing on the same corner as yesterday evening: missing one of her front teeth, sticking her dirty hand out into the path of every person who passes.

Twelve hours since she arrived at Kennedy Airport. In another three days, she'll be back on a plane again, heading home to Phoenix. The backyard immaculately landscaped, the small clean pool—everything spotless, even more so now that she's the only one living in the town house in Scottsdale. *Are you going to move back to California?* the kids asked after Ronnie's funeral. But move to where? Southern California, where back in the 1960s, she lost the first of her husbands? Northern California, where half a century ago she left behind the unmarried version of herself? What did the kids think the twenty years she'd spent in Arizona had been? An extended visit?

All of life is an extended visit. There's no visiting within the visit. She reaches the corner. She might have returned to Southern

California had Patty Ann really needed her. She might even have moved into that big house in Venice with her and Glenn, helping out with the two younger boys. But even if Isaiah hadn't joined his father, living in that canyon, he still would have grown up. Lucas would have grown up, too. And where would that have left her? An old lady living with her middle-aged daughter, nothing to do, no one to do it for?

The beggar woman is muttering something, moving toward her. A yellow car beams up Amsterdam Avenue—a taxi. She thrusts a hand out, like she's seen on television and in the movies. The taxi swerves dangerously to the left, cutting off other traffic, screeching to a stop beside her. She opens the door and slides in before the begging woman can get any closer.

"Broadway and One Hundred and Sixteenth Street," she says. "And try to drive less like a crazy person, please."

The driver—a dark-skinned man with a turban wrapped around his head—turns to look at her. "Okay, lady." He peels back into traffic. She takes hold of her armrest as they dart uptown along the streets of New York City.

At least she won't be late for Kenny's graduation ceremony. They all offered to come fetch her: Kenny, his girlfriend—although she hasn't met her yet—and even Molly, in her own fashion. *I can't get free before noon myself, Aunt Barbara, but I can have a car waiting right in front of your hotel. I'll give instructions to the driver.* Sweet of them, of course, but she can get there on time and in one piece by herself.

Don't worry about me, dear, she told Molly. *I made it to seventy years old. I can make it two miles north in New York City.*

The cab veers wildly to the curb and jerks to a stop in front of Columbia University's tall main gates. The sidewalk teems with people. She pays the cabdriver, tipping him what she hopes is a correct amount, and picks her way through the gaggles of girls, tippy in high-heeled sandals beneath graduation robes, and anxious parents. Everyone graduating from Columbia's undergraduate and graduate schools is part of this morning ceremony. There will be a second, private ceremony for the medical school this afternoon.

Dr. Kennedy Gannon Rosetti.

Just thinking those four words makes her heart leap. She's come two miles uptown and a lot further than that to get her grandson here today.

She parts friend from friend, husband from wife, making her way toward a campus guard, her entrance ticket safely tucked inside the navy blue purse she bought special for this occasion. It's been years since she had a flock of kids following her, but, like living through earthquakes, the physical memory of those decades never leaves her. How much easier it is to move through crowds as just one person! A warm hand lands on her shoulder.

"Grandma!"

Kenny's face is flushed and happy. In his free hand, he wields an outlandishly oversize latex glove, some sort of totem for the graduation ceremony.

"Kenny! How in the world did you find me in this mess of people?" His light blue gown with black trim, the emerald green sash around his neck, and the velvety black mortarboard set off his clear eyes. The robe accentuates his height—the one physical attribute he clearly got from his Gannon genes. But he inherited something still more important from them. She has to catch her breath. Four generations of doctors, starting with Michael's father. She straightens his cap. "My, my, don't you look like a swell!"

A tall girl with close-set blue eyes and olive skin homes in on them. "It's kismet!" the girl says, revealing a set of showily perfect teeth.

"Grandma," Kenny says, "This is Jennifer Cohen. Jennifer, this is my grandma."

She takes Jennifer's hand. So this is the girl her grandson likes.

Jennifer has thick dark hair that hangs almost to her waist. Her flowery, thin-strapped sundress does nothing to minimize a massive bosom. There's something different about her, something unlike girls back in Arizona. Not uncomely, just different. Kenny's been in New York seven years now, studying in Columbia's joint MD-PhD program.

"I am very happy to meet you, Jennifer," she says. A group of students brushes past, jostling her new purse. Not only does it go with her trim peach-colored pantsuit, it also has a secure closure so no unwanted hands can slip into it. Nonetheless, she tucks it in under her arm.

"And I you, Mrs. McCloskey. You're just how Kenny described you, except even prettier!"

She laughs. "Flattery will get you everywhere with me, dear. Kenny, shouldn't you be in there already? With your classmates? Lord, look at all these people! What a mess. How am I ever going to get a seat?"

"Stay cool, Grandma. Jennifer will take care of you. Did you bring binoculars like I told you?"

"Don't tell me to stay cool," she says. "You may be a doctor now, but I am still your boss."

Kenny laughs. He bends down and kisses her cheek.

She and Jennifer have to walk around the block and enter the campus via the gates on West 114th Street, pressing their way through the hordes of people.

"Did you sleep all right? Is your room okay?" Jennifer asks.

Her room is nice enough, with a view of the steep blue-green rooftops of the American Museum of Natural History and a cushion of leafy trees. But so small! No wonder New Yorkers are always busting their personalities out all over, living in such small spaces. "It's dandy," she says, skirting around two girls tearfully hugging, then skipping a little to keep from falling over a stroller. "Everything is dandy."

Inside the 114th Street gates, the campus stretches as long as a football field. A podium has been set up on the stone steps in front of a beige-colored dome-topped library, and rows of folding chairs line the lawns and walks facing it. There seem to be thousands of them.

"You have one more year, Jennifer?" she says.

"Yes! One more year and, fingers crossed, I'll be here wearing my own cap and gown."

"In social work? You'll be a doctor of social work?"

Jennifer nods. "A PhD from the School of Social Work."

They've walked up to the middle of the sea of chairs now, toward the division between visitor seating and the seating for the day's graduates. The world around them is a flurry of excitement. People taking seats, taking pictures, taking stock of where they are on this May morning in 1996 that means so much to them.

"Kenny told me you met working with some of the same patients. But social work—you're not a medical doctor. I didn't quite understand that."

"We were both volunteers at the Gay Health Advocacy Project. I also want to focus on AIDS work. So no, not a medical doctor, but I do work with medical patients." Jennifer pauses, then adds, "I'm particularly interested in working with the families of HIV-positive patients, though."

Well. Kenny never told her that.

"That's nice," she says and turns away before Jennifer can say anything further. This is a great day, a happy day! Nothing can spoil it.

There are two side-by-side chairs toward the very front of the visitor seating that seem to be empty. She points. "Come on."

When Kenny called to say he'd be returning to Arizona for his residency, she almost jumped for joy. When he specified that the residency would be in infectious diseases down at U of A in Tucson, and that he was going to pursue clinical AIDS research, it was like the wind being knocked out of her. Tucson, not Phoenix? And after all these years of study, after earning both an MD and a PhD, he wasn't going to be a medical doctor, like his grandfather, his great-grandfather, his uncle? Instead, HIV research? Of all medical ailments, did he have to choose that one? *That's nice,* she said. *There's that nice outdoor museum in Tucson.* She's avoided the subject since.

"I don't believe those are free," Jennifer says. "You see those—"

She pushes her way forward again. New Yorkers aren't the only ones who know how to hustle. "Oh, thank heavens!" she says to the middle-aged man seated beside the two empty seats. There's a little sweater on one and a doll on the other. "I was just about giving up on catching so much as a glimpse of my grandson's graduation."

"I'm sorry," he says. He gestures to a third empty chair on the other side of him. "My wife is just letting the girls run around a bit until the ceremony begins."

"Lucky you!" she says, "Getting to sit back and relax while your wife does all the running after the children. Well!" She picks up the tiny sweater. "They must be little, too. Two years? Three years?"

"Olivia's going to be three in July," he says. "And—"

"Three in July! So she didn't have a ticket." She hands him the sweater and sits down, reaching next for the doll. "Don't worry. They'll be happier on your laps anyhow. They'll see better and squirm less. I know. I raised five of them. Six, if you count my grandson." She places the doll in his arms. "He's the one graduating today."

By the time the wife is back, she and the guy are regular old friends. Small and sharp-faced, with a sleek dark ponytail, the wife looks set to kick up a fuss, but the husband stops her: "Dina, this is Barbara. She's flown all the way here from Arizona on her own—"

"Twice widowed," she says, shaking her head.

"—to see her grandson graduate from the medical school."

"His mother couldn't come," she explains. "No one else in the family could come. One of my sons is with the army, and another has a farm and couldn't leave it. My third son—or, actually my second son—isn't with us anymore."

"I'm sorry," the woman says, looking suspicious, as though something more is about to be asked from her than is possible to give.

"I miss him every day," she says. Because what else is there to say? "And then my youngest daughter is over somewhere in Africa. Working. So she couldn't come, either. My grandson has a few younger brothers, but he didn't grow up with them—because he grew up with me, see. And his brothers couldn't come all the way from California, anyhow. That's where they live. Which means I'm on my own. But I wouldn't have missed this day for anything."

"Well, congratulations." Looking overwhelmed by all this information, the woman takes one of the kids onto her lap and extracts a box of cinnamon Teddy Grahams from her bag. The other kid clambers around her knees until the man thinks to pick her up also.

"Second wife," she whispers to Jennifer. "Kid from first wife graduating today." Not all stepparents show the kind of love and interest Ronnie did for her children. It was a blessing, and she's aware of it. In a way, Kenny was the kid they had together. Whatever

241

people may now want to say about her and Ronnie, they can't say he wasn't a good stepfather and step-grandfather.

"Here's the program, Mrs. McCloskey," Jennifer says, handing her a thick piece of white paper.

The crowd is beginning to still. She settles in her seat. The ivy-covered stone buildings rise up around them, so handsome, so stately, so solid. Here she is at an Ivy League graduation—could her parents have ever imagined this? And Michael! A fourth Gannon doctor. How would it be if, instead of Jennifer, Michael were here beside her? White-haired, but still tall and blue-eyed and handsome? Because Michael would have never stopped being handsome—the first thing she thought the first time she lay eyes on him was he was the handsomest man she'd ever seen, even propped up in his hospital bed and so underweight, his skin yellow from the jaundice, spotted with red dry patches from the malnutrition.

Will you come back again tomorrow?

You bet. I'll come back to see you as often as you'd like me to.

But if Michael hadn't died, if he could be here, she wouldn't be. Because everything would have been different. Patty Ann would never have married a loser at eighteen to keep him from being drafted and then dived into a second marriage with that monster. Michael would never have let any of that happen. Patty Ann would have gone to Vassar, and then who knows? Maybe Patty Ann, always so bright, would have gotten her own medical degree right here at Columbia.

And Kenny—apple of her eye—would never have been born.

The thing about life is it is so damned confusing. Such a web, each piece of it dependent on something else, something that can be as tiny as a smile from a stranger or as huge as heart disease. The good all tangled up with the bad.

Bells toll. The crowd quiets. Horns play, followed by orchestra music. Grouped by school, the graduates begin to file down the stone steps flanking the library to their respective places before the podium. Extracting the binoculars from her purse, she scans the beaming faces coming in waves, the unending flow of blue cloth. One cluster of kids carries foreign flags; another brandishes newspapers. And there they are, the medical school students, with their oversize latex gloves!

That's him!

And then her vision of Kenny is swallowed up again as the graduating students pour into the central square of the campus, up the steps, across the walkways.

She lays the binoculars in her lap and opens her commencement-.day program. There are a lot of graduates. This is going to take a while.

"May I?" Jennifer says, pointing to the binoculars.

"Of course."

The program is a nice weight. The lettering is handsome. Traditional elegance, like one would expect from a college in the East. Jeanne used to send her notes on similar paper from Vassar.

Poor Jeanne. The last time she came East it was for Jeanne's funeral, two years ago. A quiet affair: Molly and her family, Francis and his pregnant wife, two former colleagues from Vassar, one former student, and the assistant to the oncologist who had treated Jeanne's breast cancer. And, of course, she and Kenny.

She opens the program. The list of honorary-degree recipients starts with:

WYNTON MARSALIS, COMPOSER, MUSICIAN, TEACHER

Toward the end, Ronnie would listen to a recording of trumpet solos played by Marsalis over and over. She came both to hate and love those elegant concertos.

Don't you get tired of those?

I'm listening to them welcome me upstairs.

And how do you know you're going up*stairs?*

He turned his head to look at her, slowly and painfully. She and Ronnie had always joked so much; it hadn't occurred to her that he might take her words seriously. She returned his gaze and took his hand in hers. She squeezed it.

If anyone will be welcome in heaven, it will be you, dearest.

That's all she ever said. They never spoke further about it. But she knows he understood, at that moment, that she forgave him. No matter what mistakes he might have made or what dark secrets he might have struggled with—even if he might have strayed once or more—Ronnie was a good man. She's been lucky, really. Most women don't get one good husband. She got two.

MARK O. HATFIELD, UNITED STATES SENATOR FROM OREGON

ANDREI KOZYREV, FORMER FOREIGN MINISTER OF RUSSIA

SADAKO OGATA, UNITED NATIONS HIGH COMMISSIONER FOR REFUGEES

"Pff," she says, shutting the program. Times change. The Japs *tortured* Michael. For more than a half century, Russia kept the entire US spooked with the threat of communism. Now Kenny's school is handing out graduate degrees to their people like doughnuts from a welcome table.

"It's slow getting started, isn't it?" Jennifer says. "It's such a big school. Almost nine thousand students are graduating today."

Nine thousand. That's how many "fire balloons" the Japanese launched across the Pacific, hoping to strike North America. Each balloon contained a bomb.

The only way is not to think about it. About any of it. Sissy, who is supposed to be an expert on the subject, working over there in Africa, says the path to resolving conflict is through recognition and truth. She couldn't agree less. Nothing erases the past. The past will always be around longer than the present. The solution lies in moving on.

"Yep," she tells Jennifer. "A lot of happy kids. A lot of happy parents."

"And grandparents," Jennifer says, smiling.

"And grandparents."

Horns blow again. The graduates are seated now, and older men and women in cloak and gown, less steady on their feet, appear at the door of the library. A voice over a loudspeaker introduces them with due pomp and circumstance: the representatives of the alumni anniversary classes, the faculty, and on and on until the president of the college takes his place by the dais.

"Daddy. Can't see," the little girl sitting on her neighbor's lap says.

"There's nothing to see yet," he tells her.

She takes the binoculars back from Jennifer and hands them to the little girl. "These are magic," she says. "Stand up on your daddy's lap. Now, don't drop them, and don't put them in your mouth."

Finally they play the opening song, "The Star-Spangled Banner."

"Put your hand over your heart," she says to the little girl, tapping her hand against her own thin chest. The girl smiles, excited to be part of a ritual or just to have a reason to move, and flings her left hand in the region of her right shoulder.

She catches the father's eye and gives him a steely look. He quickly switches his daughter's hands, then slips his hand over his heart also.

"Honestly," she mutters. To think she had a brother, two husbands, and two sons fight for the likes of this. And one of those husbands came back on a slow path to dying. And one son and her brother never came back at all. Not alive, anyhow.

And then there were all the other, connected casualties, like Francis's friend and even, in a way, Patty Ann. All these lives rearranged or even ended. It's easy to say, "Don't dwell on the past"— and she does say that all the time. But it is harder in practice not to do so.

"O say does that star-spangled banner yet wave..."

But things *are* getting better with Patty Ann. That's something to remember. Between Glenn's stonework and the rent from the house's extra bedrooms, their money problems seem under control finally. Patty Ann even says two fancy boutiques, one on Melrose and one on Montana, have begun stocking her Beachswept jewelry, and Glenn sold one of his sculptures to the private collection of a famous actor—she'd never heard of him, but that doesn't mean anything. And Sean has his job and, it seems, a girlfriend. The other two boys are a bit more of a mess, but they're still young; there's time for them. Look at Francis! He didn't come into his own until well into his thirties, and then he became a family man and from one of his songs alone must have made a million.

"In our enthusiasm to save money and to make money..." the president of the college is saying, talking about health care in America, comparing it to the savings-and-loan debacle. Thank God she didn't lose anything in that. Thank God she and Ronnie didn't have to rely on Medicare, either. It cost an arm and a leg those last months, keeping him home, hiring home health care. For the first time in their two decades of marriage, she saw Ronnie completely naked helping the nurse get him into the bath, to slip him into clean pajamas. Poor Ronnie—he'd always been such a modest man. But at least he didn't have to face the endless scrutiny of being in a hospital. People whispering about him. People saying things.

"We need a new contract today, where everyone gains—not just a few..."

Jennifer is clapping loudly, her hair and breasts swinging. A pleasant young woman, but what a physical spectacle girls make of themselves nowadays, tossing their vim and vigor all over the place. A sparrow skims the air over their heads. He doubles back and alights on a lamppost, letting out a brilliant trill. Who is he calling to amidst the thousands of humans on this campus this morning? Above, the sky stretches clear blue, streaked with ribbons of white cloud. The little girl has fallen asleep, one arm and one foot flung onto her lap. She pats the child's chubby ankle aimlessly, smoothes her skirt down over her pink tights. The sweet thing is the same age as Francis's daughter. She'd have liked to see Mia while she was East. She would have liked to see Francis, too, for that matter. But now that the fuss over his music has died down, he prefers his privacy up on that farm in Massachusetts, and she has to accept that.

How sprawled her family has ended up! Patty Ann on one coast. Francis on the other. Mike smack in the middle of the country, in Texas. And Sissy—not even on the continent. At least Kenny will be in Arizona.

The degrees are being conferred now, the dean of each school introducing a mass of graduates and formally requesting that the president of the university bestow diplomas on them. The actual diplomas will be handed out in the individual ceremonies this afternoon. For now, graduates of each school rise in turn by their places, while related members of the audience seem to rise along with them, a spirit of shared elation as buoyant as the bright spring air. Each dean tries to say something funny, something to set apart their throng of optimistic hearts and faces, and no one jeers at the goofy jokes and awkward attempts to be clever.

The family next to her cheers. The little girl wakes and touches her hand milkily.

"It's all right," she says. "They're shouting because they're happy."

The law school dean steps away from the podium, and a new bunch of students rise from their chairs. Their necks are flecked with deep green; it's the medical school!

She lifts the binoculars and scans the standing graduates; they are to the right of the dais, toward the front, with their backs to the thousands sitting behind them. They sway and clap, and she is sure she'll be able to pick out her Kenny. *Kennedy.* Twenty-two years ago, he sat beside her, a skinny seven-year-old clutching a torn sweater of his mother's in the place of a stuffed animal as they drove away from his parents' pitiful hovel in Los Angeles, through the desert, toward her and Ronnie's comfortable home in Arizona.

Give me his brother, too, she told Patty Ann. *Give me Sean also.*

No. Sean needs to stay with me.

Then Patty Ann married Troy and suddenly wanted Kenny back. But she'd been smart enough to make Patty Ann sign over legal guardianship. *It's just a formality,* she'd said, *in case of an accident or something. We can tear it up later.* She wasn't so uneducated as people might think.

How Patty Ann yelled at her when she refused to return Kenny. *Go ahead,* she told Patty Ann. *Shout as much as you like. Kenny is staying right here, where he is safe and happy.* During the worst of times, Patty Ann would call in the middle of the night, three sheets to the wind, shouting about Luke, shouting about Kenny, virtually incoherent.

Kenny would have been torn to bits trying to protect his mother in that household. Instead he grew up with Sissy walking with him to school and Ronnie taking him to his baseball games and helping him patiently with his math homework. A sweet boy in a happy household. He would never be here today if she'd sent him back to Patty Ann. That's the real reason Patty Ann backpedaled on coming today, not Glenn's wrist surgery. They've called a truce over her keeping Kenny, finally. Neither of them wants to reopen old wounds.

"I respectfully request, sir, that you grant these degrees, along with the rights, privileges, and responsibilities thereto attached..."

She scans the backs of the graduates again. That's Kenny! Boxing the air with his latex glove!

"I solemnly swear by whatsoever I hold most sacred that I will be loyal to the profession of medicine..."

She lifts a white-gloved hand to her mouth. A little sob, like a hiccup, escapes.

"...and just and generous to its members. That I will lead my life and practice my art in uprightness and honor..."

"Mrs. McCloskey, are you okay?" Jennifer whispers, hand hovering over hers.

"Congratulations, and welcome to the profession of medicine!"

"Of course I'm okay, dear. Haven't you ever seen a grown woman cry before?" She's earned these tears. She stands up proudly.

———

For lunch, Kenny has reserved a table for them at a large Mexican restaurant on Broadway. Cheerful approximations of southwestern life hang on the ceilings and walls: brightly colored sombreros and ponchos, brilliantly red plastic chili peppers. A waitress, noting Kenny's cap and gown, congratulates him, then reels off the day's specials like a train barreling through a tunnel.

Everything seems to happen quickly in New York City. Pedestrians walk quickly; even the squirrels dart around like their tails are on fire.

"It's not fancy, but I thought the theme would make you feel at home," Kenny says. "And Jennifer loves southwestern cuisine. She can't wait to try the real thing."

So Kenny is planning to bring Jennifer out to Arizona, at least for a visit. "It's a perfect choice for lunch," she says. "Best of all, I won't have to pretend to know how to speak Spanish."

"Your Spanish is not so bad, Grandma."

"When I went to buy my new purse"—she lifts it up for them to see—"the salesgirl kept showing me bags made from canvas. She was very pretty but not very good at speaking English. I kept telling her, 'No, no, I only want to see leather.' Finally I lost my patience and said, loudly and firmly: *¡Basta! Lo que necesito es de Cuervo.*"

Kenny breaks out laughing. "*Cuero* is leather," he explains to Jennifer. "My grandmother was announcing that what she needed was some tequila."

"By then, I *did* need a shot of tequila." She takes a gulp of her margarita, delivered already by the waitress. Fast, fast, fast—New York City. The margarita isn't quite right, though. Ronnie became a real expert at them, mixing them every Friday evening. After Luke died, Ronnie never made a daiquiri again. He understood she'd always associate the taste with life before.

Life before, life after. She's had a few of those.

"Did you know that tequila can be used in the treatment of colds, irritable bowel syndrome, and even colon cancer?" Kenny says, sipping from his Diet Coke. "Seriously—it's the cactus it's made from, the blue agave. It helps deliver medicines to the intestinal tract and can kill toxins."

"Seriously—we're going to talk about bowels at the lunch table?" she says, raising her eyebrows at him, taking another sip. It may not be the best margarita ever, but it's cold, and she hadn't realized how hot and thirsty she got out there during the ceremony. New York has its own kind of heat.

Kenny looks chastened. "I just thought it was interesting. The Mexicans have used it medicinally for centuries."

"Kenny just can't stop practicing medicine," Jennifer says, smiling. "Even while having lunch. He was born to be a doctor."

She licks her lips, sweet and salty. "Then why doesn't he practice?"

Kenny frowns. "I will be practicing medicine, Grandma."

That's another thing margaritas can do—make one's tongue slippery. "Well, whatever you do, I'm sure you'll do it well."

She looks around brightly. But Kenny—dear, earnest Kenny—is not going to be put off so easily. She's stepped right into the den of snakes, and there's no escaping. It's almost as though Kenny has been waiting for a chance to talk about this with her. Probably he has. God knows she's done her best to avoid it.

"My own father," he says, "last time I saw him, he hit me up for fifty dollars. I was *nineteen*. I didn't let him know I'm graduating from medical school today. I'm not sure even where I'd reach him. But *Ronnie* was always there for me. He always had my back; he was better than a father. Certainly better than my father."

She *really* wishes she hadn't brought this up.

Kenny takes a breath. "I want to give something back. I won't be able to help Ronnie, but maybe I can help others who have AIDS, in his honor."

Although she knew it was coming, it hurts, hearing her grandson put it out there like that. She sets her drink down. "Now, hold on just one minute, mister. Your step-grandfather died from non-Hodgkin's lymphoma. That was the official cause of death. You know that."

"Yes, but—" Jennifer starts, then stops and fingers a tortilla chip. She shoves the salsa dip toward her.

"Grandma," Kenny says.

The waitress returns, balancing three heavy plates on her arms—

"Here we are!"—and doles them out, giving her Kenny's fish and Kenny her steak.

"Here we are, indeed," she says. She switches the filet of fish for the sizzling strips of sirloin, picks up her knife, and carves into it. Charred on the outside, the inner flesh is pink and tender. Her and Ronnie's relations, such as they were, always were swift and in the dark. So different from . . . Oh, my God—*Michael*. She didn't know bodies could feel the way he made hers feel; so many years ago, and still, when she closes her eyes, she can almost *feel* him. But who's to say her experience with Ronnie wasn't the more *normal* one? And they *did* have relations. It happened.

And yet. The sudden string of illnesses, the cancer. The doctor treating Ronnie didn't ask her—her, a lady in her sixties—to be tested for HIV for no reason. She's not an idiot. Something happened, sometime, somewhere behind her back. And it probably didn't happen with another woman. She *knows* that. The truth is she knew all along, like it was a pact she and Ronnie had. A pact of silence. Ronnie *was* different. Patty Ann said so from the start. But she needed him, and, in his way, he needed her. And in the end, they did love each other. Not in the same way as she loved Michael, but in their own way.

She can't fault him when she willingly signed on for that silence. She's *glad* he never told her what he was doing, if he was doing something. If he had, she would have had to leave him. How stupid that would have been. They were happy.

"Your step-grandfather and I were married longer than me and your grandfather. We had a real marriage," she says. "I don't appreciate anyone suggesting otherwise, especially not my own grandson. Ronnie was a good man and a good husband." She gives him that look, the one that over the years has told him there will not be a second piece of cake or another half hour of television. "Kennedy.

We're going to leave this subject now. If Ronnie chose to take something private to his grave, we can give him that much."

She's had almost seven years to think about this. Ronnie can lie peacefully in the cemetery in Scottsdale. She's not going to remember him for something she never knew. She's going to remember what she did know.

"So Jennifer," she says, "Kenny says you are from here."

Jennifer doesn't miss a beat, just smiles and nods, as though they hadn't just aired their dirty laundry in front of her. The girl will make a good social worker.

"Right here, in Manhattan."

"And your father was a dentist."

"Orthodontist. How'd you know?"

"Hmm," she says. "Just a lucky guess."

Jennifer flashes those perfect teeth again. "My parents would love to meet you while you are here. If you can find the time, I mean."

"Of course," she says, and smiles back. The conversation about Ronnie is over.

Jennifer swallows a forkful of lettuce. "Kenny told me he doesn't look like you, but when you smile I see a resemblance."

"Kenny is tall like his grandpa and has the same hair color as his father. But he looks most like my side of the family." Those misty mornings in San Francisco so many years ago, her father and brother fishing from the pier while she wandered along the shore looking for clams or saltwort. Many a time, a wave would get the best of her, knocking her down—*Papa,* she would cry, her mouth full of salty water, her freshly washed and ironed dress ruined, knowing a slap on the rear awaited her at home. Her father and brother would turn to look, and she can see her brother still, fishing line in his hand, grinning down at her. "He looks like his great-uncle Tomas. Or how I think Tom would have looked, had he lived to be a man."

"That was my grandmother's brother," Kenny explains. "He died during World War II, in France."

"I'm sorry," Jennifer says.

"A lot of boys died," she says.

"Well, hello, Aunt Barbara!" And there is Molly, as tall and cheerful as ever, wearing a navy blue tailored suit with leather sneakers, making her way through the restaurant to their table, then bestowing hugs on everyone. "Congratulations, Kenny! Nice to see you again, Jennifer. Ugh, I'm so sorry I couldn't get out of this deposition any earlier."

"We started without you," Kenny says. "Jennifer was famished."

Jennifer shakes her head and smiles.

It is *love* between these two. Something tells her she is going to get to know Jennifer much better.

Molly pulls out the fourth chair. "Tell me everything!"

After Molly has ordered, Kenny and Jennifer describe the ceremony step by step, reliving each speech and each stride toward the podium. She interjects "It was wonderful" or "So exciting" every once in a while, and Kenny beams in response. Any earlier disagreement seems to have been forgotten. Molly smiles and nods good-naturedly to everything in between bites of her tacos.

Suddenly Kenny stops talking. He holds up a finger. "Hey, listen. There's Uncle Francis's song, in Spanish."

Wafting over the din of the restaurant: *Y sobre los mares ondulados, nos alcanzamos. Y sobre la tierra quemada...*

She may never have really mastered Spanish, but she understands each word perfectly: *And across the rolling seas, we reach our hands. And across the scorched earth...* After all, she's heard the original enough times in English. And not just on the cassette she's kept in her car for something like eight years now—for a while, it was impossible to enter the grocery store without hearing it. Or to turn on the television once they used it for that commercial. Funny to think that of all her children, quiet, reclusive Francis would end up being the famous one.

"He seems happy on his farm," she says. "He and Georgina. I don't think he's even interested in making a second album."

"He never enjoyed performing," Molly says, shrugging. "He had a tale to tell, and he told it. It wasn't ever about the money."

Molly probably knows better than she what goes on with Francis. Always so simpatico, those two, and then Molly became his lawyer. But at least she has a phone number she can call on his birthday now, an address to which she can send a Christmas card or present for little Mia. At least she knows he is safe. For a long time, even after he reappeared, she wondered what she could possibly have done to Francis to make him disappear for so long. One day she realized it was he who'd done something to himself. Things have been easier since.

"How are you, Aunt Barbara? Keeping out of trouble?"

She drinks the last of her margarita. "Why would I want to keep out of trouble?"

Molly laughs. "Have you been to visit Mike recently?"

"Hmm. You know, although Mike is staying on the base now, he's still working some mighty long hours. And Holly has her ladies' clubs, and Mike the third's getting ready for his last year of high school. And the two younger kids—Bradley has football, and Melissa is very involved with the Boys and Girls Clubs of America. They're busy."

"Aw, not too busy for you, I'm sure. They love when you visit."

She sets her fork and knife down neatly on the right side of her plate and folds her napkin in her lap. "To tell the truth, Molly, I don't really like Fort Bliss. I don't like to be there."

Kenny and Jennifer exchange glances, swiftly, but not so fast that she doesn't see them. Apparently Kenny has told his girlfriend everything about *everything* in their family. Ronnie, Francis, *and* Luke. Well, never mind. From what she's observed so far today, they'll be married once Jennifer graduates.

Molly nods. "And Patty Ann? Do you visit her in LA often?"

"Sometimes."

"And Sissy? Any plans for her to come home for a visit in the near future? God, I feel as though I haven't seen her in ages. Maybe a decade! Not since...I don't know when. What is she now? Thirty-five?"

"Thirty-four." She's going to ignore the temptation to say the obvious, the thing that's on her mind more and more nowadays— if Sissy doesn't find someone soon, it'll be too late for her to have a family. By the time *she* was thirty-four she had four kids already. But Sissy doesn't seem to have the slightest interest in settling down. Sissy doesn't seem to have the slightest interest in coming home to live, either. "It's a far way to travel from Africa, and her job there keeps her very busy. Lots of conflicts to resolve! I don't see her much myself, either."

"Well, it's nice Kenny will be back in Arizona."

Molly adjusts the shell on a chain around her freckled neck—it looks strikingly like one of those made by Patty Ann, and her diamond solitaire engagement ring and pavé-diamond wedding ring flash a little under the lights of the restaurant. Molly's husband is also a lawyer, a tall man with a receding hairline and an unexpected sense of humor. Kenny and Jennifer are, she's pretty sure, holding hands beneath the table. Maybe they've interlaced their fingers. Everyone so happily married or happily unmarried or happily soon to be married. Everyone so busy. Back in Scottsdale, two widowers are courting her. It's nice to get the flowers, but neither of the men actually interests her.

"I'm planning to offer to head the library angels," she announces. "You know, the volunteer staff at the library." In fact she had no such plan until this very moment. But as soon as she says it, she knows that's exactly what she's going to do once she's back in Scottsdale. "The woman doing it before has decided to go back to school and get a degree in library science."

"Have you ever thought about that yourself? I mean, going back to school and getting a college degree? People do it at all ages. That's what the School of General Studies is at Columbia," Kenny says.

"Are you going to be a snob, Kenny, now that you have all these fancy degrees behind you?"

Molly nods. "I'd say your grandmother has gotten more than her share of education just by living through this last century."

Kenny looks mortified. She pats his hand. "Jennifer," she says. "I just want you to know that Kenny and I don't usually argue this much."

"I know," Jennifer says. "Kenny has had too much cola."

They all laugh. Jennifer will be a good addition to their family.

She motions to the waitress and pays the bill while Jennifer visits the restroom and Molly and Kenny discuss plans for tomorrow. Molly has invited them all to her house for lunch, with her husband and two little daughters.

"The girls are excited to see you!" Molly says once they are out on Broadway. The sidewalk swarms with other graduates and their families. A speck of dust flies onto her eyelid. She rubs it away, resting her hand against a makeshift table by the curb, piled high with paperbacks. Another table next to it has a selection of sunglasses and sun hats. The man and woman behind the tables are laughing about something. So much life teeming on the streets. New York really isn't like Scottsdale.

"I packed some prickly-pear jam," she tells Molly. "I'll bring it tomorrow."

"Great! Prickly-pear jam on bagels!" And then her niece has disappeared into a taxi and down the broad avenue.

"Should we find a taxi, too?" Kenny says, taking her arm. The private ceremony is at the Columbia University Medical Center, even farther uptown. "Or brave the subway? The subway is a little faster, and it goes straight there. And cheaper, of course. But it'll be hot and noisy."

She smiles up at him. "The subway, obviously."

Hot, humid air slams them as they descend the subway steps. A piece of newspaper attaches itself to one of her kitten heels. She brushes it off and hurries to board the arriving train close behind Kenny, slipping into a seat across from him and Jennifer. With a screech, the subway sets off, propelling them uptown under the streets of New York City. Kenny and Jennifer touch hands just briefly. A very young woman next to them fusses with a baby girl in a stroller, all pink baubles in her hair and half-toothed smiles. One of those smiles lands in her direction, and she smiles in return. Her reward is a burble and an even bigger smile. The mother looks up and smiles at her also.

A strange sensation, like she's hurtling through life itself, comes over her. She sees herself at about Kenny's age back in Southern California many years ago, Michael alive and well by her side, all the kids asleep in their beds. Everything on earth just as it should be. She could never have imagined life would go so off course, become so complicated. Why can't life just run like minnows through one's fingers, moving fast but bright and tickling? Why does it have to be so full of darkness and shadows?

She shakes the thought away.

When she gets home, she will step up to take over the volunteer program at the library, just as she said she would. She'll introduce some new events, too. Book groups—maybe two, one for adults and one for children. She could find a teenager, someone fun, for the kids and find someone lively for the older group also. She's not suddenly going to pretend she herself is much of a reader. Luke was the reader in the family, and Sissy is. Patty Ann, when circumstances have allowed it. Michael liked to read, too, especially poetry. That's how they met, after all—she offered him reading material. And Ronnie! He just tore through magazines: *National Geographic, Scientific American. Life,* when they still published it. Both *Time* and *Newsweek.* She still gets some of the magazines, with his name on the labels. Every two years, she finds herself writing a check to renew the subscriptions.

"Next stop," Kenny mouths over the roar of the subway.

"Already?"

A cookbook book group, though—that's something she could do. That would be fun, even. She could choose a different cookbook each month and, at the meeting, members of the group would all bring in something they'd made from it. It wouldn't have to be just women, either. Lots of men like to cook. They'd probably think it a good way to meet the ladies. But would it be okay to have food in the library? She'd have to—

"Grandma." Kenny is reaching for her hand.

The subway has stopped. She jumps to her feet. Up the stairs they go, into the sunshine.

"I should have bought a hat off that stand!" she says.

This next ceremony is in the garden of the medical center. It's cooler here, shaded and quiet. They take their seats, and a soft feeling of peace comes over her, and a new string of images from years earlier appears in her thoughts, of Kenny and Ronnie, of Kenny and Sissy. There was a fierceness in the way Sissy took Kenny into the fold back then, a determination almost greater than her own to protect him. It's a shame Sissy couldn't be here today. Africa! What a place for a girl who couldn't step into the Arizona sun without acquiring a dozen new freckles.

When she gets back to Scottsdale, she's also going to invest in a home computer. Kenny says he and Sissy communicate through "e-mails." She's going to find out what those are. Why shouldn't she and Sissy communicate through e-mails also?

On the podium, a kindly-looking man with square gold-rimmed glasses is being introduced by the dean of the medical school. She's been so busy daydreaming she completely lost track of the proceedings.

"Who is he?" she asks Jennifer.

"Dr. Lonnie Bristow, president of the AMA. He used to be a spokesman on the AIDS crisis for them."

She thinks for a minute. "Do you think Kenny is making the right decision, Jennifer? Going into research?"

"He'll be great," Jennifer answers firmly.

She folds her hands in her lap. A year after Kenny came to live with them, about when Patty Ann took up with Glenn, Kenny started wetting his bed. No matter how much she scolded or teased or pleaded, he couldn't stop it. *Look, Barbara,* Ronnie finally said. *I know you're the one with the experience raising kids. But let's have Kenny sleep in our bed. I'm willing to bet he'll never again have an accident.* For the following week, Kenny slept in the big bed with her while Ronnie slept on the sofa. Never once did she wake up to wet sheets. At the end of the week, Kenny went back to his own bed, dry as the desert around them.

She was what? A grandma? A mother? A grandma-mother? She never thought of Kenny as one of her children. He was always Patty Ann's son. But she loved him as though he were her own child. And Ronnie loved him like a father would have.

All her life, she's wanted to believe in the truth of order. But life is more like a crazy juggernaut of possibilities, like one of those incomprehensible charts of the nervous system Kenny brought home over the holidays to study, synapses shooting in every direction. How can there be order? Somehow she met a nice man from church who was willing to throw in his lot with hers, even though hers was weighted with five kids and a mountain of bills and his was so light. It was wrong of her to think earlier of Michael at Kenny's graduation; it is Ronnie who should be here, with all that gentle pride he carried silently around with him, helping little Kenny earn his Boy Scout badges, learn to do the crawl down at the community pool. To combat his bed-wetting problems.

Ronnie wasn't Michael. *He was Ronnie.*

"I'm sure Kenny will be, too," she tells Jennifer.

The ceremony ends, and they find their way into the reception. Kenny guides her through the crowd, introducing her to friends and professors, always using the same words: "And here is my grandma, Barbara McCloskey. Without her, I wouldn't be here."

And each time she thinks: *And without you, I wouldn't be here, either.*

Because every relationship, from the most intimate to the most fleeting, has the power to change the course of life until, after a while, life becomes a Tinkertoy accumulation of connections: her long-dead father-in-law back in Massachusetts—the broken World War I vet she only once met but whose nonetheless uncrushable belief in humanity and sense of duty triggered Michael's decision to enlist during World War II after the bombing of Pearl Harbor; the day she volunteered to come through the ward where Michael was convalescing, peddling books and magazines she herself had no interest in reading; the night Patty Ann allowed a good-for-nothing greasy boy to drive her home, then sat in his car kissing him until she, with Sissy on her hip, came out and banged on its window; the ex-marine who shot Kennedy, making LBJ president, who then ended new draft exemptions for married men, which compelled Patty to marry that useless boy, and then to have a baby with him, and then to hand that baby over to her to raise . . .

And there he is standing in front of her, a full-fledged doctor.

She squeezes Kenny's arm and nods toward Jennifer, chatting with two young men in robes. She can hear them teasing and coaxing her to continue, with Kenny, to a party after the reception is over. "Jennifer seems like a sweet girl. When are you going to get hitched?"

Kenny laughs. "One celebration at a time, Grandma!"

She pats his arm. "You know what? I think I'm done here now. I'm going to go back to my hotel and leave the two of you with your friends."

"But, Grandma, our dinner reservation—"

She looks at her hand, veined now but still slim and delicate, on his arm. "You have dinner with your young woman. Really. We had lunch together. And we'll have lunch and dinner together tomorrow. I think you should get to do both—celebrate with your family and with your friends. And frankly, I don't want to celebrate with your friends." She gestures at the crowd of young women and men in their cocktail dresses and sober dark suits and smiles. "They look kind of boring."

Kenny laughs again. "Oh, Grandma. Are you sure?"

"Kenny, am I ever not sure of what I want?"

They make up a paper-bag dinner for her in a little Spanish grocery store—Jennifer's idea, but she doesn't protest. She doesn't argue either when Kenny hails her a taxi. She slides into the back, placing the paper bag on her lap and her handbag neatly next to it. The taxi heads down to the highway, racing along the Hudson

River, thick and gray-blue in the late afternoon sunshine. Cars bob in and out of the lanes; on the other side of the highway, heading uptown and out of the city, the traffic is almost at a standstill. The taxi exits the highway and heads back onto the streets of New York. People of all ages emerge from subways, doorways, newspaper-and-tobacco shops, on their way home from school or work. Somehow, trees with pale green leaves manage to grow through the cement of the sidewalks. Garbage piles out of trash containers that should be emptied. Squirrels hop on top of them, vying with sparrows for the spoils. The taxi pulls up across the street from the hotel, pauses, and throws itself into a U-turn.

"My," she says, extracting her wallet to pay the driver. "Do you charge extra for the thrill element?"

The driver laughs. "For you, young lady, it's on the house."

Barely has her foot hit the ground when a couple comes up to claim the taxi. The streets are alive. Nannies walk with their young charges, returning from ballet class or tennis lessons. Women trip along wearing business suits with sneakers, like Molly was— probably those same kids' mothers. There are men on the street, too, but at this moment the females seem to dominate.

Down on the corner, the woman missing a tooth is still begging. She walks over to her. "Here," she says, holding out the paper bag with her dinner. "Have this."

The woman opens the bag, examines the oversize club sandwich, banana, and bottle of apple juice. "I don't drink juice with my food. I'm allergic. I drink soda."

She shrugs. "Take it or leave it."

The woman closes the bag and sticks her hand out. "You got some money so I can bring something home to my kids?"

She reaches into her purse and takes out a twenty-dollar bill. The money will probably go into the woman's veins. But just for this moment in time she wants to believe it will buy a couple of cans of Campbell's soup, a loaf of bread, and a bottle of milk for some hungry children. She wants to think all kids everywhere have the possibility of a second chance.

She turns back toward her hotel, walking slowly, taking in the dawning of the evening. In a little while, she may venture out on her own, try one of the many restaurants lining Columbus Avenue. Right now, though, it's beautiful here, with the lights turned on against the white stone of the museum.

BOOK FIVE

2015

If your skin could sing
Like branches under full moon
Oh the shine, the shine

—Erin Hollowell on Twitter, 2015

Sugaring / April 9, 2015

Francis

THE KNOB ON THE sugarhouse door feels cold and damp to his bare hand as he pulls it shut. He took his gloves off when the last of the sap had turned to syrup, the filtering was finished, the golden liquid poured, and the season was over for the year. He'll come back to finish cleaning up in the morning.

Outside, a silver-dollar moon spills light over the melting snow and patches of frozen mud. His breath smokes away from his mouth. He'll turn sixty-three this year. His back hurts like hell, and one of his wrists sports an oozing slick gash where he managed to burn it on the evaporator. He and Georgina can't afford more than one hired hand during sugaring season now, and they can't allow Mia to keep coming home to help. He used to feel jubilant at the end of the last day of sugaring for the year. Now he just wants to crawl into bed, drag the quilt up over his head, and sleep for a week. The only thing harder to imagine than not entering that sugarhouse again next early spring is the thought of entering it again.

Still, at least this year won't have been the worst. Last year, a big seed year with erratic weather, was. Or 2012, with that sudden heat wave. The snowfall here in New England this year has been pitiless, but on the good side, nights stayed cold long enough for them to gather 6,500 gallons, up more than five hundred from last year. The day his profit goes under $7,500 is the day he's sworn he's going to give the whole thing up. They should get at least $1,000 more than that this year. Which means he'll be at it again come next March or, if the winters return to getting shorter, next February.

He runs a hand through his hair. There was a time when he didn't own a bank account. Now he has an accounting firm in his head.

It must be 2:00 a.m.

When he and Georgina first took up sugaring, money was still pouring in from his music. Slowly that torrent thinned to a stream, then to an occasional dribble. It was okay, though—they had the interest from Georgina's trust. For that matter, they still had Georgina's trust; soul-sucking 2008 hadn't happened. For all those years, sugaring was mostly a diversion: they'd risen above Georgina's past, they'd risen above his past, they'd ridden the wave of his sudden success to create a new life for themselves and the baby they had coming on a big old farm in the hills between Massachusetts and Vermont, and they had to do something with it both for tax purposes and their sanity. Waiting for that perfect early spring combination of frozen night and thawing day, tapping the maples, collecting the sap, boiling it down, dividing it between the containers, and then bringing it around to stores and fairs to be sold gave a sense of order to their life. Everything else on Iona Farm was pinned to the sugaring: the strawberry fields they put in a few years later, the apple orchard they eventually bought next to the property.

And Georgina loved it. She thought it was hilarious. *Who would ever have pictured me doing this?* she would say each time sugaring season came around, tossing one of his too-big-for-her heavy wool plaid shirts over her leather pants and cashmere sweater. For those six or seven weeks during sugaring, she'd stay clean as a whistle, rolling up her sleeves to pitch in like anyone else. It wasn't even a struggle. They'd throw a whopping backyard party when it was over, inviting the whole township, little Mia running through everyone's legs in oversize boots, a maple-walnut sticky bun in her hand and sugar parentheses in the corners of her mouth, the sound of the creek rising in the background. Those were good times.

It's been a while since they held one of those parties. Now they're lucky if sugaring season lasts five weeks. The winters aren't cold enough or they're too cold, and the thaw comes too suddenly. The rhythm is off, and in protest, the maples aren't giving up sap as they once did. Mia says the problem comes not only from the weather but also from acid rain and chemicals in the groundwater. She flirted with environmental science before deciding to study law like her Aunt Molly. She also, somewhere along the line, stopped running between everyone else's boots and slipped into helping with the sugaring.

And that's the other problem. With this winter's relentless snowfall, so deep not even the hardy snowdrops could make their way through the drifts, so persistent the earth has remained blanketed with white when it should be dusted with dusk-blue hepatica, Mia is helping later than expected—too close to her final exams. He shouldn't have let her. No amount of maple syrup is worth it.

On the other hand, if she's going to need funds now for law school, how to help her without that little extra bit from sugaring?

Money.

The light is on in the old barn. The first couple of years they lived here, a local farmer rented their west pasture and old barn for his herd of specialty cows. But Georgina hated those cows; she said watching them lumber around, their mouths endlessly chewing, made her feel more existentialist than Sartre and Camus put together. *It's enough to drive a person to drink,* she said.

269

When Georgina says things like that, it's a good idea to listen. As soon as the farmer's lease ran out, he had the cows removed and converted the pasture to a strawberry field. The barn has since been used to store extra sugaring equipment and hay for packing around the berries.

Mia is inside, sitting cross-legged next to the electric heater with a weathered leather-bound diary in her hands.

"It's your grandfather's medical log. Nothing private," she says quickly.

He scratches his arm, confused as to what she could be doing still in here. They've been working like dogs since morning. "Aren't you tired?"

She shrugs, her slight shoulders poking out of her down vest. Her face is pure Gannon—the same sharp cheekbones, heavily lashed blue eyes, straight brow—but she's inherited Georgina's delicate frame and unpredictable sense of humor. A few years ago, a cub reporter working a "where are they now" story appeared at the farm. *What do you consider your greatest creation?* the reporter asked, expecting no doubt a doleful nod to a song written almost three decades earlier.

What a silly question.

"For every patient he saw," Mia says, "he noted down the date, time, name, address, complaint, diagnosis, treatment recommended, and payment. All by hand, in the most perfect cursive."

"That would have been your great-grandmother," he says, dropping onto a hay bale. They'll have to wait for all the snow finally to be gone to start planting this year's strawberry crop and lay this hay, which means when the time comes it will need to be done fast. "She handled all the patient interfacing for your great-grandfather's medical cabinet. She even drove him to see his patients."

"That's so cute. He visited patients in their own homes?"

His grandmother died of polio the year he was born, and his grandfather died shortly after. He never met them. His father had one picture of them, a tall and somber couple. *Cute* is one of the last words he would have used to describe them.

"Hmm."

"Look at this: March first, 1933. Ten a.m. Elizabeth Creedy. Oak Tree Hill. Bleeding. Miscarriage. Cod liver oil. Basket of seven beets."

"Where did you get that?"

Mia shuts the diary. She pulls her knees in to her chest.

The diary must have been in one of Aunt Jeanne's boxes, stuck behind the old evaporator he still hasn't managed to sell. A few weeks after her funeral, Molly lugged them all up here in the back of her station wagon. *Hang on to them, will you? Until I have time to go through them?* That was about twenty years ago. They never seem to get around to it when Molly brings her family to visit.

Behind the old evaporator is also where Georgina stows her empty bottles.

"You find anything else interesting?" he asks carefully. Georgina has done pretty well since Mia was born, but she slipped up this winter. And then Mia was home before he could get the bottles over to one of the farther-away townships to recycle. At twenty-one, Mia is too old now not to notice when her mom hasn't been sober; she must have gone looking for the evidence.

She stares at her knees. "Hidden, not interesting."

What is there to say? It's an endless battle, Georgina's lifelong battle. His battle for her. They couldn't hide it forever from their daughter.

"You did find the diary, though. That's interesting."

"Yeah, it is. It's like this perfect little historical capsule. The illnesses, the payments, the tiny villages. It's funny how you ended up back here. Almost exactly where they lived."

Are we looking for your father? Georgina said in that laserlike way of hers when they started hunting for property in the area, all those years ago. He hadn't realized it until she said it, but of course that was exactly what he was doing.

"Your mother and I thought New England would be a good compromise between England and California—we'd both get a little something familiar."

"I'm glad you bought right here."

"You wouldn't want to have grown up a California girl?"

Mia smiles. She gets up, brushing hay from her jeans. "I did find one other thing." She disappears behind the old evaporator and then reappears with a big bundle in plastic, lugging it between her two arms. "What's this? It looks like there's a guitar inside."

His rosewood guitar, still carefully wrapped against the sea.

Thirty years, and he hasn't touched it.

"Yeah," he says. "There's a guitar inside."

She pulls a corner of the plastic open and wrinkles her nose. "It stinks."

The smell of the brine returns to him; it swells in his heart as the waves once did around him. He's an old man now. Such a different man. And still that scent drags him back.

"So what is it?" Mia says.

"Like you said. An old guitar."

"Broken?"

"I don't think so."

"So why don't you use it?"

"Just don't."

"But you've kept it."

People lead these lives and then pray their kids don't end up living anything like them. So they pretend their lives have been clean until either the lies catch up with them or the kids see through the lies. He doesn't hide his past from Mia; he's told her what seemed right for her to know. In a way, his past is her past, too, or at least her heritage. His father was a World War II prisoner of war who managed to survive hell in the Pacific, then died anyway when he was a boy, and his mother remarried and moved to Arizona. She is still going strong, but her second husband died from AIDS years ago. That's why Mia's much older cousin went into AIDS research and why her grandmother became such an important fund-raiser for AIDS research in her state when not overseeing the volunteer programs at her local library. His older sister stayed behind in Los Angeles and is still there running a renowned—and expensive— artist's retreat on Venice Beach with her third husband. His younger sister works and mostly lives in Africa, but he's not sure exactly where—he left, and when he got back, she was gone. He never really got to know her as an adult. He had two brothers who went to Vietnam. One came back and worked as an army doctor until retiring a couple of years ago in Texas. The other didn't.

After college, he split for Europe and spent some time bumming around, which is when he met her mother. And he met a man there with whom he rowed from Scotland to Ireland. They encountered a terrible storm, and the man died, and he wrote an album about it, with a song that became very successful.

That has always seemed like enough for Mia to know. Because, on the other hand, his life is his and no one else's. There was no reason to tell her what he was doing when he met her mother on a dance floor on the Spanish island of Mallorca. Or about *why* he left for Europe—about how he had a friend growing up he spent all his time with who also went to Vietnam and came back alive but still didn't survive. All these years later, it's still hard to think about.

"Can I look inside?" she says.

"If you want."

She hunts around for a pair of gardening shears and slits through the bundle. His old guitar case, faded but still pristine, emerges from the multiple folds of stiffened, yellowed plastic. She lays it on its back and opens the clasps.

The warm rosewood glow has dimmed, and there's a hint of rot around the sound hole. Diminished and, yet, still beautiful. The hours he spent crouched over this guitar, so many years ago. In their house in California and then in the one Ronnie bought in Arizona. On countless squares and train platforms all over Europe, busking. On the beach in Scotland where he met Rufus.

Mia looks at him, waiting. He picks it up and plucks a string. The sound is awful. He plucks again. The brittle string snaps.

"Is this the guitar you wrote the song on?" Mia says.

He shakes his head. "This is the guitar I wrote the song about."

"You'll have to change the strings. Maybe there's one..." She turns back to the case, flipping open the pick box. "Hey, what's this?"

She pries with her finger and slowly pulls out a small faded photo.

With the door shut, the air in the barn is still, timeless. He could be anywhere, anytime, back fifty years ago jumping off a pier in Santa Monica alongside his best friend. Or flipping burgers, grease spattering onto their arms. Or swimming in a muddy lake while Joan Baez sings in the distance.

"That's you! Carrying the palm leaf. Look, you are all there."

He takes the photo into his calloused hands. So many years lie between the Palm Sunday when Eugene snapped it and this day, here. His father was still alive. But then some were lost. And some more were born.

"Not all. Your aunt Sissy wasn't even born yet."

"Oh, yes, she is there, too. Look at Grandma."

There's his mother, so young, her lips painted red, her hair prettily curled, her stomach round and hard in the last weeks of pregnancy. Sissy was born barely more than a week after this.

He touches the photo with a blistered finger. "You're right. We're all here." They had just gotten home from Palm Sunday mass. Eugene was waiting on the doorstep. "Even my best friend. He was the one who took the picture."

"Your best friend? You mean as a kid? What was his name? Where's he now?"

He hasn't done everything right in his life. He's done a lot that was wrong. The first half of his life, he felt like a marionette with strings pulling him in every direction. He wanted to be a hero, like his dad, then failed every test he was given. But he's a husband and a father, and he has just put up almost 6,500 gallons of syrup. In the end, he's done at least that.

"His name was Eugene. He died during the Vietnam War. He killed himself."

Mia puts her hand in front of her mouth. "Oh, Daddy."

"I forgot it was in there," he says. "All those years I was carrying this guitar around, I never noticed it. Here: do you want it?"

Mia accepts the yellowed photo delicately, as though it's more than mere paper, a piece of history she is taking into her fingers, as though it is a butterfly that might either fall to dust or suddenly fly away. She looks up at him. He nods. She slides it carefully into his grandfather's medical diary.

"You can keep the diary, too," he says.

She holds it close to her chest. "Are you going to get this guitar fixed?"

He shakes his head.

"The past is the past. There are no resolutions," he says. "There are just stories."

Mia doesn't ask him to explain. Instead, she leans her head against his shoulder.

He puts an arm around her. Her body becomes weightier, and soon her breathing is rhythmic with sleep. He leans back against the hay, cradling her.

"We were an American family," he says softly.

His eyes grow heavy, and he closes them.

Pressure from Georgina's hand on his shoulder awakens him, the light of the sun slanting in through the open barn door behind her.

"Darlings," she says, her still-blond hair feathery around her face, a tall pair of boots on under her nightie. "It's time to come in."

Acknowledgments

A sea of thanks

to Judy Clain and Gail Hochman,

to Reagan Arthur and all the smart, hardworking people at Brandt & Hochman and Little, Brown & Co., starting but not ending with Amanda Brower, Liz Garriga, Julianna Lee—who designed this book's beautiful cover—and Betsy Uhrig,

to Anita Chaudhuri, Susan Jane Gilman, Eva Mekler, and Mina Samuels,

to James Laurence Farmer, David Foster, Dorian Frankel, Beth Phelps of Sweetbrook Farm, the Phoenix Public Library, Ed Roston, Richard Roston, Laurel Zuckerman, and, of course, my mother, MaryAnn Roston, in/of the United States,

to Sheila Friel of Imagine Media Productions, Anne and Norman Rowe, Janet Ruddock, Robin Ruddock for sharing boatloads of goodwill, time, and his seemingly limitless maritime knowledge, and Anne Wilson for sharing the story of her own currach voyage, in/of Northern Ireland,

to Ash and sleepy Quinn, on the Isle of Mull,

to David of the Heritage Garden Café, Sarah of the Heritage Center, the watercolorist, the minister and the minister's wife, Wendy and Rob MacManaway of the Argyll Hotel, and the crofter who showed me the way—literally, on the Isle of Iona,

to Kevin Byrne, Rodger Meiklejohn and Kathryn Edds, Dell for the chat, Sarah for the cake, and Lucy Hamilton and Bee Leask for the craic, on the Isle of Colonsay,

to Gillian Rodger and Grant Thompson of Historic Scotland, Katrina of the National Trust for Scotland, and Dru Heinz and the International Retreat for Writers at Hawthornden Castle, through whose fellowship I first encountered Scotland,

to Jim Gallie, Erin Coughlin Hollowell, and Country Joe MacDonald,

to Elizabeth Coleman, Jenny Colman and her lovely family, Carolina Garcia, Susan Malus, Pam Moore and Charlie Rose, Stephen Morallee, Chris Reardon, Louise Farmer Smith, and Ronna Wineberg,

to whoever that guy was who carved up a full smoked salmon on the train to Oban, Scotland, and shared it out amongst all of us fellow passengers,

to Susanna and Laura for all,

to Antti for everything.

About the Author

Anne Korkeakivi is the author of the novel *An Unexpected Guest*. Her short fiction and nonfiction have appeared in numerous publications in the United States and Britain, and she is a Hawthornden Fellow. Born and raised in New York City, she has lived in France and Finland, and currently resides in Geneva, Switzerland, where her husband is a human-rights lawyer with the United Nations. They have two daughters. Please visit her at annekorkeakivi.com.